Gro
Grossbach, Robert,
A shortage of engineers
$ 24.95
1st ed.

A SHORTAGE
OF ENGINEERS

Also by Robert Grossbach

NEVER SAY DIE

EASY AND HARD WAYS OUT

SOMEONE GREAT

A SHORTAGE OF ENGINEERS

Robert
Grossbach

ST. MARTIN'S PRESS
NEW YORK

www.stmartins.com

Design by Kathryn Parise

LIBRARY OF CONGRESS CATALOGING-IN-PUBLICATION DATA
Grossbach, Robert.
    A shortage of engineers / Robert Crossbach.—1st ed.
       p. cm.
    ISBN 0-312-27554-4
       1. Aerospace engineers—Fiction. 2. Aerospace industries—Fiction. I. Title.
    PS3557.R64 S48 2001
    813'.54—dc21

                                                                2001019272

First Edition: July 2001

10   9   8   7   6   5   4   3   2   1

o|°   To my wife, Sylvia, and my children,

Mitchell, Elliot, and Jennifer

CONTENTS

ENGINEERING JOKE:

During the French Revolution a doctor, a lawyer, and an engineer were all led to the guillotine chopping block to be executed. The doctor went first.

"Face up or face down?" asked the hooded executioner.

"Face down," said the doctor.

The executioner nodded, then released the rope that held the suspended blade. But to everyone's surprise, the blade seemed to bind in its tracks, and nothing happened.

The executioner shrugged. "An act of God," he said to the doctor. "You are free to go." He called the lawyer. "Face up or face down?"

"Face down."

Again, the blade was released . . . and again it failed to descend. "Once more, an act of God," said the executioner to the lawyer. "You are free to go." Finally, it was the engineer's turn. "Face up or face down?"

"Face up."

"All right," said the executioner, but just as he readied to release the blade, the engineer cried out.

"Wait a minute, wait a minute—I think I see the problem!"

A SHORTAGE
OF ENGINEERS

1

URINARY STYLES AND STRATEGIES

n the men's room near the Transmitter Lab there are four sinks. The first has no running water. The second has no powder in the soap dispenser. The third does not drain. And the fourth has a big cardboard sign over it, OUT OF ORDER.

The fourth is the only one that works.

I learned a great deal about that particular men's room, since I spent a substantial portion of my first month's employment in it, making coffee. I happen to be a coffee addict, six cups a day, min., a habit I'd developed during four years of engineering school. You can't do consecutive all-nighters on differential equations and thermodynamics without some kind of chemical stimulant. And, of course, the caffeine craving remains even after you graduate—which I'd done a little over three weeks earlier. Student in June, engineer in July.

Well, not much of an engineer. Not that first month anyway. I'd started on a Monday, July 10, 1989, driven into the vast cement parking lot at 7:45 A.M., found it, to my surprise, very nearly full. (I didn't know, then, that production people started at 7:00 and that many engineers came in a half hour early and stayed three hours late.) I parked near the rear and wended my way through the rectangular maze of cars until I'd traversed the nearly quarter-mile distance to the building's entrance. The structure was a two-story-high, two-block-square, featureless brick slab. A defense plant, all its windows were opaqued to the outside—never could tell when the enemy might be peering in.

I looked up at the sky, fresh morning blue, sun-scrubbed, with several high cirrus clouds. The realization struck me that I would spend the following eight hours in the concrete block-house, missing the warm solar bath, the beach, the trees, missing them this day, the next, the one after that, and so on, until I retired, 45 yrs. × 240 working days/yr., ten thousand eight hundred days under the pale fluorescents, while outside the sun shone. I pushed through the door.

The guard at the lobby desk issued me a plastic badge with the word TEMPORARY between two red lines, then phoned someone in Human Resources. Presently, a gray-haired, penguin-shaped woman appeared, called out, "Zachary Zaremba?" and, when I responded, led me through a side doorway. We walked down a short corridor, passed some cubicles, then paused at the open entrance to a small room. Inside, clustered at one end of a walnut table, were three people: a young man of roughly my age, a fiftyish man, and a young woman. At the other end of the table was a twenty-one-inch TV and VCR. "You go in here," said my escort, adding non sequiturially, "They don't let you smoke anymore."

The older man had thinning brown hair and wore a blue suit and striped yellow tie with a tiny, strangling knot. He introduced himself as Herman Lerner, head of Human Resources, and explained that he was going to give us our incoming briefing because "the girl"—he indicated the sixtyish woman who'd brought me in—"needs to set up some equipment." He then proceeded to show us a ten-minute video extolling the broad-based product lines of International Instruments ("Look any-where—we're there"); had us fill out W-4 forms; life, medical, and dental insurance forms; and patent assignment forms.

"This doesn't really seem fair," observed the young lady, on receiving the latter.

She was an Asian girl (actually Eurasian, I learned subse-quently) with shoulder-length, carbon-black hair, sculptured, delicate chin, and crimson, bow-shaped lips. I had fantasized making love to her within minutes of entering the room, crude bent-over-the-table, hiked-up-skirt stuff that is not in my real-life nature but that, as with most guys I know, is often featured in mental film productions. (I realized a year later that, while enjoying the cerebral cinema, I'd entered ten deductions on my W-4 and consequently owed a huge income tax bill.)

"I'm not following you," said Lerner.

"This says anything we discover, if there's a patent, it belongs to the company," said the girl. I noticed she had perfect teeth.

"That's right," said Lerner.

"It doesn't seem fair."

"It's a standard agreement. All companies have it."

The girl's eyes widened. "What if we don't sign?"

Lerner looked at her very directly. "Then you can't work here."

The girl nodded slowly.

"Is that a problem,"—he looked down at some papers— "Ms. Li?"

She didn't answer, but scrawled her signature on the form and pushed it back toward him. He looked at the other guy and me. "Anyone else have an issue with this?"

"Not me," said the other guy brightly. He was a bulky, fleshy fellow with black-framed glasses outlining a very white-skinned, glabrous face. He signed the form with a flourish and I read his *Warren Kushner,* as he shoved it back toward Lerner.

"Personally, I agree with the young lady," I said as I too signed the form and slid it over, knowing I really didn't give a shit and was only trying to curry her favor. She glanced at me, but otherwise showed no reaction.

Lerner launched into a detailed talk about insurance coverage, 401K plans, and tuition reimbursements—and I quickly blanked out—until his conclusion about how he hoped we'd think of II as our second family. I'd had enough problems with my first; I didn't need another one. And besides, your family doesn't make you sign patent agreements, unless they're quite unusual.

When there was no response to Lerner's call for any questions, he proceeded to lead us into a second room, where the secretary who'd escorted me in was fussing over a camera.

"Ms. Leeping will take care of your badges now," he said, backing toward the entrance. "And just remember, if you need me for anything, be it professional or personal, my door is always open." He left.

"His door is always open," echoed Ms. Li, while Kushner sat down in front of a white screen. She tried to make it sound like some idle musing, but the mockery bubbled right through.

My badge had a red background, signifying a confidential security clearance, the lowest level. (Gorbachev could probably have gotten one.) The Secret status the company had applied for would take three months to obtain. In the photo, my eyes bulged behind my glasses and my mouth was a flattened slit; it seemed to me I looked like a frog.

"I have a question about the accidental death and dismemberment insurance," said Ms. Li as the three of us walked through the wide asbestos-tiled corridor afterward. "What if somebody dismembers you intentionally? Are you still covered?" Her speech had not the slightest trace of an Asian accent.

"I guess you're asking whether the 'accidental' is from your viewpoint or someone else's," I said.

"Yes."

"And what if you're dismembered *and* die?" said Kushner. "Do you collect twice?"

"Or does it depend on which happened first?" said Ms. Li.

"We should put these things to Lerner," I said.

She smiled at me with those perfect white teeth. "I go in here," she said, pausing before double doors with an overhead sign, SOFTWARE ENGINEERING. "Nice meeting you." And she disappeared inside.

Kushner and I continued on as instructed: down the long hall past the corridor with the MRB sign, right turn at the vending machines, past SECURITY, the CREDIT UNION, and the REPRO ROOM, right turn up a ramp, and left at the elevator to RF ENGINEERING (RF stood for Radio Frequency), where someone named Marie was expecting us. It felt like three-quarters of a mile.

"They should give you roller skates," gasped Kushner, who was breathing heavily and perspiring. "Not that I know how to skate."

"I guess you're not in shape," I offered. We pushed through a door into a long room partitioned into cubicles.

"Well, I'm in *my* shape," said Kushner, "which is the only one I've got."

A woman emerged from an opening in the partitions. "Hi, I'm Marie. You must be the new people." She was mid-fortyish, with that crimson hair color found nowhere outside a chem lab.

Kushner and I introduced ourselves.

"Well, Warren, you're going to be in W5"—she gestured toward the rear of the room—"and you'll be reporting to Mr.

Sklar, who's—well, I'll take you in there and introduce you."
She turned to me. "Zachary, uh, Mr. Meissner hasn't quite
decided yet on your first assignment, so for the time being
you're going to . . ." She motioned outside the door we'd
entered. "They have your desk in a new room they're setting
up." Back to Warren. "Warren, if you'll just wait right here, I'll
walk Zachary to his area."

"Take it easy," I said to Kushner, as Marie and I went out the
door, turned right, and then left into a thirty-by-thirty-foot
room, completely bare except for a desk midway along one
side wall.

"Mr. Meissner did want to speak to you," assured Marie,
"but he's very busy today." She handed me a stapled document. "He suggested you can look over this."

I advanced uncertainly toward the desk.

"If you need anything, supplies, you just come to me," said
Marie. "You know there's a cafeteria, right?"

"Yes," I said, approaching the desk as if it were some
archaeological artifact.

"See you later," she chirped as she left.

I sat down at the desk.

No one spoke to me for the remainder of the week, except
for Marie, who, on Thursday, came to give me my time card.
"You charge job 102.4," she said. "Put down forty hours."

"What's 102.4?"

"Overhead."

Riddle: What has its feet on the ground but is overhead?
Answer: Me. I read again and again the document Marie had
given me: *Response to RFP #469137-M.* RFP was an Air Force
Request For Proposal. The 197-page booklet described the
operation of an Identity, Friend or Foe system, IFF in the jar-
gon. The idea was that someone on our side would beam a
coded microwave signal (the "interrogate" signal) at a vehicle—

say, a plane or tank or helicopter—and the vehicle would then beam back a coded answer. If there was no answer, or if the answer was wrong, we'd blow it up, the assumption being it was an enemy. Friendly vehicles would have the right code. The proposal had separate sections for the power supply, transmitter, receiver, digital electronics, software programming, and mechanical/thermal stuff. I understood about twenty percent of it.

I had brought some textbooks with me from Ann Arbor, weighty tomes on digital circuits and electromagnetic waves, and I tried going through them to find some relevance to the proposal, but there was very little. The texts were all theory and derivations and careful citing of source material; the proposal pulled formulas out of the air, gave no explanations, offered no references other than in-house computer simulations. It didn't take me long to give up.

In the second week I began going to the cafeteria at lunchtimes. (I'd eaten at the local McDonald's and Burger King the first week.) The cafeteria was open from exactly noon to exactly one. They didn't kick you out at one, but they let no one else in. The food was not bad—salads, burgers, pizza—and reasonably cheap. I usually sat alone, not because I'm unfriendly (though I am somewhat reticent) but simply because I didn't know anyone. The vast preponderance of co-lunchers were men, mostly middle-aged, mostly growing a bit paunchy, shoulders slumping, hair thinning, dressed in drab slacks and stained ties, talking techie stuff, or lawn stuff, or mutual funds, or retirement.

No sex, drugs, and rock-and-roll here.

Rarely even sports.

Thursday morning I went to see Marie. "I finished reading the proposal and I really don't have anything else to do."

She looked up from a pile of papers, indicated a tin on the

left side of her desk. "Would you like a cookie, Zachary?" Her eyes widened hopefully. "They're chocolate chip, baked 'em myself."

I reached into the tin, extracted one, bit into it, struggled to suppress the gag reflex. The taste was that of not-quite-dry plaster of paris. (My father is a dentist; as a child, I'd sampled the material on several occasions.)

"Excellent," I pronounced.

Marie beamed.

"Uh, as far as the proposal . . ."

"Oh. I know Mr. Meissner definitely intends to speak to you. He's just been swamped with the new project and all. . . ." She made a notation on a yellow pad. "I'll remind him again."

I started wandering the halls in the middle of the third week. The plant was vast, the corridors labyrinthine, the rooms like chambers in some elaborate fantasy adventure game. The CAD LAB with its gray-tiled floor, neat rows of computers, "D"-sized sheets dripping line by line from Hewlett Packard plotters. The glassed-in MICROWAVE INTEGRATED CIRCUITS LAB with its CLASS 10 CLEAN ROOM sign and white-gowned, shower-capped workers hunched over the microscopes of ball- and wedge-bonders. The PLATING ROOM, with its tanks and conveyor belts and steaming vats of acrid chemicals. The steel-caged ELECTRONIC STOCK ROOM, crammed floor to ceiling with shelves of electronic components. ASSEMBLY AREA ONE, with its hundreds of (mostly female) blue-smocked employees chained to metal benches, soldering components to printed circuit boards. (The chains were real, not metaphorical; the operators were grounded to prevent destruction of sensitive electronic parts by static electricity.)

It was Medieval Land meets Science Fiction Land, as frightening and foreign as a Kafka castle or an insect hive.

Early Wednesday morning they took away the vending machine where I'd been getting five of my seven daily coffees, and I began to go nuts. I quickly checked several other vending machines I'd located in my travels . . . and they were gone too. It was a policy shift, I realized, some arcane management decision, but this hardly assuaged my growing panic. *Coffee.* I *needed* coffee.

I grabbed two cups in the cafeteria at lunchtime, felt okay till about three P.M., visited the cafeteria again in the hope that the new management policy might include reopening it for snacks now that they were otherwise unavailable. But no. (Management initiatives, I was to learn, generally involved removing options, not creating them.)

When I left the plant at five P.M., tired and zombie-eyed, I drove directly to the local hardware store and bought one of those one-cup immersion heaters that plug into the wall. The next day, armed with a jar of instant Maxwell House, a cup, a spoon, and the heater, I marched into the office full of confidence. Who needed International Instruments. I'd take care of the problem on my own. At nine A.M., when my at-home breakfast coffee was just beginning to wear off, I rose from my swivel chair, strode through the corridor to the nearby men's room, and filled my cup at one of the sinks.

I had two things in my favor: I took my coffee black, no milk, no sugar, so I required minimal supplies, and I had a steady hand, so returning to my room with a nearly full cup posed no difficulty. I sat down at my desk, dipped the immersion heater coil into the water, clipped the plastic body to the cup's rim, and, holding the plug, bent to find a socket.

There was none.

I'd forgotten a basic: an extension cord. You always needed extension cords. I looked around the room to locate the outlets. And looked. And looked again. And traced the entire periphery in a squatting position to confirm what seemed to be impossible.

There were none.

How could they build a room without outlets??

I dialed Marie. "Marie, this is Zack Zaremba. I—I'm not sure where to begin here, but . . . my room appears to have no electrical sockets."

"Ohh, is that right," she said agreeably. "Is the lighting not adequate? Do you need a desk lamp?"

"No, the lighting is fine. I just—"

"Are you thinking, then, of a computer? Because the computer people, they usually install their own power, but your room was just built recently and I don't think they've gotten around—"

I told her why I needed the outlet.

There was a moment's silence. Then: "Well, I understand, Zachary, but you know, technically, it would be a violation of company policy for you to make your own coffee anyway."

"It would?"

"The only snacks and beverages in the plant are supposed to be furnished by our vendor, Foremost Foods. They're the ones who run the cafeteria. We used to have a contract with a different company, but we recently made an exclusive deal with Foremost. Have you been to the cafeteria yet?"

"Yes I have, but they're not open when I want coffee."

Another long pause. "Ohh. Well, I think Foremost is supposed to put in new vending machines. I could find out for you. . . ."

"Well . . . it's okay. You don't have to." I didn't see much point in knowing the information. "Thanks anyway." I hung up.

And then I remembered. I'd noticed a socket in the men's room. Intended, undoubtedly, for electric razors. Or for the maintenance guys to plug in their floor waxers. An outlet next to the right-end sink.

Company policy be damned, I needed that coffee.

And so began my time in the Transmitter Lab lavatory. I'd

take my Maxwell House, my heater, and my cup with me and do my business at the sinks, while various people wandered in to do theirs at the urinals and in the cubicles. The sinks were near the entrance, oriented so that they faced the interior; the water took about a minute to come to a boil (ten seconds more and it would bubble over the cup edges); the human mind cannot help categorizing. I offer these informational bits in partial explanation of why I began classifying people according to how they urinated. The process was entirely subconscious; it took place largely during the sixty-second boil. Show a human enough geometric figures and, regardless of size or spacial orientation, he or she will soon begin identifying them as triangles, rectangles, et cetera, abstracting thereby (without necessarily knowing the figures' names) the essential features of the geometry.

I began, of course, with the *One-Hander*, by far the most common type, your basic unzip, wait-a-second, here-it-comes kind of guy, relaxed, casual, with a shake-it-twice-then-tuck-it-back-in dismount.

(The urinals, I should note, were the sensible chest-to-floor type, not the kind that end three feet above the ground, which require short people to stand on their toes and little kids to retreat to toilets.)

The next pisser species was your Delayed Responder, a One-Hander who did a lot of staring at the ceiling, probably tried to picture running water, and eventually peed in a series of short, squelched bursts. The Dribbler was a subspecies who concluded the process with excessive penile whipping and squeezing, leaving the room finally with a fly area decorated by an array of dark spots. (I'd read once about prostate problems in older men; I supposed this might be an indication.)

The Two-Hander felt the need to have additional control over his dick. Should one arm suddenly become paralyzed or palsied, be seized or yanked, or otherwise prevented from controlling a powerful wiener determined to go its own way, the other could act as a fail-safe to prevent urinary sprays from flying everywhere.

The Surveyor was constantly glancing sideways to check the equipment and functionality of the guy next to him.

The No-Hander was either irrationally confident of an unwavering stream or terminally lazy. Let the drops fall where they may.

The Loners could not urinate in the presence of others. They fell into two classes: Fakers, who'd flush after thirty seconds and zip up ostentatiously, and Retreaters, who withdrew into cubicles. Subcategories of the latter included those who left the door open or closed, or stood facing the toilet, or who sat down on it (Girlie-Man Retreater).

The Usurper was the opposite (in some sense) of the Retreater and a variant of the No-Hander; he folded his elbows over the urinals adjacent to his own. He not only required his, but part of the next guy's as well.

I noticed after a week that my classification system was becoming a labeling system. I'd pass someone in the hall and think, Retreater, or I'd see someone at a cafeteria table and observe, *Dribbler.* And the labeling system soon became judgmental in other areas besides liquid excretion: The Delayed Responders were repressed and uptight; the Surveyors had inferiority complexes; the Retreaters were timid; the Two-Handers were controlling and excessively cautious. I developed a theory of Urinary Styles and Strategies, corporate life reflected in a men's room mirror, where Usurpers competed for managerial ascendancy; Two-Handers wrote detailed memos; Dribblers hemmed and hawed and told reluctant lies to No-Handers, who confidently believed them; Retreaters had job-stress-related nervous breakdowns, Fakers falsified data, and Surveyors resented higher-salaried peers.

My first week on Long Island, I'd stayed in a Holiday Inn in Shoreview, five minutes away from International Instruments. Then I'd rented a three-room, garden-type apartment there (interestingly, Shoreview was neither on a shore nor offered any particular view), sharing it with a guitar player whose ad I'd seen on a Foodtown bulletin board. Occasionally, weekends, I'd travel into Manhattan, sometimes to explore, once to see my roomie perform at a club. After my fifth week at work, I began to feel like one of those homeless babblers I'd seen around Penn Station: My days were spent wandering the halls, reading random passages from my old textbooks, making coffee in the men's room, sipping it slowly at my desk. Lunchtimes I'd eat in the cafeteria, take walks, sit in my car and listen to the radio. Afternoons were a repeat of the mornings. Occasionally I'd hear a few words that seemed applicable to what I was doing, only to discover I'd been talking to myself.

By week five I began weighing my shit.

Indirectly, of course—I'm no pig. I'd discovered, in a corridor that led to SHIPPING AND RECEIVING, a doctor's scale (the type with the sliding weights) standing in an alcove. I presumed it a relic from some managerial dynasty of the past, artifact of a leadership that felt itself enlightened and progressive because it provided the means for employees to keep fit. An on-premises weight room would have been a likely concomitant, along with handouts promoting healthy diets and twice-yearly dental visits. The walk from my desk to the scale took at least eight minutes, and so was an excellent time killer, which suited my purposes. It quickly escalated from an occasional visit to an everyday occurrence to a three- or four-times-daily ritual. It wasn't long before two of the trips happened to be sandwiched around a fairly massive defecation (now, *there's* an enticing image)—and I noticed the loss of mass.

My shit, on that day, weighed three-quarters of a pound.

On the next day it weighed about a half pound. Two days later (I didn't go on the day in between), I deposited a whopping one pound plus. I took pains, both literal and metaphorical, not to pee while I shat, since the weight of urine would contaminate the purely fecal readings. Urine weight was a subject for a different investigation. (This was how I now thought of the process: a scientific exploration.) By the next week I began plotting a histogram of the data, shit weight by intervals (e.g., 0–¼ lb.) on the horizontal axis, number of samples that fell into the slots on the vertical axis.

It was remarkable to me that here I was, into the seventh week of a job that was paying me $120 a day simply to show up, sit at a desk, make coffee in the men's room, and weigh my shit. In saner moments—after watching a ball game, just before falling asleep, after a game of "horse" with an imaginary opponent—I realized: I was going nuts.

I was, quite simply, losing my mind. Like a prisoner in solitary confinement. On Thursday of week seven I returned at three P.M. from my fifth walk to the scale to find a note on my desk from Marie: *Please see me.* I headed immediately for her area. (Her desk was in an open space between partitions.) I knew what she would say: They had overestimated the workforce requirement, there simply was nothing for me to do right now, my departure would include a week's severance pay and extension of the medical insurance till the month's end. She looked up at my approach and smiled sweetly.

"Oh, Zachary, I'm glad you got my message."

"Yes. Yes, I did."

She lifted her eyebrows. "Well, the time has come."

I nodded. "Yeah, well, I, you know, I figured . . ."

"Mr. Meissner is ready for you now."

THE BOYS IN W5

The floggings will continue till morale improves.
—HANDWRITTEN SIGN IN ENGINEERING OFFICE

Anton Meissner had a round, ruddy face, beady black eyes, and thin oily black hair combed sideways across his scalp. He looked up as Marie and I entered.

"Mr. Meissner, I have Zachary Zaremba for you," she said quietly, as if presenting a donut. She exited immediately, closing the door behind her.

"Zachary, good to meet you finally," said Meissner. He extended a palm without rising and I strode forward to shake it. I'd seen him in the men's room: Two-Handed Delayed Responder. He proceeded to introduce me to a second man in the room, a hunched, gray-haired individual, whom I would come to know as either Whispering Bill or Bent-Over-Bill. Bent-Over-Bill (Dribbler) sat in a straight chair in a corner; he nodded his recognition, a handshake clearly too much effort.

The office was an eighteen-foot square; a window opened on a sunken interior courtyard one story below. Snuggled within the square were Meissner's walnut desk, a conference table, and two tan file cabinets. On one wall was a large oaktag chart labeled AIR. Various technical tasks filled the chart's left edge and spawned, from little triangles, a series of horizontal lines that spanned twenty-one months' time, as registered by "Jan's" through "Dec's" across the top. The lines also ended in triangles, but these were upside down.

"Have a seat," said Meissner, indicating a metal folding chair facing him.

I complied.

"All this time, you're probably wondering: 'I'm sittin' here yanking my pud, what the hell did they bother hiring me for?' " He grinned. "That about right?"

I grinned back, simultaneously shrugging and tilting my head at forty-five degrees, i.e., diffident, but aware.

"I presume you've read the proposal, probably sick to death of it."

Diffident, but aware.

"Anyway, that's what we got here." He lifted an index finger in the direction of the chart. "That's what you're going to be working on."

"Air," I said, reading the letters atop the chart.

"Advanced Interrogator/Receiver," said Meissner. "Billion-dollar contract."

"Billion dollars," said Whispering Bill. His voice was a hoarse rasp.

"So tell me . . . Zack," continued Meissner, "what school you graduate from?"

"University of Michigan," I said.

"Ah, Michigan. Good university, good engineering school. Great football team they got up there."

"Very often, yes."

"Fine team," wheezed Whispering Bill.

"I should've had your resumé in front of me," said Meissner, "but those Human Resource people . . . well, you know
how *they* are."

Diffident, but aware.

"So, uh, what areas are you mainly interested in, Zack? Any
technical subjects you find particularly exciting?"

"Well . . . really . . . I just want to do creative work. I'd
like . . . I mean, I became an engineer because I'd like to do
something, to understand something no one else ever has
before. I'd like to build something new."

"He wants to be original," rasped Whispering Bill.

Meissner stood up. "That's good, Zack. Excellent. And
believe me, you'll absolutely get your chance. That's just the
kind of people we want here." I rose too, as did Whispering
Bill. We both sidled toward the door. "Bill here is gonna show
you the ropes," continued Meissner. "Bill's one of the finest
engineers on my staff, heads up a whole bunch of things, but
most particularly Power Supplies." At the door. "You like power
supplies?"

"Nothing works without 'em," I offered.

Out the door.

"You're gonna do good work," said Meissner.

"Thank you," I said. "Nice meeting you."

Whispering Bill and I began walking through a wide aisle
amid the cubicles. The cubicle walls were six feet high, covered with some kind of felt material to which, at intervals,
were tacked or taped various papers: "1989 Vacation Schedule," "Science Fiction Club Meeting Notes," "Blood Drive," et
cetera. Bill's hunch bent him nearly double; he had an excellent view of his shoes, but very little else.

"That's Meissner," he said. "Runs the whole AIR project.
Reports to Ingrassia. You know Ingrassia?"

"Uh, no. Not really."

"Chief engineer. Him and Sanders brought in AIR."

"I just hope it wasn't polluted," I noted. There are certain stupid things I can never resist saying.

Whispering Bill made a sound somewhere between a rumble and wheeze. "That's a joke," he pronounced. "I don't mind it, but don't say them in front of the higher-ups. Those people have no humor."

We came to a cross aisle, made a left, then the first right, entered a large cubicle with a sign W5. None of the four men inside looked up as Whispering Bill led me to an empty desk. "This is yours," he said. "You can bring your stuff from the other area. Any supplies you need, paper, pens, that type thing, just ask Marie." He indicated a neat pile of 8½-by-11-inch sheets on the desktop. "Meissner wants you to start on WRLs. Ask one of the guys to show you what to do. When you finish those, come see me."

"Where are you?" I asked.

"Two cubicles down," he whispered. "Come out, make a right." I guess my face must've shown my uncertainty. "You'll be fine," he added. And left.

I sat down in the swivel chair in front of my new desk. I faced a wall on which was tacked a large sheet (so-called "D"-sized) with the schematic of a complicated-looking circuit. I pivoted . . . and saw Warren Kushner smiling at me.

"I was wondering whatever happened to you."

I had wondered the same about him. I'd seen him only once since that first day; he'd entered the men's room just as my water came to a boil. (He was a toilet-facing Retreater.) "They put me in this big area by myself," I said, "and never gave me anything to do."

"Zee mushroom philosophy," piped up a short, jowly man at the next desk. He wore a shapeless beige sweater and brown, scuffed shoes. "Management policy for engineers. Don't give zem any light, let zem eat *merde*, and even so, zey get bigger!"

The thirtyish man to his right rolled his eyes and brushed ineffectually at a lacquered pompadour. "He means, 'Put 'em in the dark, feed 'em shit, and watch 'em grow.' Edouard hasn't quite mastered English yet; he's only been in this country thirty-four years."

"Soon I go back to Paris."

"Ron Wonderbury," said the pompadour, coming over to shake hands. Wonderbury was a *Surveyor*. He indicated the Frenchman. "And this is Edouard Boulot."

"Welcome," said Boulot, smiling, "and my condolences."

"Why—"

He pointed to the sheets on my desk. "WRLs."

"Wire Run Lists," said Kushner.

I squinted at the top paper, which was divided into columns headed "Designation," "Color," "Gauge," "Length," "From," Dwg.#," "To," and a final "Dwg.#."

"Zere are two thousand miles of wires in zat plane," said Boulot. "You will know every inch."

"It's not a plane, it's a platform," intoned the last man in the room. "The military doesn't have aircraft, ships, or tanks anymore, only platforms." He returned his gaze to something on his desk. He was a bearded fellow, fortyish, heavyset, with black hair combed straight back and baggy trousers—I'd seen him several times in the men's room, a No-Hander.

"Is this for the AIR project?" I asked the room. "That's what they told me I'd be working on."

"The WRLs aren't for AIR," said Wonderbury.

"Never believe what they tell you," said the *No-Hander*, writing something on a piece of paper.

"Jim, 'ee is very cynical," said Boulot. "Almost as much as

myself. 'Ee is what-you-call a 'Job Shoppair.' You know what zat is?"

"Mercenary," called Jim, before I could answer. "Hired hand."

"Shopper Jim will be gone in three weeks," said Wonder-bury. "Hardly even pays to learn his name."

Shopper Jim's mouth stretched into a slow, mirthless grin. "That's what the Directs always say. Fact is, I'll be here longer than you, Wonderboy. I'll be watching when they lay your skinny ass off and you stumble out into the parking lot with all your stuff in cardboard boxes." He raised his left index finger. "But I promise you, I will not gloat."

---

o

The WRLs were indeed mind-numbing. I had to check that each "From" and "To" on a sheet, as designated by a letter and number (e.g., E11, or J33), correlated with the schematic circuit diagram that contained the wire. Some wires started on one schematic and ended in another, so I'd have to look up both sheets. I got the schematics from the REPRODUCTION DEPARTMENT, which was responsible for all released drawings and which, over its window, displayed a handwritten sign summarizing its business philosophy: *This is not Burger King. You don't get it your way. You take it our way or not at all.*

I'd lean on the ledge of the four-foot-square opening, fill out my "Request for Print" form, slide it into the time/date stamper, and then wait three days until I'd be called to pick up the photocopy. There were boxes on the form marked Urgent and Ultra-urgent and on several occasions I tried checking one or the other or both, but it never made any difference: The prints always came back in three days.

Every two hours or so Whispering Bill would come in and ask, "How you doing on those WRLs?" and I would reply,

"Well, I have these," and hand him the stack I'd completed since his last visit. In rare instances, say once in three hundred connections, I'd find an error, which I'd check in red and correct. "That's good," Whispering Bill would say. "Good catch." And then he'd scurry out.

"You just made his day," Shopper Jim commented on one such occasion, two weeks into my WRL work.

"Really? I would think that would upset him."

"No, no. See, he takes that and runs right into Meissner with it and that justifies both their salaries for the past month. Also, it gives Meissner reason to scream at whoever made the mistake—not that he needs a reason—which he loves to do."

Kushner and I had got into the habit of having lunch together in the cafeteria. Kushner had graduated from Brooklyn Polytech, lived with his mom in Westbury, and had already submitted his application for grad school.

"I really think you need a masters to get ahead in this business," he would comment. "Everybody got a BS, you have to distinguish yourself." He'd puff his cheeks. "The thing is, I really don't know if I can handle it. I mean, both the school and the work. Sklar already told me he expects heavy overtime."

Kushner reported to Marvin Sklar, the "box" engineer for the AIR transmitter. The AIR hardware was divided into four units—transmitter, receiver, digital processor, and power supply—each of which had a cognizant or "box" engineer responsible for its operation.

Kushner stroked his forehead. "Maybe I shouldn't go to school, maybe it's a mistake."

Kushner worried a lot. He ate tofu and various sprouts, nuts, leaves, and beans every day for lunch and worried that he would get cancer. He worried that his car wouldn't start when he came out into the parking lot after working late. He worried that he wouldn't be able to do his assignment to

Sklar's satisfaction and that he'd receive a bad review. But most of all, he worried about women.

We were admiring the rear end of a callipygous red-haired Purchasing secretary as she stooped over the next table.

"Look at that," I said. "If I could just slide my hand six inches up the back of that thigh, a mere fifteen-hundredths of a meter, I would be happy for a week. I'd live on the *memory* for a month."

Kushner seemed pensive, distracted, or at least as much so as anyone could with an alfalfa sprout dangling down the side of his chin. He leaned over the table. "You wanna hear something really sick?"

The girl's skirt hiked up even higher. "Absolutely." I certainly wasn't looking at him.

"It seems unbelievable . . . but I haven't even had a date."

I raised my eyebrows. "You mean since getting out of college. . . ."

"I mean . . . ever."

"Ever?"

"You think I'm abnormal?"

I forced my eyes to swivel in his direction. "Well . . . quite possibly. But I wouldn't worry about it. You, uh, I mean, you like girls, right?"

"Oh, yes, yes. I worship them. I have quite an extensive pornography collection, which you're more than welcome to come up and see. Of course, I'm horribly tortured by the thought my mother might find it, even though I hide it in fiendishly obscure places."

The redhead had straightened and was now swiping ineffectually at her hair while conversing with a friend, her large nipples straining through her bra to pucker the soft cotton of her sweater.

"I'd rate her a two," said Shopper Jim, passing by our table.

"Two? Isn't that—"

"The number of Clydesdales needed to pull her off my face."
He grinned. "That's Barbara. Quite lovely, but more germs than
a petri dish—or so I read in the Accounting men's room."

Kushner had stiffened at Jim's approach. "The thing I
don't understand," he said, as if he and I had been talking
about it before Jim interrupted, "is that Sklar told me the job
was already three weeks behind. How could that be? We just
started."

Shopper Jim moved away. "One piece of advice," he called
back, swiveling his gaze from Kushner to me. "Jim's first rule
of engineering: Don't take it too seriously." He walked off.

"He once told me he never talks about work during lunch,"
whispered Kushner. "That's why I changed the subject, so he'd
go away."

"You don't like him?"

"I donno . . . he makes me uneasy."

"What about what he said—about not taking things seriously?"

Kushner shook his head. "Look at him, what does he have?
He's forty-something, no pension, no security. . . ."

"Where's he from?"

"I donno. Some western state, someone said. He's a
migrant worker."

"He told me yesterday that your only security ever, unless
you're already rich, is your ability to get the next job."

"Well, of course, he has to justify himself."

Shopper Jim claimed to know a great deal about nearly
everything, or, as he would put it, "What you need to understand to get by in engineering, The Way Things Work."

"The Way Things Don't Work is to follow procedures," he
explained one morning when he saw me filling out a Request
for Print form at the REPRO window. He ambled over, leaned

his bulky frame across the ledge inside the opening, and called to a sullen, haggard-looking woman at one of the desks. "Rosemary. Hey, lover!" The woman looked up. "See you a sec, Rosie." The woman rolled her eyes. "Just one sec." She reluctantly rose and shambled toward us.

Jim put his arm around me. "My young friend here is getting daily reaming from Bent-Over-Bill 'cause he doesn't turn around his WRLs fast enough."

"Six million stories in the Naked City," said Rosemary.

"Isn't it eight million?" I whispered.

"Yeah, but Rosie's heard two million," said Jim.

Rosie smiled, showing rows of intermittent teeth.

"See, at first he thought the Repro Department was just slow, you know. Inefficient. But I explained to him: Zack, these people are the most abused, unfairly treated, put-upon people in the whole place. The company would drop stone dead without these people, but they get no acknowledgment whatsoever. You should be happy you get anything at all."

Rosemary looked at me for the first time. "What you need?"

"Uh, uh . . . 402937, Rev. D."

"What size is it?"

"Uh, I believe . . . 'C.' "

She shuffled away, into another room. Three minutes later, she returned. She flipped the neatly folded print onto the window ledge. "This the one?"

I looked at it. "Yeah. Hey, wow. Thanks."

She spun without a word, and returned to her desk, and pointed at Shopper Jim. "Don't think I'm not on to you, you oily, fraudulent dickhead."

Jim smiled. "Understood?" he said to me as we walked away.

"Understood," I replied.

I began to alternate the days on which I'd lunch with Shopper Jim with those I'd eat with Kushner—or rather, they began to alternate themselves. I'd usually sit next to whomever I spied first, and the remaining person would invariably choose not to join us. On my "Jim" days, we'd occasionally go out to eat, Jim pulling me up from my chair and leading me out of the plant and into his blue 1974 Plymouth Fury with the bashed-in left rear fender. "Lunchtime," he'd say. "Gotta have a change of scenery." Which nearly always turned out to be a Burger King or McDonald's, Jim ingesting pickle-lettuce-tomato-onion-ketchup-relish-dripping Big Macs, me neatly biting into absolutely bare fish fillets on a bun.

"Fussy eater," Jim noted the first time we ate out.

"Right."

"No vegetables."

"Right."

"Never?"

"Never."

"You're gonna die."

"So're you."

"Not me," said Shopper Jim.

On the way back to the plant we'd frequently see Boulot, walking by himself. He'd always pleasantly refuse Jim's offer of a ride.

"Man needs to walk off his craziness," said Jim. "Lotta anger there, lotta bitterness. Man's a powder keg, actually, type you read about shows up with a machete one morning, hacks his colleagues to bits."

"Sounds like someone to stay away from."

"Oh, no, he's a nice guy. Smart, cultured, sense of humor. I like Boulot."

One day, when I was doing the driving, Shopper Jim noted my Wiffle ball bat on the back seat. "Wanna play?" he asked.

He must've seen my skeptical look. "Hey, I ain't *that* old. I play games. I listen to Metallica . . . once. I like sports."

We played against the south wall of the International Instruments building and Jim actually wasn't bad. I myself can make the ball take off, dip, and curve like it was on a rubber band, and Jim still managed to hit a reasonable number of pitches. Of course, since I was twenty years his junior and something of a Wiffle fanatic, I generally came out ahead in our three-inning games.

"Good for you," said Jim, after his first loss. "You got talent. Means you won't be completely bereft when you leave engineering."

"How do you know I'll leave engineering?"

"Well, (A) you have nontechnical interests, and (B) your general awareness exceeds that of a flatworm. Those people generally get out."

"And what about yourself?"

Shopper Jim narrowed his eyes. "I'm working on it."

After the fifth week on WRLs, I decided they were worse than doing nothing at all. I found myself reverting to old habits: walking the halls, weighing myself every two hours, drawing out random stationery items from the OFFICE SUPPLIES window. Along with defecating, the latter constituted one of the day's great pleasures: I'd discovered that engineers could ask for nearly anything in this realm and not be questioned. You filled out a form with your name and department number (2134 for Microwave Engineering), listed the thing you needed, and—just like that—Sandy or Pat or Sue actually walked back through the long rows of neat steel shelves and got them for you. No questions about why you required twelve Pink Pearl erasers over the past week, or four boxes of staples, or seven quad-ruled pads. You were an engineer—you must need them. It was a giddy, dizzying sensation—legalized stealing, really—and, for the brief instants of the transaction, made me feel truly professional.

But it was not enough. No matter how many pencil boxes, Post-It pads, and loose-leaf binders bulged out my desk drawers, the WRLs gave me a perpetual headache. Each day I took two extra-strength Excedrins at nine A.M., two more at two P.M.

"Very bad for your stomach," Kushner noted. "You'll have ulcers before you're twenty-five."

"But I won't have a headache."

I needed an outside activity, something to look forward to. Each evening, I'd drive back to my apartment, cook myself some rudimentary supper—Swanson's Hungry Man fried chicken TV dinner was typical (of course, I didn't eat the little *corn* section), or Elio's frozen pizzas; read *Newsday* (which, to my undying irritation, offered really scant coverage of the Pistons, Redwings, Tigers, Lions, or even my beloved Michigan Wolverines); then sprawl on the couch, hook my thumbs under the waist of my jeans, turn on the TV, and watch glossy-eyed and slack-jawed, while scarfing up Mallomars, Bugles, and Dr. Brown's cream soda, and filling the room with hundreds of belches and farts. All in all, a pretty good life—although my roomie was quick to point out its deficiencies.

My roomie's name was Angelo Belpanno, although I called him Phantom, since I saw him so rarely. He was a guitarist and kept musician's hours, out all evening, back when I was sleeping, sleeping when I left in the morning. He was about twenty-six, and the only times we ever intersected were on weekends, when he'd awaken about four P.M. and hang around for two hours before leaving. One day, I found a note from him on the table, a one-line message. I'd gotten these in the past with such advisories as, *Rent due 7/1,* or *New roll paper towels under sink,* but this one was different. It read, *Get a life.*

"What does this mean?" I said to him the next Sunday.

"Self-explanatory, I believe," he said. He'd just emerged from the bathroom and stood shirtless, towel wrapped around his waist.

"How do you know I don't already have one?"

He shrugged. "Do you?"

I considered for several seconds. "Well . . . no."

He nodded. A comb appeared in his hand and he began running it through his shoulder-length hair. "You seeing any women?"

"Not really."

"Didn't think so. Want me to fix you up?"

"Well . . . that would be very—"

"That I can do, but that's not the whole story. You like sports, right?" He didn't wait for confirmation. "I mean, I seen you read *Newsday,* you start from the back. That's a sign. You watch all kinda games on TV."

"Okay . . ."

"You should coach a team." He must've seen my expression. "Kids' team, any kind. Baseball, football, basketball—that's what you should do. I'd do it if I had the time. You like kids?"

"I donno, some. I used to be one."

"That's what you should do. Very rewarding."

And then he went back in the bathroom and shut the door—before I could talk to him more about my real interest, the women.

Although I was put off by the Phantom's smugly condensed prescription for improving my existence, my pique was tempered by the realization that he was probably correct. When, later that day at the Shoreview Library (another outside-work hangout) I saw a bulletin-board poster advertising for coaches for the Shoreview Soccer Club, I decided I would apply. I wondered if the fact that I'd never played the game or even seen a single match would prove an insurmountable impediment.

Fearful of complete inadequacy, I proceeded to take out six books with titles ranging from *Coaching Youth Soccer* to *Soccer: Advanced Defensive Formations.* I'd always believed you could learn everything by reading.

On the Friday before the Labor Day weekend, Bent-Over-Bill came to my desk and told me I'd checked my last Wire Run List.

"New assignment for you," he rasped. "AIR project. Want you to tabulate the currents."

I stared at him blankly.

"You talk to each of the box engineers, you ask about all the active components in their units, tell them you need to know the maximum current draws. I'm handling the AIR power supplies, gotta have that info."

I still didn't move.

"This comes right from Meissner himself," he added, invoking the name of the deity. And then he turned and left, taking my final WRL with him.

3

SOFTHEADS, HARDHEADS, AND DICKHEADS

Who's the dickhead?
—SIGN UNDER MIRROR TAPED TO WALL ADJACENT
TO DESK OF SHOPPER JIM

The first box was the transmitter; Kushner took me over to the lab area to introduce me to the Cognizant ("Cog") Engineer, his boss, Marvin Sklar. When you see electronics labs in the movies they always show these high-tech white-tiled rooms with dozens of rack-mounted instruments bristling with LED readouts and intricate computer displays and manned by intense, serious, smocked, and hair-netted workers. Real labs are quite different: The instruments are very often falling-apart pieces of shit; the premises are strewn with cables, connectors, adaptors, tanks of liquid nitrogen, half-eaten tuna sandwiches, papers with scrawled circuit diagrams, clips, staplers, soldering irons smoking in their coiled-cage stands; and the people—if you consider techs and engineers in that category—wear the same clothes as anyone else. It is true that some are intense and meticulous, but others, who accomplish the same or more useful work, are often relaxed and slovenly.

The Transmitter Lab at II was about twenty feet wide and forty long, with three rows of peeling, two-tiered wooden benches that extended nearly the length of the room and that were interrupted by one cross-aisle. Sklar's chief technician, a short, grinning Asian introduced by Kushner as Gung Ho, greeted us at a bench near the entrance.

"Mist' Sk'ar, he over there," said Ho, indicating a steel desk crammed against a rear wall, where a burly, hairy-armed, balding man was talking animatedly on the phone.

"Whatcha workin' on, Gung?" asked Kushner.

Ho pointed to a small circuit board on his bench. "Boss say, 'Now you work this,' so I do. Oscillator, ten gigahert'." "Gigahert' " was Gung's rendering of the frequency in gigahertz, billions of cycles per second. The oscillator was a generator of high-frequency power.

"Ten gigahertz?" said Kushner. "That's not for AIR. . . ."

"No, not AIR. Special project." Ho winked theatrically.

At that moment, we saw Sklar hang up the phone and we started down the aisle in his direction. Kushner introduced me when we arrived.(Of course, I already knew him from the men's room: Usurper, and I told Sklar my assignment.)

"You'll have to give me two or three days," he said brusquely. "The shit's piling over my ears."

"That's fine," I said. "I'll come back to see you on—"

The phone rang before I finished. "Marvin Sklar," said Sklar, snatching up the receiver. He listened a moment. "No, no, this *is* MES Technology." Another pause, then, his voice becoming all creamy and mellow, "Yes, we *do* produce custom oscillator designs." Buttery laugh. "I see. Well, it's just that we currently have several major subcontracts with them, and I'm on the premises a lot, so I've been leaving an extension here as a forwarding number."

Kushner and I started away. "Is what was going on there what I *think* was going on?" I asked.

Kushner shrugged. "If you think he's running his own business, then . . . yes. Quite so."

---
o

Sam Hsu was the cog engineer for the AIR receiver.

"A Boy Named Hsu is what they call him," said Shopper Jim, by way of preparing me to interface with the Receiver head. (Engineers did not speak to or meet each other, they interfaced.) Jim was currently working for Hsu on the receiver front end, the part that first detected the microwave signal that the potential target beamed back. "The only thing you need to know about Hsu is that he's a dick," Jim added.

"That's his evaluation of everybody," said Wonderboy.

"And it's usually correct," said Jim.

"Invariably ignorant," said Wonderboy.

"Invariably foolish to say aloud," said Kushner.

"Invariably true of most Americans," said Boulot, popping two Chiclets in his mouth. "So why even point it out?"

Wonderboy whirled to face him. "If you hate this country so much, Boulot, why don't you just go back to France?"

"I will," said Boulot. "I am planning." He chewed the gum ferociously. "Of course, I hate ze French too."

Thus prepared, I went to see the receiver cog engineer. A Boy Named Hsu (*Two-Hander*) stared out at me through rimless spectacles as I made my request. "And when am I supposed to do this?" he asked when I'd finished.

"I . . . I don't know. Whispering Bill said as soon as possible."

"I don't take orders from him."

"Well . . . he said this came from Meissner."

Hsu's head moved laterally to and fro on his neck, a weed waving in the wind. "Already, I work Saturdays, Sundays— when do I have time for this? In my sleep?"

"I don't think this'll take that long. He just wants the current from each supply."

"Current from each supply? I have three supplies—plus twelve, minus twelve, minus five. I have, maybe, ten components hooked to each. So: For thirty components, I need to find how much current they draw, worst case. I have to look up each spec. How long does that take?"

"I—I guess I don't know."

"No. You don't know." He rose from his desk. He stood barely over five feet tall; the finger he jabbed at me was navel-level. "You want me to find the currents, you get a memo from Meissner. In writing."

I shrugged, nodded, reported the conversation to Whispering Bill, returned to Hsu the next day with a single-line printed page. It read, *Kindly supply Zachary Zaremba with the information he requests at your very earliest convenience.* It was addressed to *All AIR Cognizant Engineers* and signed *A. Meissner.*

Hsu read it wordlessly, then strode from the cubicle (a small but private one) and walked down a short hallway to a lab area. Unsure if I'd been dismissed, I tagged along. Hsu stopped at a bench where Shopper Jim was discussing the Jets with a bearded tech. Hsu handed Jim the memo.

"You do this," he said, then turned abruptly and left.

"Rude little fucker, isn't he," said Jim.

○

The remaining box engineer was a pleasant, bony, mid-fortyish man with rotting, mossy teeth and a face full of wens, blebs, and other tumorous growths. His name was Herbert Scheisswig, but the technicians called him Medieval Man. Medieval

Man was in charge of the AIR processor, the box that sensed when somebody pushed the interrogator button, looked up that day's code in its memory, sent pulses to the transmitter telling it to produce microwaves in clusters corresponding to the code, compared the receiver's detected response from the target to that day's correct answer, and then, by means of lights and beeps, notified the operator (after thirty or so repetitions of the sequence) whether to shoot the target down. This from a six-by-four-inch box, a half inch thick, that was also responsible for detection of operating faults in all the other boxes, the so-called Built-In-Test or BIT function.

And all overseen by someone who looked like he ought to be polishing visors for Sir Lancelot.

"Yeah, I can do that," said Medieval Man, after I'd made my request. "You understand, though, that there's still major uncertainty in the software requirements, so if the Softheads all of a sudden determine they need three times the memory, the effect is gonna ripple through the hardware."

Processing was divided into two groups of people: Hardheads, who designed, combined, and powered the semiconductor chips; and Softheads, who wrote the digital code that made the chips work. The two groups, I was to learn, disdained each other's functions and were forever at odds.

Medieval Man motioned me to follow, then walked from the small DIGITAL LAB, where we stood, to a few yards down the corridor. He pushed and held open a pair of double doors and I peered inside. The room was vast and darkened; approximately 75 people sat at computer terminals, men and women, 150 pupils fixated on illuminated screens, 750 fingers scratching with rodentlike energy at the keyboards.

"This is what we're up against," said Medieval Man.

Shopper Jim later told me that Medieval Man reported to the head of Software instead of vice versa, an inversion of logical responsibility brought about by corporate politics. The double doors swung shut.

"I'll get you your currents, uh, Zaremsk—"

"Zaremba."

"—but I'll tell you right now, I don't have a good feeling about this."

I let him know I understood his unease and would convey it to my superiors.

<hr>

°

The first practice was on a Tuesday, the second week in September. I found myself on a middle school soccer field surrounded by seventeen six-year-olds. One of them, Eric, was the son of my assistant, Ed Nowicki. Ed had assured me immediately on arrival that he knew absolutely nothing about soccer and was just there as a general Good Samaritan to help out.

"So you don't have to worry about me trying to, you know, take over any of your authority or trying to run things."

"Well," I said, "that certainly is a relief."

Thirty yards distant, another coach had begun loudly addressing his team of first-graders. "All right, everybody, listen up!"

I remembered that phrase from my own Little League coaches, who seemed to use it constantly. Listen *up*, as though that final direction would clinch even more attention than the unadorned command, ensure even more enthusiasm.

"All right," I told my group, "I'd like everyone to sit down— that's it, form, like, a circle, and just relax."

Reluctantly, haltingly, the group complied.

From the duffel bag I'd brought, I pulled out the rolled-up oaktag diagrams I'd made and began to unravel them. I held up the first of the drawings. "This is a soccer field," I began. "The rectangles at the ends represent goals"—a boy with glasses began tearing out clumps of grass—"and the circles represent players."

"What is 'represent'?" asked Cory, a boy missing two front teeth.

"To stand for something."

"What is 'stand for something'?"

"Like, the rectangles, they're supposed to be"—I pointed to the goalposts at the ends of the field—"those things over there."

"Oh," said the boy. "But it doesn't look like them."

Two boys in the back had stood up and were walking around. "Let's move on," I said. "And everybody please sit." I began to explain about the object of the game, about not using hands, about *lines*—forward, halfback, fullback—everything I'd read in the books. I noticed the other coach had his team up and running, kicking to each other in two-man drills, passing. A few of his kids, watched by his assistants, were taking shots on goal.

"We wanna play!" shouted a blond-haired boy on my team after fifteen minutes.

"Yeah, we wanna play!" echoed two others.

"We *will*," I promised. "We will. But first we need to understand the game."

I explained about corner kicks and goal kicks and the goal box and when a goalie could use his hands, and I was just getting into offsides when I realized that the half of my team that didn't have their heads lolling and that weren't fidgeting uncontrollably or fighting were running somewhere in the grass with Ed chasing them.

"All right!" I said suddenly, catching Ed's pleading gaze as he returned to the group with three runners in tow. "Let's all stand up now and do some stretching!"

Lots of pre-exercise stretching was what the books had recommended. We stretched, and then we did light calisthenics, and then we ran as a group around the field, and by that time an hour and a half had gone by. Then I took out the soccer balls, gave a demonstration with Ed of proper kicking form when making a pass (we both were awful and uncoordinated beyond words; my only hope was that our observers were too young to realize it), then paired off the kids to practice their own passes.

Five minutes later the other coach approached. "Hey, you guys wanna scrimmage?"

"Maybe next time," I said. "We're working on fundamentals."

He grunted something and walked back to his team.

I had just lined up my own group to begin taking kicks on goal when I noticed cars beginning to arrive in bunches. Practice was over, parents were coming to retrieve their kids. I watched them walk from their vehicles, young mothers, mostly, a few fathers, one elderly fellow I guessed was a grandfather.

"Before anyone leaves," I shouted, "I have some handouts." I walked among them, hurriedly distributing photocopied pages summarizing the materials I'd covered in the lecture.

A few of the parents waved as they left, as did some of the kids; others simply walked off. I heard one kid whisper loudly, as he passed by with his good-looking mom, "This coach stinks! We didn't do anything!" The mom tactfully put a hand over his mouth and smiled at me pleasantly.

I had to wait about ten minutes before the stragglers finally got picked up, until at last Ed and Eric and I headed toward our own cars.

"A disaster, huh?" I said as we came to the curb.

Ed pursed his lips. "Can't tell," he said. "Don't know anything about soccer."

———
o

One day about two weeks later, Marie came into our cubicle and announced that Meissner wanted to see us all immediately in Conference Room F.

"I wonder what's up," I said to Boulot as we walked through the halls.

"He probably wants to give everyone a raise," said Boulot, grinning.

"One thing you know," said Shopper Jim, "management doesn't call sudden mass meetings to announce good news."

"Is that a rule?" I asked.

"Just an observation."

The conference room was twenty feet long and held a single large rectangular table. The box engineers were all seated before we filed in. Meissner was at the head of the table with Bent-Over-Bill next to him. "Close the door," he ordered Wonderboy, the last man in.

He waited until the rustling of papers and scraping of chairs subsided, then opened a folder in front of him. "This meeting is going to last about five minutes and cover two subjects. First subject: Top management of II, in their wisdom, has decided to institute a rating system for all degreed engineering personnel. A numerical value ranging from five to ten will be given each employee based on performance evaluations by supervisors and an assigned essay. Employees receiving eights or better will be considered on a fast track to management positions."

Boulot whispered to me, "If we do well, we can be like him."

"Why is the lowest number a five?" asked Kushner, who was taking copious notes on a lined pad.

"Because anyone rating less than that, we don't want around," answered Meissner. A few arms shot into the air, but he motioned them down. "There'll be a handout that'll answer all the questions." His eyes blazed. "Second subject, much more important. You all know Zack over there"—I felt my chin drop and eyes widen—"has been taking a survey of the currents drawn by each box. Well, the results are in and they're not good: Add up the total and it's more current than we've got, more than the supply." He scanned the faces. "We need to cut down, gentlemen. We need to cut down by twenty percent."

There was a long silence. Then:

"I don't know about the rest, but for the processor it's impossible," said Medieval Man. "I got a certain number of chips, they each draw a certain current—that's it. *Finito.* I might need even more chips before the Softheads finish."

"My box too—fixed," said A Boy Named Hsu. "The receiver has the minimum number of components, it needs every one, it already hardly draws anything. How do I cut down?"

"Ditto here," said Sklar. "The whole transmitter development is geared to maximizing efficiency, minimizing current. You can hope, but you can't count on it."

"I'm in the same position," rasped Bent-Over-Bill. "Same position. All the power supplies optimize efficiency. Optimize. You do what you can, but it's the same position."

Meissner's face had grown rigid; small muscles writhed near his temples. "So it can't be done, is that what you're all telling me?" Gazes dropped; the surface of the table suddenly became intensely interesting. "Maybe I should just go upstairs and tell Ingrassia that we're going to miss the AIR current spec, is that what I should do?"

No answer.

Meissner's face began to flush. "We are not even three months into the program and already, already, I am hearing we can't do what we promised. A problem presents itself, and our reaction—we just throw up our hands. Not even a pause, not a hesitation, not a thought about how it *might* be possible to solve. No, we just shrug and say, 'No way'."

Heads had bowed even farther. Lines of sight had dipped below the table, onto people's laps, their ties. All except

Shopper Jim, who was looking back and forth from Meissner to some kind of chart.

Meissner's face was now quite ruddy; his entire head had seemed to enlarge, as if expanding to accommodate the inrushing fluids. "Well, I will tell you something," he said. "That is unacceptable. You say the current can't be reduced— I say that is unacceptable. Unacceptable!" He pounded the table with his palm; I felt my heart race. "International Instruments will not be placed in a position of disgrace by engineers too lazy or too incompetent to solve a problem. And I personally will not tolerate a staff that would do that!"

Suddenly there was a knock on the door, which opened before anyone could respond. Gung Ho stuck his head inside.

"Sorry, interrupt. Mist' Sk'ar, phone call for you, he say very important."

Sklar looked up. "Well, can you—"

"For MES Technology."

Sklar looked back and forth from Gung to the red-glowing Meissner. For an instant, Sklar's muscles tensed as he started to rise from his chair . . . and then thought better of it. "Take his number," he said with unnatural calm. "Tell him I'll get back to him."

Gung closed the door.

"Therefore," resumed Meissner, "you *will* find a way to reduce the current draw. Each of you. Every box without exception will require less current. I don't care what it takes, how many hours of work, nights, weekends, holidays, you will exhaust every possibility on this." He was trembling. "Now, is that clear?"

Silence.

"Is it?"

Mumbled assents.

"Good. Then our meeting is concluded."

4

GAMES PEOPLE PLAY

Bureaucracy is a giant mechanism operated by pygmies.
—HONORÉ DE BALZAC

So in your view Meissner was not terrifically upset," I said to Shopper Jim when we'd returned to our cubicle.

"Oh, no," said Jim, "not really. See, you need to compare it to his normal demeanor, which is highly irate. He's just a pissed-off kind of guy."

Shopper Jim shrugged, then opened his notebook and pulled out the paper I'd observed him looking at during the meeting. He held it up and I could see now it was a color chart, gotten from some paint store, no doubt, twenty squares ranging from pale pink through deep crimson. "See," said Jim, "I compare this to his face. The brightest he reached was"—he indicated patch #14—"*blushing rose.* That's just concerned. When he gets to"—he pointed to square #19—"*volcanic flame,* then I'd consider some flesh-colored earplugs."

"So you don't think the spec on current is that big a problem."

"He doesn't think anything's a problem," chimed in Wonder-boy. "Zaremba, you have to understand—this guy doesn't care."

"It's true I don't give a nanoshit," said Jim, "but that is apart from the fact that specs are a self-canceling game. Especially military specs."

"In what way?" I asked.

"In all ways," said Boulot.

"Let me explain the genesis of Jim's Third Rule," said Jim. "Begin with the Air Force. The Air Force requires a certain performance for a system. But it knows, if it goes out for a bid with what it needs, the vendors are gonna whittle it down, say it's too tough, come back with exceptions in a lot of areas. So what it does, it tightens all the specs by twenty percent before they're released. Now the vendors take a look. The fact is, on any new system, especially one pushing the state of the art, when an engineer reads a spec, he has no fuckin' idea if he could do it or not. So the engineers try to be conservative and cut back twenty percent just like the Air Force figured. But the managers, they wanna win the job. They *have* to win the job or else they're gonna get laid off because there'll be nothing *to* manage. And they're worried about the competition. How'll it look if you say something can't be done and your rival promises to do it. So the managers browbeat and bully the engineers, who, being largely gutless sheep, eventually cave in. Except at the better companies, the ones with smarter managers and braver engineers. These bid the job with exceptions to the specs, and, because they're realistic and understand the difficulties, at a higher price.

"Now the Air Force evaluates the responses. Cheaper and no exceptions versus expensive and many exceptions. Naturally, being a major bureaucracy and wanting very much to believe in Santa Claus and the Tooth Fairy, they choose cheaper and no exceptions. Now move ahead two years.

Cheaper and No Exceptions finally admits it can't meet the spec—it's over by twenty percent—plus the price it estimated is too low. It pleads, cajoles, threatens even to go out of business. The Air Force looks at its options: Two years have gone by; to start off with somebody else, somebody who might not even do any better, is unthinkable. And besides—let's face it, they didn't need that extra twenty percent anyway. It was padding! They hem and haw, give Cheaper and No Exceptions a hard time, but eventually relax the specs and permit an upward adjustment in price. Now, of course, Expensive and Many Exceptions is indignant, but what can they do? By this time they've either learned their lesson and are busy lying like crazy on the next proposal, or they're out of business."

He grinned. "Thus, Jim's Third Rule: You can't make anything, at least not to spec." He paused. "Of course, Jim's Fourth Rule very often saves the day."

"The fourth rule being . . ." I prompted.

"You can't measure anything. Turns out, when you really deeply investigate the accuracies and errors involved in microwave measurements, most of the time no one can determine whether something meets spec or not. Least of all the military. So this works well for all sides."

"He's got everything figured out," said Wonderboy. "The only thing he can't explain is why he's not running the company."

"It's because I don't want to," said Shopper Jim.

———
o

We got our uniforms the second week in October, black shorts and orange shirts with ironed-on numbers and QUEENS COUNTY SAVINGS BANK in tiny letters on the back. The kids were extremely excited about the outfits—fighting and jockeying for position as I handed them out, showing far more enthusiasm than in any of the practices. I myself had a hard time imagining the cheer: *Go Bank!* or something equivalent.

Our first game was a week later on a crisp, sunny autumn Saturday at three P.M. It was a home game on the fields of Shoreview Middle School and the parents were out in force, arrayed along the chalked sidelines, seated on the grass or multicolored lawn chairs, split into distinct factions: the Queens County Bank people and the Sevarino's Hardware people. The Sevarino's coach was the guy I'd declined to scrimmage against at our first practice. I felt at an immediate disadvantage: I pictured droves of hairy-armed, blue-collar Sevarino workers easily whipping any number of timid bank clerks.

"All right, let's take some goal kicks!" I yelled to my team as I dumped a bag of soccer balls onto the grass. Ten minutes later the game began. Within a minute, Sevarino's had scored, three of their speedy little forwards bunching up to dribble through my entire team and ultimately punch it past our pudgy, immobile goalie, Kevin.

"That's okay, Kevin!" I shouted. "Don't worry about it."

"He let in a goal," called our center forward, Michael Hoffman, as if no one else were aware of it.

"The *team*," I called to Michael. "The *team* gave up the goal."

"But he didn't even try for it," said Michael, which was true.

"All right, let's get it back!" shouted Ed, my assistant.

The Sevarino's parents were cheering crazily. Their team scored the next time by leaving a "hanger," a kid who remained back near our goal while our team was taking the ball past midfield going the other way. The ball got nudged loose by a defender, kicked ahead a few times by a knot of Sevarinos, then finally reached the "hanger," who, unguarded (or un*marked,* as the soccer books called it), easily put it past our goalie.

"He let in *another* goal," called Michael.

"He was offsides!" I said to Ed.

"Yeah, but didn't you say there *was* no offsides for these kids because the league felt they couldn't understand the rule?"

"Well . . . yes, but . . . but . . . it's not fair to take advantage of that. It's teaching them the wrong thing."

"Let's get it back!" shouted Ed.

At the quarter, down 3–0, I switched positions for my team, inserting the kids who'd had to sit out the first period, moving others around. I'd planned it all out meticulously beforehand: Each kid would play several positions; everyone would get the same treatment regardless of skill. I put our goalie, Kevin, at center fullback, put Michael in goal. The second quarter began.

"Look at that," noted Ed regarding Sevarino's, "he's keeping his team exactly the same, except for two fullbacks."

I shrugged. "He wants to win."

A minute later we were down 4–0, a cluster of forwards and halfbacks overwhelming Kevin and barreling the ball past a diving Michael.

"Let's get it—"

"Don't," I said to Ed, putting my arm on his shoulder.

He nodded. Sevarino's scored twice more before the referees blew the whistle for halftime. A man carrying two plastic bags came over to where my team was seated on the sidelines.

"Juice," he said, pulling out paper cups from one of the bags and two plastic containers from the other. I helped him dispense the liquid. "I'm Michael's father, by the way," he said.

"Hi."

"Looks like we're gettin' beat pretty good."

"So it would seem."

"You know why?"

I knew he would tell me, no matter what.

"Because they're all bunching up on the ball and powering it through. We need more of our kids on the ball to hold 'em off."

"It's the wrong way to play," I said. "I'm trying to teach them position, to move in lines."

"But we're getting killed!" said the man, spilling one of the drinks.

I scrambled positions again in the third quarter; Sevarino's made only minor changes. We were behind in the final period 9–0 when Michael, from a halfback position, took the ball most of the way down Sevarino's right sideline. I could see his father running alongside him outside the chalk stripe, red-faced, shouting instructions ("Left! Left! Cut back! Go right!") while Kevin, now at center forward, puffed along behind. Just outside the goalie box Michael stopped and took a kick, which the Sevarino's goalie easily blocked. Kevin, meanwhile, had tripped and was lying on a patch of dirt ten yards behind.

"Michael had no help!" yelled his father, as I ran onto the field to tend to the weeping Kevin.

The league was supposed to issue first-aid kits to the coaches (it said so in the handouts they gave us), but of course they never had, so I'd bought my own at a local pharmacy. I dipped a piece of gauze into my water bottle and cleaned a mixture of dirt and bright red blood off Kevin's left knee.

"I know it hurts," I said softly, "but you'll be fine."

He struggled to control his sobs, puffy cheeks streaked with perspiration and tears. For the first time I noticed a hint of epicanthic fold in his eyelids: Somewhere in his background was Asian blood.

"You did fine," I said. "You held your position."

A few of the other kids had formed a circle around us and were staring. "All right, everybody," I said, "he's okay. Nothing to see. Go back to your spots."

They gradually dispersed. Watched by the referee, I daubed

some Bacitracin from my kit on Kevin's knee, then covered it with a Band-Aid. "You're all set," I said.

"Thank you, Mr. Coach," he responded.

"You wanna come out, take a rest?"

He hesitated, then shook his head.

I nodded to the ref. "Then we're ready to go."

The final score was 10–0. At the end of the game the two teams lined up and shook hands, as is the custom. "Sorry to run up the score," said the other coach, as we met at the end of the lines. "I mean, I couldn't tell them not to try, could I?"

"You did a great job," I said.

My team began to scatter. "Don't forget, next practice Tuesday!" I yelled.

"Don't be sad, Coach," said Scot, whose mother wore four-inch heels when she picked him up at practices. (Her paths across the grass were like a cultivator's: ideal for seeding.)

"I'm fine, Scot," I said. "We'll improve."

Alan Gunderson, the tallest kid on my team, pulled away from his father's hand. "Coach, you know what meteorites are?"

"Well, I—"

"God's turds," he said, then ran to catch up to his parent.

Ed and I began gathering in the practice soccer balls and then I told him it would be okay if he and Eric left, I'd finish taking down our goal net and pack it away. He seemed relieved. I walked over to the goal and began uprooting the hooked plastic stakes that anchored the net to the ground. I glanced up once and saw most of the parents had departed, gone to their cars at the edge of the field. Finally, I rose, started to reach toward the horizontal bar to remove the masking tape that held the net top—and realized I was too short. I crouched, leapt, caught on to the bar with one hand, managed to tear off two pieces of tape. The parent who'd put the

net up had been thorough (probably an engineer); I saw I'd
have to repeat the process at least four times.

When I came down from my third jump I heard a voice
behind me.

"I want to thank you."

I turned to look around.

"I'm Kevin's mom."

She was in the process of standing up, having just knelt to
check Kevin's leg. To my amazement, I recognized Lilah Li,
the girl from my orientation session in Human Resources.

"You're . . . Hi."

"Hi."

"Did you say—"

"Ya, I'm sorry I didn't get to talk to you before this. I've
been working late nearly every day. My neighbor's been taking
him to the practices."

"Oh . . . oh."

"I saw how you took care of him. I wanted to run out onto
the field, but, you know boys, even at this age, to have their
mother show any concern—he would've never forgiven me.
Am I right, Kevin?"

"Mr. Coach did a good job," said the boy.

"Yes. A very good job," echoed Lilah. She was wearing tight
jeans and a man's plaid shirt; her hair was tied back with a
blue scrunchie. She was so beautiful I could barely speak.
"And something else," she continued. "You put him up
front . . . and left him there even though you were losing by a
big score." She swallowed noticeably and her eyes seemed to
widen. "That was—that showed me something."

"I just let 'em play," I said awkwardly. "They all paid the
same registration fee."

She began moving away. "The other coach seemed to feel
differently."

I shrugged. I leapt to tear the last piece of tape off the net and it came down around my ankles. "Kevin's dad here?" I asked, for reasons I could not imagine.

She was fifteen feet away. "Kevin doesn't have a dad."

I stopped to gather up the net. "Sorry," I said, not knowing if I should be, if the guy had died, or divorced her, or just left, or if Kevin's conception had been immaculate.

" 'Bye, Mr. Coach," said Kevin.

" 'Bye," I called.

"Maybe I'll see you at work," called Lilah.

I rose. "I'll look for you," I said. I watched them walk all the way to Lilah's Corolla, their shadows rippling in the waning October sun, until I was alone in the middle of the field.

―
o

Whispering Bill assigned Boulot and me to handle work on the AIR power supplies. We would re-engineer them, where possible, to produce higher currents and we would design racks of Special Test Equipment, STEs, that would enable production-scale quantities to be tested efficiently.

"Gotta order the parts first," breathed Whispering Bill.

"But we 'ave no design," said Boulot.

"Parts have a three-month lead time," said Bill. "Can't build anything without parts." He coughed several times.

"But eet makes no sense."

"Well . . . I agree," gasped Bill. "But Meissner says we gotta order the parts. It's on his milestone chart."

Boulot threw up his hands, turned in my direction. "You see 'ow eet works. Eet's like that game—what is that game?— the retarded man . . ."

"You think Meissner's retarded?" rasped Bill, bending over now.

"He means Simple Simon," said Wonderboy, who'd been

eavesdropping. Wonderboy always seemed to be listening in on everyone's conversations.

"Yes, yes, Sample Seemon," affirmed Boulot. " 'Order parts'—no one does anything because it makes no sense. Anton *says,* 'Order parts'—then we jump because 'ee 'as to fill some box on 'ees stupeed chart."

"Just do it," said Bill, and left the cubicle.

"This was not the way you learned in school, eh?" said Boulot to me. The question was rhetorical. "First you order parts. Then you do a design. Then you decide what you are trying to make." He laughed, tugged at his tie to loosen it, then rotated it on his neck so it hung between his shoulder blades. "This ees 'ow I dress from now on," he said. "This ees 'ow we do things at International Instruments." He undid his belt and removed it, rethreaded it through his pants loops so the buckle rested just above his ass. He shrugged. "Now, we proceed."

Over the next few days I worked with Boulot to create new parts lists. We began with old designs from previous projects, the designs, in fact, that had been bid for the present job. Boulot went over the schematics with me, spreading them out on his desk, explaining the functions of each transistor, resistor, capacitor, and coil, making rough estimates of new parts. He was very tutorial, very professorish, and described the circuits in a clear, intuitive way.

"Take your plus fifteen. You put in *vingt-huit*—twenty-eight volts, you want fifteen volts out. Now, if thees twenty-eight is, maybe, twenty-nine, twenty-seven, sometheeng not exact, you still want fifteen out. Your output current goes from one hundred milliamps to five hundred milliamps, you still want fifteen volts out. So. To do thees, you need a transistor"—he pointed—"thees one. You see, thees current gets more, it puts more voltage 'ere"—he indicated the base terminal—"you 'ave more current 'ere, and so from the collector to emitter, 'ere, you 'ave a lower voltage drop. You see?"

"Feedback."

"Yes! Feedback! You sense"—it sounded like *sants*—"what is 'appening, and you compensate. We go through eet." And he wrote out the equations describing the voltage drops and currents around the circuit.

It was like being back in school with one of those rare enthusiastic professors, someone who took a pure, childish delight, not in his own vast knowledge but in the elegance of what he was showing you. And there was a lot to know, more than just the *regulation* Boulot was describing and the *ripple* I'd learned about in my electronics classes—the amount of residual alternating voltage that remained superimposed on the direct voltage output—but other things that could cause subtle malfunctions.

"The problem," said Boulot, "ees that feedback can be negative, as I 'ave explained, or positive, which can cause the circuit to oscillate, produce a 'igh frequency. That is very bad. Interferes wiz everything."

"How do you tell if it's going to oscillate?"

Another thirty minutes of explanation. Referral to textbooks. I'd taken circuits courses in my junior year, including feedback circuits, but retained mainly the odd names—Nyquist's criterion, Bode plots, Nichols charts—and lost much of the sense. Feedback could vary continuously, not only in strength (amplitude) but in the angle at which it added to the original signal. Its exact nature depended on how every component in the circuit would behave at different frequencies, a complex phenomenon, particularly since some of the components had values that depended on the strength of the very signals they were influencing.

"What does this mean?" I asked, pointing to a notation on

one of the circuit diagrams. There was a little rectangular box next to a capacitor. The lettering in the box read, *OMIT B.*

"I donno," said Boulot, shrugging. "Maybe someone, 'ee thought you don't need zat part."

Toward week's end we began to build a new list of components, "based," according to Boulot, "on nussing, not a design, not a calculation, not a single test in zee lab. Imagined from a dream."

The form for the parts list was called a BM, Bill of Materials. "Bowel Movement," commented Wonderboy. "That's what it really is."

" 'Ee never deals wiz zees things," said Boulot. " 'Ee 'as no bowel movement."

Wonderbury was in the Systems Group, the department responsible for the overall performance of a system and its function and interaction with all the other equipment—friendly and enemy—on the battlefield. The Systems Group mainly did computer simulations and studies; Wonderbury was the liaison to the AIR project's Radio Frequency (RF) Group.

"On the contrary, here's mine," said Wonderboy, indicating a D-sized chart on the wall over his desk. The chart listed each component in the transmitter and receiver chains, along with the power levels, noise levels, and signal distortions they produced. The final column showed cumulative results from input to output.

"Looks like that tells you everything," I noted.

"Everything," echoed Wonderboy.

"Nothing," said Shopper Jim, looking up from whatever it was he was working on. "It's all lies."

"The computer doesn't lie," said Wonderboy. "I can't help it if you guys can't put the right components together."

Shopper Jim started to say something, then closed his

mouth midthought. "You're not worth the energy," he commented instead, returning to his calculations.

"Meissner judges the BM by weight," said Boulot. He held up the single sheet we'd completed. "Ten grams will not do eet."

"I once had a BM that weighed a pound and a quarter," I noted brightly. I proceeded to explain how in my early weeks I'd weighed my fecal output.

"So what?" Wonderboy said. "I've taken dumps that weighed *five* pounds."

"Wow," I said. "That seems . . . Jesus. Did you piss when you shat? Piss can be very heavy."

"No piss," declared Wonderboy

Once again, Jim looked up. He pulled a bill from his wallet. "Wonderbutt, twen'ny says that's impossible, even for someone as full of shit as you."

"I see," said Wonderboy. "And how do you propose to prove your case—by shoving measuring instruments up my ass?"

"Please," said Jim, "we're engineers here, we'll settle the issue by calculations."

"You can't *calculate* my particular capability."

"Of course not. We'll simply take average sizes and volumes and assume your own capacity isn't more than, say, three times that. Does that sound reasonable? The point is to show that a five-pound shit simply is not possible, even for a systems engineer."

Wonderboy ran a Chapstick over his lower lip. "You also need density information. How you gonna get that?"

Shopper Jim raised his eyebrows. "Let's assume that feces is on the borderline of floating. We've all had shit that floats, we've all had shit that sinks, sometimes even within the same batch."

"Mine rises in the air," said Boulot.

"Now," continued Jim, "if a piece of shit has its top surface tangent to the water—i.e., if the water volume displaced is equal to the volume of the turd—then by Archimedes' principle the weight of displaced water equals the weight of the turd. . . . and so the density is about that of water. I propose this as a reasonable approximation." He glanced around the room. "Agreed?"

Wonderboy said nothing. Gung Ho and another tech had entered the cubicle.

"So whaddaya say?" said Jim, thrusting his bearded chin under Wonderboy's smooth jaw. "You gonna back up your statement or just admit it's no more accurate than that chart on your wall?"

Wonderboy hesitated, looked around, noted the half dozen pairs of eyes focused on him.

"Three times average," repeated Jim. "Anywhere in there, you win. That's an average-*size* guy taking his maximum shit."

Wonderboy exhaled. "All right," he said finally, "let's do the numbers."

Suddenly I felt anxious. I presumed Jim was basing his judgment on my reported pound-and-a-quarter, but what if something was wrong? Suppose the scales had been off, or not sufficiently precise, or I'd misread them, or . . . or my shit capacity was simply abnormally low. My technical credibility with my peers would be greatly diminished.

"Let's begin with diameter," said Wonderboy.

Shopper Jim extended a meaty index finger. "How about . . . mmm . . . three-quarters of an inch?"

Wonderboy pulled a metal ruler from his desk. "How about inch and a half?"

"No way."

There was silence. Then one of the techs, a balding late-fiftyish man named Ben Nussbaum, said, "Gimme the ruler."

Wonderboy handed it over.

"I'll be back," said Nussbaum.

Ten minutes later he returned to the cubicle. "Inch and an eighth," he announced proudly, proffering the ruler back to Wonderboy.

"Did you wash?" asked Wonderboy. Then, not waiting for an answer, he added, "Put it on the desk." He returned his attention to Shopper Jim. "Nussbaum is shorter than average. He has a smaller intestine."

"I'm five-ten," said Nussbaum.

"He's taller than you," said Jim to Wonderboy. He narrowed his eyes. "Tell you what, I'll give you inch-and-a-quarter, how's that? Remember, the volume goes as the square of the diameter, so this is a tremendous concession."

Wonderboy considered. "Accepted," he said finally. "Now, what about the lengths?"

There was a moment of silence. "Can call ribrary," volunteered Gung Ho. "Reference desk have everything."

"Excellent!" said Jim. He turned to Wonderboy. "You want to monitor?" He held the earpiece halfway between Wonderboy and himself as he dialed Information.

When the reference librarian came on, Jim introduced himself. "Hi, this is Dr. Charles Fogblatt of Cornell Medical Center. I'd like to get some information on the large intestine."

As we all stood there awaiting a response, I thought, Look at them—at us—how we approach a problem. This casual disagreement over shit, this "investigation," these engineering approximations, were going to cost International Instruments hundreds of dollars. It was the work of crazy people.

There was a three-minute delay, then Jim began relaying aloud the relevant phrases.

"Reference source is the *CIBA Collection of Medical Illustrations*, volume 3 . . . four segments of the large intestine . . . only two contribute immediately to fecal output . . . descending colon averages twenty to twenty-five centimeters in length . . . sigmoid colon averages forty centimeters in adults . . . rectum simply stores the feces . . ." Another two sentences, then, "Thank you, that was terrific. Our bowel patients are in your debt."

He hung up. "Twenty-five plus forty, sixty-five centimeters," he said. "Time to rock-and-roll."

Boulot, holding a calculator, stepped to the cubicle's blackboard.

"Density of water is 62.4 pounds per cubic foot," said Jim.

Boulot wrote it on the board.

"Divide by 1,728 cubic inches per cubic foot."

Boulot wrote; *62.4/1728 = .0361 lbs. / in³*.

"Volume of the intestine equals length times pi D squared over four. Equals 3.14 times 1.25 squared over four, then times length. Make sure to convert 65 centimeters to inches."

Boulot fingered the buttons on his calculator, then wrote, *31.4 in³*, on the board. My heart leapt as he multiplied the final two numbers. "One-point-one-three pounds is the average," he announced. "Three times average would be 3.39 pounds." He turned to Wonderboy solicitously. "I don't sink you could 'ave sheet five pounds. Not unless you were 'aving a very bad day." He laughed.

"My twenty . . ." said Jim, extending a hand in Wonderboy's direction.

"I don't concede," said Wonderboy. "I know what I did. The assumptions we used must've been wrong." He stood up.

"Hey, we had a deal."

"True, but the calculation doesn't prove you won." He stalked from the room.

"Didn't really think he'd pay," said Jim. "But it was fun to see a man who always takes theoretical results over measured ones forced to reverse his position."

―――
○

The following Friday, all the AIR engineers turned in their BMs at a department meeting with Bernie Bebber, the director of purchasing. We sat at a giant walnut table in Conference Room C, this in the carpeted management area on the second floor. The management wing had a different feel to it than the engineering and manufacturing parts of the building; the walls were paneled wood, the lighting was recessed and softer, there were a far greater number of visible females.

I noticed Bent-Over-Bill wincing just before we began. "You okay?" I asked.

"Oh, I'm fine, fine," said Bill. "Have some testicular nodules is all. Several of 'em. Nothing I'm not used to."

I was about to question him further when Meissner called the meeting to order. He flipped through our sheets, then handed them to Bebber, a potbellied, thick-lipped man whose breath came in audible puffs.

"We all understand these are preliminary," said Meissner, "but unless we order parts now, we'll fall hopelessly behind schedule."

Parts for military systems, unlike those in commercial devices, were frequently specialty items not kept in stock by the manufacturer. Since vendors had to fabricate them from scratch, often to tight specs that required extensive testing, it was quite common for some components to have 12-to-16-week delivery times.

Bebber began poring through the sheets. "The one-ohm thin-film resistors," he puffed. "Whose are those?"

Kushner looked around. "Uh, I think that's ours."

"You need those?"

"Well, uh, see, I've done some stability calculations at low frequencies and—"

"Look, I don't give a shit about the technical stuff, I don't understand that crap anyway. You need it, you need it. You got a vendor?"

"Uh, well . . ." He nudged Sklar, who was engrossed in writing something on a notepad. "Marv . . ."

"Marvin, do we have a vendor for the thin-film resistor?" said Meissner sharply.

Sklar's head snapped up. "Not yet," he said. "We're making inquiries."

"These are gonna be hard to get," said Bebber.

"What about the output transistors?" said Meissner.

"On the list," said Sklar, grinning. "We'll be fine . . . unless Motorola sells 'em to someone else."

"We'll get the Air Force to strafe their factories," said Meissner.

Bebber continued down the lists, questioning sources on particular items, but for the most part nodding his head until he came to the Power Supply area. "The J-leaded one-mic tantalums," he said. "Whose are those?"

Boulot and I raised our hands; Whispering Bill's went up an instant later.

"Those are going to be very rough," said Bebber. "Very rough. We need those?"

Boulot emitted a nasalized Gaelic chuckle. "Who can say? We put down everysing. How are we supposed to know? We don't even know what currents we will draw. We have no design."

Bebber looked at Meissner, who immediately turned to face Boulot.

"Edouard, we have *had* this discussion. Do you or do you not need those tantalums?"

" 'Ow can I answer zat rationally?"

"Then answer it irrationally!" Meissner's face had begun to

show red. I saw Shopper Jim slip his color chart out from the pages of his notebook.

"You want an irrational answer? 'Ere: We order every fucking part we can sink of because we 'ave no fucking idea what we may need. Zere's your answer!"

"Get out," said Meissner quietly, face at least 18 or 19. "No one talks like that here."

Boulot rose and strode to the door. "Fine. I am 'appy to leave." He shut the door behind him.

There was an instant's silence before Meissner turned to me. "Now, do you need the tantalums?"

"Uh, well, yes, I think we do. We definitely need the one-microfarad to supply the surge for the power amp, and Edouard said the tantalums have the lowest parasitic resistance."

Meissner turned to Whispering Bill.

"Need the low resistance," winced Bill.

"There you are," Meissner said to Bebber.

"Those are going to be rough," said Bebber. He belched. "Those are a challenge."

---
o

The Saturday following the meeting, Kushner invited Shopper Jim and myself to dinner at his mother's house. My guess was that he'd meant to ask only me, but Jim had approached the lunch table just as Kushner was popping the question and Kushner, unfailingly polite, had felt compelled to include Jim.

Kushner and his mom lived in a Colonial-style house about eight miles west of International Instruments. Mrs. Kushner was a small, energetic woman with neatly lacquered gray hair.

"I'm honored that Warren would bring home two of his colleagues," she said after the introductions. Then added conspiratorially, even though Warren was present, "He never tells me anything, never shares his work life. After all, I'm his mother, what do I know? I'll bet your mother knows what you do, Zachary."

"Not really," I said pleasantly.

"Mine's dead," added Shopper Jim.

Kushner's mom smiled uneasily; I could tell she didn't know quite what to make of our comments. "Well," she said breathily, "are we all ready for dinner?"

"I want to show them my room first," said Kushner.

We climbed up a flight of stairs to the second floor. It felt, somehow, like the house was too small and delicate for our presence, like it was a dollhouse invaded by human-sized beings.

"This is mine," said Kushner as we entered a small bedroom. There was a single bed, a walnut dresser, a matching desk with a populated chessboard on it, worn light blue carpet. On the walls were a Scotch-taped poster of Patrick Ewing, diplomas from Westbury High School and the Polytechnic Institute of Brooklyn, and a Certificate of Participation in the Westbury Marching Band.

"You play an instrument?" I asked.

"Tuba," he said. "I was terrible. I liked to march, but I could barely play a note."

"You need to move out," declared Shopper Jim.

"Why?" said Kushner. "You think so? I don't pay any rent."

"You need to move out," said Jim.

Kushner closed the door. The three of us seemed to fill the whole room. Kushner dropped to his knees, fished for something under the bed, finally emerged. "Look," he said.

It was a large nock-hockey set.

"Wanna play?"

Jim and I just stared at each other.

Kushner turned the set on edge, loosened two wing nuts, and removed the back panel to reveal a narrow hollow. Inside were four magazines. Kushner removed two, *Bare* and *Pink Pussies,* and handed them to us. "Whaddaya think?"

I thumbed a few of the pages. "Nice," I said.

"You need to move out," said Jim.

There was a knock at the door. "Warren?"

Kushner, in a spasm of energy, seized the two magazines and stuffed them back in the set. "Ma, don't—"

The door opened and his mother leaned in. "I just wanted to tell your friends that dinner will get cold unless we eat it now," she said sweetly.

Kushner stood in front of the set, blocking it from her view. "I was showing them my nock-hockey," he said. "We'll be down in a minute."

She shut the door.

"Case, I believe, closed," said Shopper Jim.

The dinner was pleasant enough; I imparted the basic background info all parents require—graduated so-and-so, lived in such-and-such state, only child, father a dentist, mother a teacher, no steady girlfriend.

"That's lovely," said Mrs. Kushner. She turned to Jim. "And how about you, Jim?"

"Cal Tech, Arizona, no sibs or parents, divorced." He smiled.

"I see," said Kushner's mom uncertainly.

Actually, this was more than Shopper Jim had ever told me, and I was quite impressed by the Cal Tech credential, unless, of course, he was lying, in which case it was an impressive lie.

"And how long have you been at International Instruments, Jim?" said Kushner's mom.

Jim chomped down on a roll; a dozen crumbs fell into his hand. "Year and a half."

"And do you like it?"

For a moment, Jim stopped chewing and looked directly at her. "Mrs. Kushner, engineering is a horrible occupation. No one in his right mind *likes* it. I do it for the money. I don't work for II and I don't want to. Someday soon I'm planning to leave."

Mrs. Kushner sat up, looking very much personally offended, "Well . . . despite what you say, I'm sure not everyone feels that way." She turned to Kushner. "I know Warren doesn't. How about you, Zack?"

I really wasn't in the mood to tell her what she wanted to hear, but neither did I wish to make her uncomfortable. "I've only been at it a few months," I temporized.

"Well, I know Warren is very enthusiastic. Am I right, War?"

Kushner's eyes seemed defocused. When he responded, it sounded almost like he was thinking, not talking aloud. "I wanna be good at something. I'm a hard worker. I want people to say, 'He's a good engineer.' I'd like to do one thing, just one thing . . . well." He quickly looked around, then down at his plate.

"He's even asked me to help him with his Goals and Aspirations essay."

"Ma-aaa . . ."

"His what?" said Jim.

"It's a thing you're supposed to write for the Fast Track Management Program," said Kushner. "Ma, he's a Job Shopper, they didn't give him one."

"What about you, Zachary?" asked his mom. "Do you have one?"

"I might," I said. "I may've lost it."

"Well, Warren has been working quite diligently on his. I help him mostly with the grammar—you know how engineers have trouble with English."

"Illiterates, most of us," said Jim.

"Barely speak," I added.

Kushner's mom turned to Jim. "I really don't understand why you're so negative," she said. "I think engineering is a marvelous profession. I was reading the other day where they project a shortage of engineers into the year 2000."

Jim grinned. "Shortage of engineers?"

"That's what the article said."

Jim paused to bite into a seeded roll. "Mrs. Kushner, you have to understand there really is no such thing as a shortage, only a shortage at a price. The people who put out those statistics have a vested interest in a steady supply of cheap technical talent. If there really were a shortage of engineers, our salaries would have gone up faster than inflation—and they haven't."

"Excuse me," said Mrs. Kushner, standing suddenly. "I've just got to check the dessert." She quickly disappeared into the kitchen.

"You're a very discouraging person," said Kushner to Jim.

"I hope so," he responded.

Going home, I sat with Jim silently in the car. (He'd driven.) I thought about Kushner in that little room of his, working on his essay, glancing up at his high school tuba picture, masturbating to magazines in his nock-hockey set. He'd tried to be open and friendly and revelatory, and Jim had been . . . Jim. I liked Jim, thought him amusing and knowledgeable, but his Kurt Vonnegut professional cynicism could grow wearing. I'd become an engineer because I thought there were rewards beyond the purely monetary. All professions had insecurities, and it was easy to be facile and breezily critical about what was wrong with yours. At that moment, held up against Kushner's Goals and Aspirations, Jim's nickel wisdom seemed like so much glib prattle.

———
o

"Preliminary Design Review," said Meissner at the Friday status meeting. "Two weeks. The Air Force will be here, people. Will we?" He looked carefully from face to face.

5

OF PDRS AND PIDOOMAS

Six phases of a project: (1) Wild enthusiasm,
(2) Disillusionment, (3) Panic, (4) Search for the
guilty, (5) Punishment of the Innocent, (6) Praise
and Honor for the nonparticipants
—POSTER FOUND IN MANY ENGINEERING CUBICLES,
AUTHOR UNKNOWN

Kushner and I were in the cashier's line in the cafeteria, he
with his bean salad and small yogurt, me with my chicken
sandwich, absolutely plain, when she came toward us. She was
wearing a thigh-high, body-clinging orange dress, sheer black
stockings, heels, and an ocher ribbon in her hair that tied the
ebony strands back into a short bun. For a moment, on her
way, she twisted sideways to acknowledge someone behind her,
so that the bulbous outlines of her breasts and ass strained and
stretched the knitted material.

"This is better than one of my magazines," said Kushner as
we drew nearly even with the cash register. "Is there a wet spot
near my fly? I think I just came."

"Tell people you spilled something," I said, quite stimulated myself.

We paid our respective $4.89 and $3.52 and headed toward
a table.

"Hi," said Lilah, intersecting our path. She smiled up at me with perfect white teeth. "I'm glad I spotted you. I wanted to ask you something."

"Oh . . . well . . . how are you?" I said lamely. My hands were full of tray. I indicated Kushner with my chin. "Uh, Lilah, this is Warren Kushner. War, this is Lilah Li."

Kushner's face had gone from his usual pasty white to very near transparent. He nodded pleasantly enough, but seemed unable to actually speak.

"You have a sec?" I asked. "Come join us."

She glanced at her watch. "I have about three minutes. But . . . sure." She followed us to an empty table, and we all sat down.

"You still brooding about Sunday?" she asked.

We'd lost our fourth straight soccer game by a fourth straight shutout, 6–0. Both kids and parents had now sorted themselves into two groups: those who were angry and thought me incompetent as a coach and those who felt sorry for me and thought me incompetent as a coach.

"I passed 'brooding' after the first week," I said. "I'm now into tortured self-doubt and catatonic depression."

"Oh, poor boy," she said, reaching over and patting my wrist. I've always been amazed at what the most trivial gesture made by an attractive female can evoke—at least in me—under the right circumstances. Kushner had been kidding about ejaculation, but I felt a real instant erection push up against my trousers. How fortunate I was to be seated, with a tabletop between my groin and terminal embarrassment. I wasn't surprised at the numbness in my legs: My circulatory system had divided my entire blood supply between my face and my penis.

"Is it warm in here?" I asked, brushing at my forehead.

"I hear the plant heating system is always broken," said Lilah.

"I don't think anything works in this building," I tempo-rized. "I know the vending machines don't."

"Really? But aren't they new?"

"Absolutely. Installed only last month by Foremost Foods. But have you ever tried them?" She shook her head. "They don't work. I've put in money for coffee three different times, got only hot water."

"But that's awful. What'd you do?"

"Oh, the sensible thing. Kicked the machine until I'd bro-ken every toe, then beat at it until my palms were bloody, then sat down and wept." She grinned. "Actually, all you do is fill out a form and give it in to Human Resources and you get your money back . . . but I wanted the coffee. So now I've returned to plan A." She waited. "I make it at my desk with an immersion heater."

"Very resourceful," she said.

I glanced over at Kushner. He wasn't eating, wasn't even moving, certainly wasn't speaking.

"What I wanted to ask you," said Lilah, "was, if you wanted, if you felt it would be of any use—I found this soccer videotape, a kind of training tape for kids—anyway, I spotted it in a video store, it was only $7.95, and, uh, I bought it. I thought Kevin would like it, but then, I was thinking, maybe the whole team might want to see it and, well, if you'd want, I could have every-one over my place and we could show it . . . if you'd want."

The sound of her voice, her face, her tongue flicking around inside her little curclicued orange lips, had really left me quite paralyzed by now, probably as much as Kushner. "That . . . yes . . . sure . . . that would be nice," I croaked, my voice, to my own ears, an exact replica of Whispering Bill's. "It's great of you to offer. I . . . I'll call the team."

"Terrific!" she said, standing up. "Next Saturday okay?

Around six P.M.?" I nodded. She moved away from the table. "See you then," she said brightly, and, nodding toward Kushner, added, "Nice meeting you."

And left.

It was nearly a minute before Kushner rcgained the power of speech. "You know her . . ." he said dazedly.

o

" 'Ee 'as, I donno, various 'ealth problems," said Boulot. We were staring at one of the Special Test Equipment panels that had just come back from the PAINT DEPARTMENT. Boulot, still dressed backward—tie knot between his shoulder blades, belt buckle at the crack in his butt—was talking about Whispering Bill. " 'Ee spends a tremendous amount of time in the 'ospital. Three years ago, 'ee was mugged, three guys, zey knife him across ze throat, after zat, 'ee talks in a whisper. Then two years ago, somesing 'appen to 'is back, I donno, somesing fell on eet, 'ee walks bent over. Then last year, 'is lung collapses, zen 'ee gets Guillain-Barré syndrome, 'ee is paralyzed for six months. 'Ee came back just before you arrive but I 'ear now 'ee has more problems."

"He said one of his testicles had nodules."

" 'Ee is a nice guy," said Boulot, "but 'ee must 'ave done somesing really bad long ago, because God is punishing 'im—not zat I believe in Her, of course."

We grabbed the panels and headed over to SPECIAL ASSEMBLIES, where they were beginning to put together our first STE. We were still missing many of the parts, of course, but the wiring harnesses were diagramed and ready to be fabricated. We walked down the long hallway past the CREDIT UNION, past the REPRODUCTION DEPARTMENT and the SECURITY AREA, turned left where the big defective vending machine squatted, then headed down another lengthy corridor past the medical forms rack, the MATERIALS REVIEW BOARD WING, the scale where I used to weigh myself, and the FIELD SERVICE WING. Finally, we turned right at the corridor that led to SPECIAL ASSEMBLIES.

On the way we passed RECEIVING, and Boulot paused at the window. " 'Ave you gotten a package for Edouard Boulot?" he asked the shirtsleeved man in the frame. " 'Eet would be from the Dale Company, a big resistor."

The man pursed his lips. Just behind him, taped to a wall, was a sign: *A lack of planning on your part does not constitute an emergency on our part.*

"For zee AIR job," added Boulot. "Job 2301-2."

The man seemed about to respond when suddenly a bell rang quite loudly. At once, a metal screen descended to fill the window frame. The man backed up several feet, sat down in a swivel chair, and rotated away from us.

"Excuse me . . ." said Boulot.

The man pulled out a *Newsday* from a nearby desk and began to thumb the pages.

" 'Aayy!" said Boulot.

No response.

"What's going on?" I asked.

"Ah, break time," said Boulot. "Zese people are union, some union sing, zat's the way eet is." He shrugged. " 'Ee won't do anysing for anuzzer fifteen minutes. We'll come back." He turned to leave, then called over his shoulder. "Hey, fuck your muzzer wiz a fire hose!" He laughed his nasal Gaelic laugh, then turned to me. " 'Ee would come and punch me, but 'ee can't, 'ee is on break."

More snickers, then we continued down the hall. We made a second stop at ELECTRONIC STOCK, a huge caged room with long aisles separating multitiered steel shelves packed with electrical components. A bald man at a peeling wooden desk looked up at our approach.

"We need forty-microfarad electrolytics," said Boulot. "One-hundred-fifty-volt tubulars, for zee AIR project STEs."

"Hold on," said the man. He began hitting the keys of a dun-colored desktop computer. "Fuckin' machine," he muttered, shaking his head. "Used to be, I had the book, took me a second. I could look everything up. Now . . . fuckin' machine . . . what was that voltage again?"

"One-fifty," said Boulot.

Suddenly the man's face brightened. "Yup, here we are. Sprague. Tubulars. Got eighteen left, no problem." He looked up. "Just give me the form, I'll pull 'em for you."

"I don't 'ave ze form," said Boulot. "But it's for zee AIR job, 2301."

"Gotta have a form," said the man.

"What form?" I asked.

"SWR," said Boulot. "Stock Withdrawal Request." He turned back to the man. "But I don't 'ave eet, what can I do? I ran out of zem."

The man shrugged. "Gotta have the form. You need forms, order them."

"All right, where do I order zem?"

"I got 'em."

"Okay, zen let me 'ave a few."

"Can't."

"But why?"

"I told you, anything you use from this room, you need a form."

Boulot rolled his eyes. "So you mean I need a form to order ze forms. . . ."

"Exactly."

"But ziss is fantastic—"

"Hey," said the man, "I didn't make the system. Maybe you could borrow one from somebody."

Boulot crossed his arms and clutched his shoulders. "Come," he said to me, "we better leave before . . . I don't know what I do."

We stepped out of the room and continued down the corridor. After a moment, Boulot said, "I will tell you what is zee strength of America. Zee strength of America lies in ignorance and apathy."

"I'm not sure I follow. . . ."

"Take ze French. We are a nasty race. Very nasty. Narrow-minded. Bigoted. Argumentative. Xenophobic. The worst traits of the bourgeoisie. But . . . stop an average Frenchman on the street and ask him to name five of his country's contemporary poets, and he can do it." The floor under our feet changed suddenly from asbestos tile to epoxy-painted concrete; we had entered the manufacturing area. Boulot smoothed one sleeve of his shapeless gray sweater, then looked up at me expectantly. "Can you?"

"Poets . . ."

"Living. Americans."

My mind flashed quickly to the few American poets I'd ever read or heard of: Poe, Sandburg, e. e. cummings, Emily Dickinson, and . . . was Thoreau a poet? I hesitated; engineers received meager education in the liberal arts.

Boulot grinned.

"Allen Ginsberg," I said.

He nodded. "That's one."

"Bruce Springsteen." He shook his head. We walked past racks of hanging smocks. Through a windowed door I could see a long room filled with wooden benches at which perhaps a hundred people—mostly blue-smocked women—were soldering electronic parts.

"But you see," said Boulot, "zese same people who know ze poets, zey cannot agree on anysing. *Anysing.* Zey argue, zey fight, zey curse, zey form zeir own political party, zey 'and out pamphlets, zey criticize ze government, zey criticize ze unions, management, business, utilities, students, foreign policy, everyone and everysing. Zere are ten million political groups, all very educated, very articulate, constantly grabbing each other's throats. And so ze country is paralyzed. It is in constant ferment, constant turmoil. It can barely keep from falling apart, and sometimes eet does fall apart.

"But in America . . . no. Ze people, zey are not interested. Ze government? Of course ze politicians are all corrupt, but zat is not our problem. We are more concerned wiz ze football game and Michael Jackson and thirty-five-inch TVs and ze barbecue on Sunday zan 'orrible boring economics and legislation. Let ze Democrats and Republicans fight it out, we go to ze movies. And so . . . ze country is stable, powerful, and productive." He sighed. "Almost makes me want to stay."

We passed the machine shop, a vast open area where gray-aproned men in goggles hunched over an array of lathes, drill presses, compressed air and vacuum lines, sheet-metal brakes, and oil-squirting, churning, numerically controlled milling machines.

Boulot put a hand on my shoulder. "You understand, I did not mean to insult you personally. I sink you yourself are very intelligent. And ze poets question was completely unfair."

I nodded sheepishly. "Why's that?" I asked as we paused in front of the SPECIAL ASSEMBLIES door.

"Because," said Boulot, "I don't sink America *has* five contemporary poets."

We went inside.

The SPECIAL ASSEMBLIES foreman was named McFarland, and right off he told Boulot the STE panels would be late. "You're lookin' at three weeks, minimum," he said, fondling the aluminum rectangles as if, under hand pressure and scrutiny, they would yield up some alien-monolith-type secret.

"Three—But why?" said Boulot. "I need zem by Monday."

"Main thing is, they gotta make the silkscreens—you know how backed up Screening is?—then I gotta get 'em drilled, then I gotta mount the parts. The last two, that's easy, but the screens . . ."

With a catlike move unexpected from a balding man in a sweater, Boulot reached out and snatched back the panels. From the corner of my eye I saw Shopper Jim enter the room.

"You know what?" said Boulot. "I make zem myself. I 'ave a stencil, I 'ave a drill, I get parts, I do everysing."

"Suit yourself," said McFarland.

Boulot turned to leave. Shopper Jim had just entered.

"See?" said Jim to me. "That's why engineers will never achieve the status of doctors."

"Because they have initiative . . . ?"

"You miss the point. Imagine a surgeon arriving at the operating room and being told by the head nurse that there weren't any scalpels left, the main overhead light was out, and the new supply of sutures wouldn't be in for two weeks. He'd just laugh, turn around, and walk out, right?"

"I suppose."

"But an engineer in the same position? No. An engineer would sharpen his own personal pocketknife, carry in three floor lamps from the lounge, raid his mother's sewing box for thin black thread . . . and then perform the operation on his own personal time. Admirable, no?"

"Well . . ."

"That's why we are where we are." He turned to Boulot. "By the way, Meissner was looking for you. He wanted to see you right away."

Boulot shrugged. " 'Ee wants to tell me what a good job I am doing."

We took the long walk, mostly in silence, back to the engineering section. Boulot declined to stop off at the RECEIVING window, even though it was open when we passed. "I get ze parts tomorrow," he said. "I allow myself only a limited number of stupidities per day."

"Shopper Jim said you have to make friends with all these people. Then they do things for you."

"But I don't *want* to be zeir friend," said Boulot. "I don't want to be *anyone's* friend. Why should I 'ave to do zat? Why don't zey just do zeir job?"

"Well . . . according to Jim, that's not how things work."

Three minutes later, we reached Meissner's office. "I be right out," said Boulot. He knocked once, then disappeared inside.

I lingered by the door. Presently, I heard the sound of rising voices, Boulot's and Meissner's. The words, though indistinct, were clipped and clearly angry. Another moment, and the door flew open. Both men were standing. Boulot with jaw tilted upward, hands in pockets, Meissner wild-eyed and face at color #19.

"End of discussion," said Meissner. "You understand that? End!"

"Oh, I understand very well!" said Boulot. "Very well."

"Good," said Meissner, muscles quivering high up near his right temple. "And another thing: You better get rid of that backwards tie shit before PDR."

Boulot stepped out into the corridor and Meissner slammed the door behind him.

"He doesn't seem like your favorite person," I commented as we headed back toward the cubicle.

"I 'ave a daughter," said Boulot. "Since my wife pass away I 'ave to drive her to school in zee mornings, and sometimes I am late, which makes heem very mad. All ze time, 'ee screams at me, I am used to eet. My daughter, she 'as been sick, I 'ad to spend time off to take care of her. 'Ee screams at me more, I don't care. Now, tomorrow, she ees in a little play in school, second grade, she is Dorothy in *Ze Wizard of Oz*. So I ask Whispering Bill, Can I 'ave off two hours to see 'er, and 'ee say, 'Yes, of course, but I 'ave to tell Meissner.' So now I 'ave my answer."

We reached our cubicle.

"But you know what? I am going to do eet anyway."

We entered the room.

"And you know what else? Someday, you will see, I am going to kill zat man." He brushed a wisp of hair back over his scalp. "I am a very tough guy, you know."

o

Eugene Baker, the one black kid on the team, held out both arms for me to inspect. "Which one you think is darker, Coach? The lef' or the right?"

"The right," I said, seeing no difference and choosing arbitrarily.

"Mos' people say the lef'," said Eugene.

We were in Lilah's apartment, the finished basement of a private house, really, that had been divided by a paneled wall into two fairly large, though somewhat dank, carpeted rooms. Along with thirteen other kids and three parents, Eugene and I were waiting for the soccer tape to begin.

"Here we go," said Lilah, pressing the start button on the VCR.

Prior to viewing the tape, I'd brought in five pizzas, and

Lilah had helped serve them on paper plates and we'd watched the kids do the things people that age do with food—drop it, fling it, stretch it, apply it to inappropriate orifices—until we and the other adults at last cleaned up. An image appeared on-screen: a group of kids in cleats and shorts, kicking a soccer ball at a netted goal while a male adult looked on. There was a slow zoom in on the adult, who turned as if just becoming aware of the camera. "Soccer is a great sport," he said, smiling, "but to enjoy it the most, there are a number of skills you need to master."

And so it went, a bit stilted and saccharine—show me a training film that isn't—but altogether not bad. There were good clear shots of the basic kicks (including the drop kick and even the bicycle kick), demonstrations of dribbling and marking techniques, a segment on heading, a segment on throw-ins, and even a pastiche on various penalties. The kids reacted in the usual dazed way—when I asked afterward if they'd liked it, they brayed a uniform, "Yesss"—but, of course, you never know with children what really sank in. (Actually, you never know this with adults either.)

On their way out, bundled in their heavy late-autumn clothes, a couple of them asked about certain things they'd seen.

"Are you gonna show us the bicycle kick, Coach?"

"No, Michael, I don't think so."

"Why not?"

"Because I can't do it." An idea struck me. "Why don't you ask your father to show you?" That would fix him.

"Okay," agreed Michael, stepping out the door.

Sean, the blond kid, asked, "What about that other kick? The one we did in practice last time."

"We did a lot of kicks, Sean."

"He means the *instinct* kick," volunteered Eric, while his father laboriously fitted each of his fingers into a glove.

I shook my head.

"The *index* kick," clarified Cory.

Still blank.

"The *insect* kick," further elucidated Eugene.

Long clueless pause . . . then, "You mean the *instep* kick?"

"Yeahhhh . . ." agreed all four.

Relief. "Sure, we'll go over that."

We were all plcased.

"Well," I said to Lilah and Kevin when everyone had finally gone, "that was nice. Thank you both."

"You're the one deserves the thanks," said Lilah. "I don't know how you deal with all these kids . . . or why, for that matter."

I shrugged. "Just a way of getting fresh air." I moved toward the closet. "Is my coat—"

"You know, you're welcome to stay for a cup of coffee," said Lilah.

"Well, that's—"

She glanced at her watch. "Kevin's TV shows begin about now"—she gave him a long look—"and he'll be in the other room, so I'm sure we won't be disturbing him."

"You won't disturb me," said Kevin, moving obediently toward the opening in the paneled wall.

I grinned. "Well, in that case . . . sure. Thank you."

I watched her at the stove, watched the tight jeans nestle between the lobes of her ass, watched her sleek black ponytail swish along her neck, watched the perfect profile as she shut off the burner, the small nose, delicate oval chin, and slim fingers as she poured the coffee. It was all I could do not to lean forward and lick her wrists.

"So . . . how do you like it at II?"

I sipped the steaming liquid. "It's okay, I guess. I have nothing to compare it to. You?"

"Same, really."

"What group are you in again . . . ?"

"Software. My degree is in software engineering."

"Oh. Right. And what exactly do you—"

"Do? Nothing. I do nothing and they pay me."

"Really? Me too." She grinned at me and, disconcertingly, kept looking. "What, uh, are you *supposed* to be doing, then?" I persisted.

"Well, right now I'm working for the Contracts Department, designing software that lets them track scheduling compliance, revisions in scope or terms, action items, documentation status, customer contacts and visits, internal charges and expenses . . . all that stuff."

"You work for Mr. Softy."

Her face lit up. "You know him?"

"Medieval Man once pointed him out to me."

"Those two don't get along. I think they're different types of jerks."

From the other room, I heard Kevin sneeze. "I'm working on AIR."

"I know."

"You do?"

"I have access to printouts from ACCOUNTING of all the people charging to a job. I saw your name."

"I'm being surveilled by upper management?"

"Not upper management, only me." She smiled.

I felt a wave of warm tension generate somewhere inside the base of my penis, spread rapidly along the shaft, then crawl up my abdomen and chest to tickle me under the chin. She'd been watching *for me*, looking for *my name*. I wondered if my face was flushing, tried to estimate what it might be on Shopper Jim's color chart. Anything above #10, and she'd notice. I glanced to my right, saw a rack against the wall filled with *Astronomy* magazines, and on the wall above it, a Bachelor of Science degree from Hofstra University.

"You interested in astronomy?" I asked, indicating the magazine rack.

"No, I just like to read the personal ads." She paused as (I guess) she caught the uncomprehending expression on my face. "Sorry," she said, shaking her head. "I don't know what comes over me. Someone says something perfectly sweet and reasonable, and I respond with this kind of cynical, wise-ass—"

"No, I like it," I said. "The New Yorkers at Michigan were all that way and . . . I think it's cool." I knew I was sounding like a Midwest hick.

"You graduated Michigan?"

"*From* Michigan. I didn't go around the campus making a regular series of marks." I raised my eyebrows and she laughed, showing perfect small white teeth.

"Touché," she said.

I nodded toward the diploma. "And you graduated, as you say, Hofstra. . . ."

"Yes. Well . . . actually, that was my second school. I went to Columbia for a year before my father stopped paying and I had to leave."

"Stopped paying . . ."

"After I had Kevin. He didn't approve."

"Didn't approve of Kevin or having a baby in general . . . or your husband?" I knew I was on the edge of prying, maybe *over* the edge, but shit, she had brought it up.

"Well, I had no husband. Kevin's father was just a friend, someone I knew but would never have considered marrying, and Kevin . . ." She smiled, staring at her hands. "Kevin was an accident. An accident I decided to have, and to keep."

From the other room, the accident sneezed five times in a

row. I was almost relieved to change the subject. "Sounds like he might be getting a cold."

"Yeah, he's had four of them already this year. The doctor said he might be developing asthma and that living in a basement apartment really isn't good for him. I think we're gonna have to get out."

"Mmm." I finished my coffee and stood up. "Speaking of getting out"—I glanced significantly at my watch—"I should be going." I'm not really sure why I said it—it wasn't like I had anything else to do—but I had more or less run out of things to talk about and felt the need to depart before blubbering incoherently. (I have always been a really bad, self-conscious conversationalist with women. I mean, you just can't say to them certain things that elicit torrents of words from guys: e.g., "So you think the Lions have a shot this year?" or "I wonder if the hair on her pussy is also red," or "I noticed that, viewed sideways, the tip of my penis looks like a fireman's hat.")

"You're sure?" she said. "There's more coffee."

I shook my head. "Thanks, no. It was great."

She accompanied me to the door.

" 'Bye, Kevin," I called to the other room.

" 'Bye, Mr. Coach."

" 'Bye, Mr. Coach," echoed Lilah, smiling.

I gave a stiff little wave, and left.

—— ○ ——

I walked through the halls with Kushner on the way to the Preliminary Design Review. Mournful eyes on the floor, shaking his head, broad butt in jellied lateral sway, there was—and I know this sounds mean-spirited—a distinctly bovine aspect to his appearance.

"It's simple, a simple simple fact."

I imagined I could hear *lowing.*

"I can't do the work."

(Mmmooooooh.)

"I'm just not smart enough."

(Mmmooooooh.)

"I work and work and study and study and I can't do it. I don't have the intellect."

He was referring to the transmitter amplifier, to getting it to function with less current. "Why don't you ask Marv to help you?" I suggested. "You just got here; he has twenty years' experience."

"Marv's *help?* Marv is the guy who assigned me the problem because he's too goddamned busy running his own business to work on it!" The cow had growled. "Do you know what he does all day? Marketing. He makes sales calls to other companies. He works on designs for things that have nothing to do with anything at II. And he has Gung Ho making dozens of these little oscillators that MES Technology is selling to some other firm. I can't even get any technician time! I mean, shit, he's receiving parts, *parts,* right here in this building—don't ask me how he does it—that he's using for his own company."

We approached Conference Room G, where the PDR was being held.

"I'm just worried about my rating," said Kushner. "I finally completed my Goals and Aspirations essay—it's thirteen pages—and now I wonder if it'll do any good."

"You wrote thirteen pages?"

"Yeah. Why? You think it's too much? How many is yours?"

"I didn't do mine yet."

"You didn't? How can you—They're due tomorrow."

"I know. I'll work on it later." The fact was, I had already evaluated myself for the Fast Track Management Program

(FTMP) and found myself lacking. I was really not suited for a fast or even a slow track to a position where I was responsible for the actions of others. I was best off the track entirely—call me a techie, or labroid, or propeller-head—where I could work on the things that interested me and not worry about running a business. And if that meant I would earn less money than my fast-track friends, and even be judged unsuccessful as a result—then so it would be.

Just outside the door of Conference Room G, there was a crimson glow, which momentarily resolved itself into Meissner's face. He was talking in intense controlled tones to Boulot, who stood before him casually chewing gum, his tie and belt buckle facing backward.

". . . will give you to three to properly attire yourself." Meissner's anger was virtually palpable; the air cloaking his body wavered and shimmered as if he stood on sun-baked asphalt. "One . . ."

"You can count to a million; I am not going to change. What difference does eet make 'ow I dress?"

"Two . . ."

"Eet is not my concern. Count to a billion, to ten thousand quadrillion, I do my job, I don't 'ave to put on my tie to please you."

"Three. That's it. You're out, you're not coming to PDR."

Chart level #20: *Lobster*. He turned to me. "You'll tell them about the power supplies."

I think I gasped.

Meissner chopped the air with his hand. "If they ask questions, you answer, that's all. Whispering Bill will do the summary presentation."

Whispering Bill, I thought, has no knowledge whatsoever of the job.

Meissner snatched open the door. "Let's go, everyone."
We entered, leaving Boulot outside.

----

o

The conference room held two hundred wooden chairs, arranged in ten rows, with a center aisle. At the front was a raised platform with a lectern that held a slide projector; a pull-down screen covered a section of front wall. In the audience, on the left of the aisle, sat representatives of the Air Force, straight-backed men in sparkling white uniforms; a number of blue-and-gray-suited civilian males; three short-haired military women. On the right of the center aisle sat representatives of International Instruments; thirty black people I'd never seen and behind them, the guys I knew from the project.

At the very back, in his own row, sat Shopper Jim, and it was toward him that Kushner and I walked. We took seats on either side of him.

"What gives?" I whispered.

"About what?" said Jim.

"About them," I answered, motioning toward the front rows. "Who are they?"

"Just folks, I imagine. Pretty much like you or me or—"

"Jim . . ."

"See the Air Force colonel in the front row, on the aisle?"

"The black guy . . ."

"He's the contract administrator for several jobs currently in-house. One day he made it known to one of the II mucka-mucks how distressed he was to look out into a company audience and see hardly any people of color. And so . . ." He made a sweeping gesture toward the first five rows.

"But where do they get them from? You mean, they just bring them in? Bring them in from outside?"

Jim just smiled. A tall, bony man with a large Adam's apple

and iron-gray hair had ascended to the podium. "Hello, everyone, I'm Vincent Ingrassia. I'm the Chief Engineer here at International Instruments, and I'd like to welcome the representatives of the Air Force as well as from our own company to this Preliminary Design Review for the Advanced Interrogator-slash-Receiver. We've got a rather full program today, and so, without further delay, I'm going to introduce Anton Meissner, the AIR project manager, who will outline for you what we have planned."

I remembered from my early days—only because he was an unusual stylist—noticing Ingrassia in the men's room as he switched literally midstream from Two-Hander to No-Handed Usurper. I had thought, at the time, he was probably schizophrenic. Meissner bounded up to the platform.

"Good morning, ladies and gentlemen. If you'll just consult the agendas that you should have found on your seats when you arrived . . ."

I reached under my ass and pulled out a printed page.

". . . you'll see that the day will be divided between a series of formal talks on the major subsystems, after which we'll break up into special-interest groups where Air Force personnel can interface directly with the cognizant members of our staff and get a detailed status breakdown in each area. The group meetings will continue tomorrow, followed by the beginning of the business and contract panels, which will extend through Wednesday afternoon." He looked around. "Now, if there are no questions"—of course, everyone was already stupefied—"I'd like to begin by presenting an overview of the AIR system." He nodded pointedly to somebody at the room's rear and the lights went out just as the front screen lit up with a slide.

"So the black people are, like, what, *rounded up?*" I whisperingly prodded Jim.

"All these things are dog-and-pony shows," said Jim. "You

do what makes an impression. Last year, I worked on a program, the contract administrator had a club foot. Come PDR, first eight rows were filled with cripples. Paraplegics, quadriplegics, quintaplegics, people in iron lungs, deaf people, blind people, microcephalics, people who were only brains floating in bell jars . . ."

Meissner's talk lasted thirty minutes and was smoothly, professionally delivered. At the conclusion, he turned the podium over to Wonderbury, who proceeded to describe the system design criteria and cost-performance trade-offs of the various modules. As he began on the receiver, I saw Jim lean forward slightly.

". . . and so for the whole chain," Wonderboy concluded, "we're expecting a noise figure of about 1.1 dB."

Jim guffawed loudly. Several people ahead of us, including A Boy Named Hsu, who was cog engineer for the actual receiver box, turned around to look. Noise figure was a measure of how much random noise the receiver added to the signal. The more noise, the less the receiver's range, a crucial performance spec. "We're already up over 1.5 dB," said Jim, "and it's gonna get a lot worse."

"Does he know that?" I asked.

"Oh, he knows," said Jim. "Course, he didn't exactly lie. He said, 'we're expecting.' Everyone has dreams."

"But what about—"

"That's in the future. He may not be here then. Or maybe the program is canceled. *You* may not be here then, or more importantly, I may not be. The Air Force may not be. So the question is, Is a lie a lie when no one is there to hear it?"

Two of the box engineers spoke next: Medieval Man on the Digital Processor, and the CEO of Marvin E. Sklar Technology on the Transmitter. Just before the lunch break, Mr. Softy, a flabby, perspiring man who in his wrinkled cotton suit, appeared to have just emerged from the steaming jungles of Panama, did thirty-five minutes on the structured subprograms, modules, routines, and subroutines that constituted the software for AIR's six microprocessors.

There was a complementary buffet lunch available in the cafeteria for all the attendees, but Jim wouldn't go anywhere near it, so I drove with him instead to our usual McDonald's. I invited Kushner along, but he wanted the executives to see him mingling and schmoozing, so Jim and I went by ourselves. On the way back, from the car, we saw Boulot out for his walk. He was wearing a leather jacket and black beret.

"Crazy man," said Jim. "Right on the edge."

In the II parking lot, with ten minutes to go before the PDR resumed, I took a football out of my car trunk and we began tossing it around. It was November, and though the Wiffle set still lay on my back seat, baseball just didn't feel right. Jim could throw the football a lot farther than I could. My hands are fairly small, and it takes my entire concentration and technique just to produce a modest spiral, but Jim seemed able to effortlessly pump it thirty-five yards or more.

"We're gonna get all sweaty and horrible," he called after I'd run a long post pattern near the guard booth.

"Right," I called back, happy to have made the catch.

Twenty minutes later, perspiring and disheveled, we entered the PDR conference room. I'd expected to be able to simply slink back to our former seats, but instead, as we opened the door, I saw Bent-Over-Bill at the podium, just as he spotted me and said, "*There* he is," into the mike.

All eyes in the room turned to Jim and me—the Air Force ramrods, the show-time black people, Ingrassia, Meissner, and all the other II-ers. I was suddenly acutely conscious of the salty film on my forehead, the tie knot at my sternum, the wrinkled shirttail hanging over my belt.

"Colonel Reed had a question," rasped Bill, who I realized must have begun his coverage of the AIR power supplies. I felt the panic start, the fluttering wings of a small insect working its way up my spine. I tried to remember the things Boulot had taught me about feedback and open-loop-gain measurements and phase margins at high frequencies . . . and found my mind a blank. I would be exposed now for all to see, an ignoramus, a sloppy, uncaring fraud. Damn Boulot, it should've been him in this spot; why had he gotten himself kicked out?

"In view of all the power supply redesign," continued Bill, "and our completion of the parts-ordering milestone, do we have any reservations about delivery from our suppliers? Particularly for the special D-connectors."

Imagine, I thought, Meissner had been right. The main concern of (apparently) everyone was not whether the parts would work, but whether they had been ordered and would be delivered. I responded in the only way I could. "The parts were ordered from a reputable, qualified vendor. There's no reason not to expect on-time delivery."

"Thank you," called a white-clad black Air Force officer sitting just in front of the lectern.

I gave a theatrically grave nod, then proceeded to the rearmost row, where Jim was already seated.

"That answer," said Jim. "A PIDOOMA, I presume?"

I scrunched my face to show my incomprehension.

" 'Pulled It Directly Out of My Ass.' Nice job, by the way."

At that instant, I saw Meissner turn and glance back at me. Lips pressed together, he shook his head twice, then returned his gaze to the podium.

"I don't think everyone shares your appreciation," I said to Jim.

o|o ECN

If God made people from nothing, where did he
get the stuff to use?
—CHILD'S QUESTION

A pparently, the PDR went reasonably well. Meissner called
a staff meeting two weeks later and handed out a sheet
that listed a number of Air Force "Areas of Concern," each of
which we'd address with an "Action Item." The latter might
range from a phone call to some Air Force functionary with
the part number of a rubber grommet to supplying a fifty-page
full-up preliminary Reliability analysis of the receiver module.
Also, since documents on the job were now proliferating like
pollen grains, any design changes from this point on would
have to be implemented by ECNs.

"What's an ECN?" I asked Boulot.

"Engineering Change Notice," said the Frenchman, with
his usual shrug/hands in pockets/nasal Gaelic chuckle.
"Anuzzer thing to make your life hell."

He walked me through our first ECR (Engineering Change
Request, the document that initiated an ECN), the substitution

of a new resistor in the +15-volt supply. We had to fill out who initiated the action (me), the date and job number, and the reason (insufficient power-handling capability of the earlier design); then complete a detailed FROM (old part number and description)–TO (new part number and description) page; then, after getting the forms signed by Bent-Over-Bill and Meissner, take them to the guys in charge of ECNs.

"Meissner wouldn't sign," said Bent-Over-Bill, a day after I'd given him the form and he'd okayed it.

"Why?"

He indicated two sentences in each of the part descriptions. "Missing two commas."

I gave it to Marie to fix on the word processor. Four hours later she returned. "Did the one in FROM," she said. "Couldn't do the other one."

"Okay . . . what was the problem?"

"Mr. Meissner's rule. Any more than one change on the word processor has to be approved by him." I guess she saw the expression on my face. "Otherwise, I guess he feels, well, people would be making so many alterations we'd be overwhelmed."

"I see. But if I waited till tomorrow, I could get the second change then?"

Her face brightened. "Oh, yes, absolutely. I'll take care of it first thing in the morning." She walked off with the papers.

Nine A.M. the next day she was again standing at my desk. I was just withdrawing the immersion heater from my coffee. She held out the ECR. "All set," she said pleasantly. Then, indicating the heater, "You know, Zachary, that's a no-no around here."

"Don't tell anyone," I whispered. I brought the ECR in to Whispering Bill.

By four P.M., he was back at my desk. "Meissner wouldn't sign," he said hoarsely.

"But why now?" I saw Boulot chuckling at his desk.

Whispering Bill pointed at the name of the former vendor in two places under the FROM description. "See that 'Goellner Electronics'? You left out the umlaut over the *o*."

I slammed down my pencil. "You gotta be kidding. Umlauts are—I don't even think they're English. Aren't they German or something?"

"Meissner's a bit of a stickler," rasped Bent-Over-Bill. "Detail man."

I rolled my eyes, then called Marie. Early next morning, after again pointing out the no-no of my coffeemaking, she handed over the changed papers. "I did the both of them without asking him," she whispered.

We were bonded in criminality.

Third time was the charm. Whispering Bill returned the ECRs with Meissner's signature.

"Now," said Boulot, "you take zee ECRs to trailer five. You look for a Chinese guy. And hold on to your head."

————
o

At the end of November, Queens County Savings Bank tied a game 1–1 with Long Island Paneling, and I took the kids out for pizza afterward. It was our seventh match, the first non-loss. Twice before, I'd also treated them after games (with few takers), but this time I'd actually seen certain improvements. Our lines had more or less moved together; there were several instances where we hadn't bunched up on the ball; Alan Gunderson had actually passed twice to Eugene Baker; and Eric Nowicki, my assistant coach's son, made his first non-penalized throw-in of the year. (Of course, our lone goal had nothing to do with any of this; Michael had simply dribbled through the entire Paneling team for a solo score.)

Our game the next week, on the first Saturday in December,

was played on an open, windswept field under a heavily clouded sky. Five minutes after kickoff a light drizzle began. I paced along the sidelines as usual, calling out directions as the teams alternately gained possession of the ball, lost it, got it back, struggled to advance.

"Jason, move up! Fullbacks, move up! Alan, watch number five! Kevin, mark your man! Get up on him, get up on him! That's it! That's it! Mark, way ta go, way ta go! Alan, pass! Pass! Eugene was open. Okay, don't worry about it. Michael, nice kick, awright! Follow it, follow it, follow it! Eric, down the line! Right down the line! Awww, Eric, it's gotta be over your head, directly over. Awright, you'll get it next time. Indirect, indirect! Steven, take it! Steve, remember, to someone on our team *first*, gotta be someone on our team. Michael's—Okay, okay, don't worry about it, you'll—Fullbacks, back! Back! All right, line up, form a wall! It's a *direct*, form a wall! Cory, all right, all right! Great stop! Way ta play goal! Yeah, punt it, gaw head. Don't be afraid, yeah . . . okay. Okay, good try!"

On the opposite side of the field I saw the usual crew of parents, bundled now against the cold, most still sitting in their lawn chairs, some sipping coffee or tea from hot thermos bottles, the usual few—Michael's father, Steven's, Alan's—running up and down the field parallel to their kids, shouting instructions. Often, the latter were the opposite of what I was calling out—e.g., "Take it yourself, Mike! Mike, all the way!"—and occasionally I'd see a kid freeze, caught in schizophrenic stasis between Dad and coach. I'd pretty much learned to accept it, annoying as it was, mainly because I couldn't do anything about it. (I'd once gone over to the parents at a halftime break and explained how difficult it was for the kids to receive conflicting directions and how the coach really needed to run the team, and though there were several nods, I knew the ones at fault would ignore me. The fact was,

I was a kid myself, I exuded neither authority nor experience and, as a result, commanded little respect. Almost, I didn't blame them.)

By the second quarter, it began drizzling harder, and the grass became slick with water. Eugene slipped while dribbling down the sideline and, in the brief time-out that ensued while the ref and I examined his ankle (it was a very mild sprain), I told Ed to check the team's cleats. "Make sure there's no mud in there," I told him. "Have them get it out with their fingers."

The game resumed . . . and then an amazing thing happened.

We scored.

Kevin with a long perfect instep kick from fullback, Cory dribbling past one of the Jack In The Box forwards, *pass* to Alan Gunderson—who slid it just inside the right goalpost. Perfect play.

The Bank parents stood up as one and cheered. I pumped my fist and then high-fived Ed, who was literally leaping up and down. The kids were all jumping around too, even Eugene, turned ankle and all.

After all this time, all the twice-a-week practices, all the practices that ended at dusk with only five kids having showed up, all the lost games, the randomness, the lack of concentration, the incremental improvements and decremental backslides, the well-you-really-can't-teach-little-kids rationalizations, the—let's face it—hopelessness. After all those weeks of urging and cajoling and shouting and turning away to calm yourself and remind yourself they *were* only six years old . . . after all that—one perfect goal.

If we did not score for the rest of the season, this would be enough.

At halftime, Lilah, the week's designated parent, brought over the drinks. The rain was now coming down quite steadily.

"Way to go, Coach," she said as she tore open the plastic bag holding the cups.

"I had nothing to do with it," I said, in the fake-humble manner of the professional mentor. "It was all the kids."

"It was great," said Lilah.

Alan Gunderson sidled over.

"Super goal, big guy," I said.

"Coach, you know what rain is? God's sissy."

"Whatever you say, Alan."

The wind blew up in the third quarter, whipping the rain in blustery swaths. After the first five minutes, the whole center of the field, which had little grass to begin with, was a sea of mud. Shallow puddles had formed in several spots near the sidelines. Most of the kids were well bundled up in winter coats, but league rules required they play in shorts, and of course no hats could be worn, since they would prevent or interfere with headers, which the kids never took. I saw some of the parents begin to look a little anxious on the sidelines.

In the next three minutes, two Jack In The Box kids slipped and fell—one had to be carried off, crying, in his father's arms—and Cory, on our team, tripped in a puddle, drenched himself over his entire body length, and had to come out. When another Jack kid slid into the goalpost and banged his head, I walked over to the referee and motioned for Ed and the Jack coach to join us.

"I think maybe we oughta stop the game," I said.

"You wanna stop?" said the other coach, a stocky guy with a brush mustache. "You're ahead."

I looked up at the sky, a dirty black blanket, and held my palms out to catch the cascading streams. I could barely see; my glasses were covered with water. "It's really pretty bad," I said, turning to the referee.

The ref was a balding, fortyish fellow in striped shirt and black shorts. "Rules say if it's just rain you keep playing."

"Well . . . yeah, but it's a pretty *hard* rain."

"As long as it's not lightning," said the ref, "rules are you play."

I shook my head. "Well . . . I donno . . . okay, but to me it looks pretty bad."

Ed and I returned to the sidelines and the game resumed. Early in the fourth quarter, the wind seemed to add another five or ten miles an hour. It was really driving the rain now, and virtually the whole field was soaked where it wasn't completely *under* the water. About half the kids seemed to be enjoying it—sliding into the puddles and opening their mouths to the rain and splashing each other—but the other half seemed quite uncomfortable and kept looking over to both sidelines at the adults.

The umbrellas had long since come out and been retracted, quite useless in the wind, and so everyone—kids, coaches, parents—was by now thoroughly drenched. When Eugene Baker got hit in the face by a kicked ball he never saw in the rain, I went back out to the ref.

"Look, this is really dangerous," I said. "You gotta call the game."

"Can't do it," he said. He looked at his watch. "Come on, there's only eleven more minutes." Ed, the Jack coach, and his assistant came over to join us.

"He wants me to stop it," said the ref to the Jack coach. I noticed Ed give me one of those are-you-insane? looks.

"No way," said the Jack coach. "We're only down one-zip. No way."

"Fellas," I said. "Look around. It's not safe. These are little kids."

"It's just rain," said the ref. "A little water never hurt anyone."

He thrust his chin out toward the children, a number of whom were splashing in the puddles. "Look at them. They're enjoying this."

"I'll give you a tie," I said to the Jack coach.

"Wait a minute," said Ed. It was the first time I'd ever seen him look really agitated.

"No deal," said the Jack coach.

"Can't do it," said the ref. "League rules."

I shook my head disgustedly and returned to the sideline. The game resumed. I watched the kids slip and slide, futilely try to advance the ball down the submerged field. A few of them had just stopped and were standing motionless, craning their necks toward their parents. Little robots, I thought. Little helpless robots.

And the parents, although a number of them now looked *very* uncomfortable, did not do a thing. Peer pressure among the adults, I supposed. No one wanted to wimp out, *to let down the team.*

I had always felt that kids' sports ought to be conducted as kids would play them if no adults were around to organize and arrange and make the rules. As I watched the little soaking robots try to run up and down the field, I knew, of their own volition, most of the kids would not have chosen to be out in *this.*

I stepped across the sideline, reached into my pocket, and withdrew the whistle I'd bought before the first practice.

"Hey!" said Ed, "what're you—"

"I'm stopping it," I said. I blew the whistle. "That's it!" I called to my team. "Everyone come in! Game's over!"

Uncertain at first, the kids began to trot over to the sideline. I patted each of them on the head. "Game's finished," I said. "Good game."

The referee came running over. "I'm gonna have to forfeit you," he said.

I shrugged.

He walked toward the opposing coaches. "Queens Bank is forfeiting," he said. "Game's over."

The Jack coach stared at me. "Hey, your call. We'll go back out if you want."

"It's done," I said.

I quickly gathered the team around me. The rain swept across us in torrential sheets. "You all did a great job," I said, "but I just think it's too dangerous and crazy to keep playing."

"Is this a forfeit?" asked Cory.

"Probably."

"What's a forfeit?" asked Alan.

"We'll talk about it next time," I answered.

I sent them across the field to their parents and began gathering up the soccer balls.

"I really can't say I agree with you," said Ed. "We only had a few minutes left." He walked away toward our goal. A moment later I saw him talking to one of the fathers as they gathered in the netting.

I headed for the other side of the field, where the remaining parents and kids were streaming toward the cars.

"How could you forfeit with us ahead?" called back Michael's father, Michael tracking behind him.

"You really blew it, Coach," called Barry Gunderson. "Alan doesn't even get the goal now."

Michael and Mike Senior were at their car. "You can't do this, Coach," called Mike Senior. "All the kids' work, and you just take it away like that. Just like that, on a whim." He shook his head, and he and Michael entered the car.

I approached my Tempo and paused near the door. The rain seemed to be letting up. Jesus, I thought. Jesus, maybe . . . was he right? The brightest moment of the season, the moment all the kids had felt good about, the payoff time—was he right? Had I erased it on a whim, out of fear, out of wimpiness, lack of heart? I felt suddenly nauseated. The water covered my glasses and blinded me.

And then I heard the voice. Her voice. Lilah's. She was standing next to me.

"What you did . . ." she said. I removed my glasses, turned to face her. The raindrops cascaded down her cheeks. "What you did . . . was just wonderful."

Our eyes locked for an instant and then she reached out, clutched the back of my neck, and kissed me. A long sweet open sucking kiss on the lips that literally left me dizzy and just about paralyzed as she walked off to her car and drove away.

○

Kushner's chin was quivering as he recounted what happened. "He didn't . . . didn't even say anything to me. Just handed me the form. Didn't even hand it, actually, just slid it across the table."

I tilted the document in question so Shopper Jim could read it.

"He rates you a seven," said Jim.

"A seven!" said Kushner, eyes red. "Can you imagine? A seven!"

"Seven is good," said Jim.

"Good? Good? How can you say that? After all the work I put in, all the time."

Kushner snatched the paper back and read aloud: " 'Warren devotes a great many hours to his assignment, stays late virtually every night, comes in weekends, holidays, etc. He is a dedicated and conscientious employee. The problem is not the quantity of Warren's time, but the quality. Not the intensity of his effort, but its outcome. The fact is he needs to work smarter, not harder. He seems to repeatedly pursue tangents not directly related to the end goal of his assignment. He travels these side roads exhaustively, obsessively documenting every dead end, every mistake, every misguided thought. He requires excessive supervision to keep on track and asks excessive numbers of questions, many repetitive, when steered in a new direction. In short, Warren lacks confidence in his own abilities, a lack that, unfortunately, seems justified. Thus, while I feel Warren *can* ultimately be a useful employee of International Instruments, I cannot, for the reasons described above, rate him a likely candidate for Fast Track Management.' " Kushner folded the paper. "Imagine . . . imagine this . . . this criminal who runs his own business on company time saying these things about me." He swallowed hard and for a moment I thought he might burst into tears.

"I still think seven is pretty good," said Jim. "Seven out of ten. That's most of the way there."

"What do you care what Sklar says?" I offered. "It's just his opinion."

"My assignment is impossible," said Kushner. "No one can do it, and he . . . he doesn't give me any help."

"The oscillator-transmitter chain *is* probably the toughest design task," offered Wonderboy (Surveyor), listening in as usual. I couldn't decide whether his tone was patronizing or sympathetic.

"And what was *your* FTM rating?" asked Shopper Jim.

"Oh, me?" Wonderboy glanced around coyly, then back to his desktop. "I got a nine-point-five."

Jim rolled his eyes. "That shows how much the evaluations are worth." He called over to Boulot. "And Frenchman, what about you?"

Boulot, engrossed in calculations, swiveled slowly. "About me? What?"

"Your Fast Track Management rating."

"But . . . I donno. Where do you get eet?"

Jim looked at Kushner.

"Marie has 'em," said Kushner.

"Frenchman, you ever hand in the essay?" asked Jim amusedly.

"You mean zat stupeed paper zey want?" He made a chopping motion with his hand. "I 'ave no time for zat, I 'ave work." He looked at me. "Zack, you handed?"

I gave a little sheepish nod. I had submitted a less-than-quarter-page (double spaced) paragraph on the last day:

Please excuse this response, but I honestly do not feel I am a suitable candidate for the Fast Track Management Program. I am interested mainly in the technical parts of the job and do not feel I would be very good at assigning, monitoring, and evaluating the activities of other people.

Boulot stood up. "Come, we see how we did."

We all, except for Wonderboy, marched out of the cubicle, wended our way over to Marie, and explained what we wanted. Reaching into a Pendaflex folder in her desk drawer, she said, "Yes, I was just about to bring these to you. Mr. Meissner completed them only about an hour ago." She handed separate papers to me and Boulot.

"So?" said Jim.

Boulot scrunched up his shoulders and laughed. " 'Ee give me a two," he said. "This is more than I expect."

All eyes turned to me. I shook my head. "I got an eight," I said, staring at the page. "It's inexplicable."

"You're in the program," said Kushner in amazement and disgust.

"It won't do any good," pronounced Jim. We were sitting at a lunch table in the cafeteria. Kushner had just announced he was planning to appeal his rating.

"It will," insisted Kushner. "I'll show Sklar he was wrong." He scarfed down a handful of vitamins; Kushner took every vitamin, mineral, and grape-leaf-shark-cartilage-yak-testicle not banned by the FDA.

"He doesn't care," said Jim, "plus he's an asshole. You're approaching this all wrong."

Kushner became incensed. "No I'm not! This happens to be very important to me, this is my career here, and—"

I held up the finger I'd been using to scrape a microscopic green particle (some errant relish?) off my hamburger. (One more such mote and I'd have to discard the thing entirely.) "Let him explain," I said.

Kushner pouted, but kept silent.

"What you must take as a given," said Jim, "is that management will always do any number of highly irrational, inequitable, and inhumane things to make your life unfulfilling, unproductive, and miserable. You're worried about your career? You *have* no career, you're an engineer. The solution is either get a lobotomy—or get out." He paused. "Even as I myself am in the process of."

I took a tiny, uneasy bite of the burger. "Get out and do what?"

"For engineers, two conventional paths. Both distinguished by zero or low intellectual content and a money-up principal goal. The first is franchisee. Lawn service, fast food, Edie Adams Cut-and-Curl, that sort of thing. I know several guys who've done it."

"And the second . . ."

"The path I myself have chosen. Night school. Tough road. One year to go."

"Oh, God . . ." I said, beginning to get a glimmer. "Don't tell me—"

"Yes . . ."

It was as if I'd bit into some cauliflower—I was that close to throwing up. "You're going to law school," I pronounced.

"Brooklyn Law," said Shopper Jim jauntily. "Four-year program."

"But . . ." Kushner's facial expression must have mimicked my own: a mixture of outrage and nausea. "You yourself said lawyers are the parasites of society. I've heard you."

"Yes."

"And yet—"

Jim leaned forward. "Consider the people who actually advance the condition of the human race, who elevate us above the animal. Who are they? Mathematicians. Physicists. Engineers. Medical researchers. Writers. Poets. Artists." He wiped some pizza crumbs off his beard. "If they're lucky enough to even get jobs, those people's starting salaries range anywhere from zero to thirty-two thousand dollars a year." He sipped some soda. "In contrast, your average scumbag six-tries-to-pass-the-bar lawyer starts at seventy, and the differences get worse from there. Engineers and physicists, the highest paid of the useful group, top out at sixty to sixty-five after twenty years. Lawyers zoom in a couple years to two hundred, three hundred; sky's the limit after that." He held out his palms. "Lawyers, apart from a very few idealistic criminal or civil rights types, are at best contract clerks churning out arcane forms and at worst sue-happy obstructionists, choking the arteries of civilization. They're everywhere, multiplying, you can't stop them, they'll destroy us all." He smiled. "God, I wanna be one."

"Jesus . . ." I said.

"You know, law school is easy," crowed Jim. "A hundred

times easier than engineering school." The grin remained. "See, it's backwards. Everything, everywhere . . . backwards." He turned to Kushner. "Don't waste your time arguing with Marv. He probably did you a favor. He pointed the way. In engineering, *the good ones get out.*"

"I suppose that's another one of your 'rules,' " I said.

Jim stood up. "Not quite. There are a few, very few, exceptions." He moved away from the table. "But it's close enough for all practical purposes."

○

Despite the labyrinthine vastness of the II facility, the ECN processing group for the AIR project had its offices in a large trailer located in back of the plant. A thin-haired, bespectacled Asian man looked up as I entered and approached his desk.

"Excuse me, I need to talk to someone about an ECN."

"Yes, you need to first see Mee."

I proffered the ECR paperwork. "Well, I've got the—"

"No, no. You have to see Mee."

"You mean you can't handle this right now? Okay. When would be a good time, then—"

"No, I don't handle."

"But you said I should see you."

"I not say 'see Yu.' "

"I don't see you. . . ."

"You do, but after you see Mee. *I* am Yu."

"You are me?"

The man rolled his eyes. "Look, we make this simple, right? First, you see Mee. Then, after, you see me. I am Yu."

I felt myself grow short of breath. "So *you* are you . . ." I said tentatively.

"Yes! Now you have it."

"And I am I . . ."

"Yes."

"And I need to see . . ."

"Mee!"

I stared at him blankly. He called over to the next room. "Tim! Hey, Timmy! Could you come in here a moment?"

Presently, a second Asian entered the room.

"This is Tim Mee," said the first Asian. "He will help you."

Drained, feeling like a child, I followed Mee back to his office.

"So what you got?" said Mee, smiling.

I handed him the ECR forms, which he glanced at, then looked up.

"His name Kevin Yu," said Mee. "He think it big joke, give people hard time with our names."

"You mean he did that on purpose?"

"Oh, sure. He does to everyone."

"Oh, well, now I feel much better."

Mee fished a form out of his desk drawer, then handed me it and my ECR. "What you must do, you make thirteen copies of ECR, then give copy plus approval form to all these people, have them sign."

I glanced at the form. It had spaces for dates and signatures from Electrical Engineering, Mechanical Engineering, Thermal Engineering, Design and Drafting, Production Control, Purchasing, Quality Assurance, Quality Control, Reliability, Maintainability, Production Assembly, Electromagnetic Compatibility, and Contract Administration. "But that's thirteen places!" I said.

"Yes . . ."

"But it's just changing one resistor. One."

"Yes . . ."

"But this is crazy."

"This is military. Everything must be documented."

"But what's going to happen when we have more of these?"

"Need more paper."

I rolled my eyes. "Jesus . . . I mean, how many of these do we already have?"

"On AIR job, oh, we running maybe twenty-five."

"Twenty-five ECNs . . ."

"No, twenty-five a week."

"Holy—"

"Oh, it get worse," said Yu. "Much worse." He waved his hand expansively. "They already bringing another trailer, hire more people."

I shook my head and started for the door. "And when I get all these signatures, I bring the form back to Yu?"

"No, not me."

I pointed my finger at him. "Don't start."

———
○

The phone rang just as I opened the door. It was Ed Nowicki, my assistant soccer coach.

"Look, uh, there's no easy way to say this," he began, "but I'm resigning my position."

The phrase didn't seem to connect to anything. I thought he was telling me—for some reason—that he was leaving his job as a data analyst at Bear Stearns. "Uh, what position?"

"You know, assistant coach."

"But . . . why?" I was stunned.

"That forfeit was a mistake."

Somehow, I didn't feel like arguing the point. "Ohhhkayyy. Let's say maybe it was. But still, is it such a big deal that you need to—"

"I'm sorry, but this is how it has to be. Eric goes to school with a lot of the other kids, I'm friends with the parents, and I'm the one has to live with them."

"Ed, excuse me, but I'm not putting this together."

"I wanted to tell you personally," he said. "My wife said I should just send you a postcard or something, but I didn't feel that would be right."

"Well . . ." I had no idea what to say. "Is, uh, Eric going to stay on the team?"

"I'm not sure. It depends on a lot of things. But that forfeit was a mistake."

I exhaled. "Okay, Ed, your resignation is accepted." I shook my head. For some reason, I added, "You'll be contacted about your severance package," and then hung up.

I looked around. The house seemed curiously bare and stark; a chill seemed to permeate the room. I spotted two pieces of paper on the kitchen table and walked over to investigate. The first was a check for $262.50 made out to me and signed by Angelo Belpanno. The second was a handwritten note from the check-writer:

Well, I'm out of here, man, got a gig in L.A. I couldn't turn down. The accompaning [sic] *should cover three weeks of rent, which should be enough time for you to get a sublet roomie. Sorry my schedule didn't let me say good-bye in person. Keep up the soccer coaching, buddy. It's good for you.*

Great, I thought, letting the paper flutter to the tabletop. The departing entertainer leaves one last piece of life-affirming advice. I wondered how he'd settled on three weeks as appropriate exculpatory payment, decided it must be a musician thing, incomprehensible to the engineering mind.

On impulse I checked the kitchen cabinet where he'd kept

a special childish curlicued plastic straw he liked to sip his chocolate milk through. Gone. So was the box of Frosted Flakes he ate in the morning and the little scale he had for weighing envelopes (he was continually sending out demo tapes and resumés). In the living area his *Guitar Player* magazines were missing from the canvas rack. I approached his bedroom door, tentatively turned the knob—despite the note, it still seemed, somehow, that I was violating his privacy. But the room was deserted; no guitar case, no sheet music stand, no plastic picks and broken E strings scattered on the carpet amid the socks and shorts.

No more Phantom, I thought. He really was gone.

Outside, through the window, I saw a haze of snowflakes swirling in the light of a street lamp. It had turned into a really lousy day.

7

LACKEYS, FLUNKEYS, AND ZOMBIES

Murphy's Law: Anything that can go wrong will
SHOPPER JIM'S COMMENTARY: TRUE BUT
INCOMPLETE. FOR SUFFICIENCY WE MUST ADD,
ANYTHING THAT *CAN'T* GO WRONG ALSO WILL.

On December 20, driving in to work and listening to 1010 WINS, I learned we had invaded Panama that morning, seeking to capture dictator Manuel Noriega in Operation Just Cause. At nine A.M., Meissner called everyone into a room and read us his own Just Cause: We would be captured (expected to work) at least one day of every weekend as well as half days on Christmas and New Year's. "No one likes it," he said, "but someone's gotta do something to keep this program from going down the toilet." He showed us his charts, indicating how we were missing milestones left and right, and also referred to the "excess current" problem, which we were still far away from solving. "The noose is tightening, people," he said, before shutting his notebook and striding from the room.

"I 'ope 'ee 'as a strong neck," said Boulot as we walked back to the cubicle. "Zee only question open for AIR is ze category of ze mistake."

"Whaddaya mean, 'category'?"

" 'Ere is ze hierarchy: error, blunder, disaster, catastrophe."

"I vote for 'disaster,' " said Shopper Jim.

"We should be so lucky," said Boulot.

That afternoon I went to Meissner's office and, concealing my nervousness, asked him if I could work all day Christmas so that I could take New Year's Day off to fly home and see my parents. "I haven't been back since I started working here in July," I told him, steeling myself for a wrathful outburst.

But he said simply, "No problem," and buried his head in some papers.

On December 24, four men in suits were ushered around the lab areas by Meissner and Whispering Bill. They shook hands with each employee they encountered.

"Who are they?" I asked Shopper Jim.

"The bosses," he said. "The one with the button eyes is Venator, corporate CEO. The one with the beard is O'Toole, some kind of financial bird. The blondish guy is Yale Sanders, exec VP for this division, and the one with the loose chin is Pepper, some other kind of VP."

O'Toole was shaking hands with A Boy Named Hsu.

"I never saw any of them before."

"They don't like to come down to the labs," said Jim. "The stuff that goes on here is messy—things don't work right, people quit, parts come in late—it makes them uncomfortable. It doesn't fit their business models."

The group was gradually approaching us. Venator shook hands with Gung Ho. I noticed that big-business executives had a certain *clean* look that working men lacked, a brushed and curried, aftershaved and bathed appearance, a *groomed* aura like that of fine stallions. And they were tall. All over six feet. I wondered briefly if the height might have somehow served a natural selection function, if the ability, say, to peer over the walls of five-foot-high cubicles had conferred a giraffelike Darwinian advantage over equally qualified but shorter managerial rivals.

The four executives had stopped, stood in a line now as Shopper Jim and I, Kushner, and Ben Nussbaum filed past them. "Merry Christmas," said each as I shook his hand.

"Merry Christmas," I responded. I knew that the notion someone might not be Christian did not enter their collective consciousness, and I forgave them for it. I noticed, and remarked to Jim, how thoroughly democratic they seemed, how their genial demeanor was the same whether they were greeting a supervisor like Marvin Sklar (who, along with a number of other engineers, had wandered into, or more likely been summoned to, the lab) or a technician like Nussbaum.

"It's not 'democratic,' " corrected Jim. "It's that everybody here is so far beneath them they don't distinguish. It's as if you were taking a tour of an ant's nest, greeting the workers." He proposed a test to illustrate his point. "We could go around again and shake their hands and they wouldn't even realize it."

We looked at each other, and I knew I had to try it. We waited a moment till two more engineers entered the lab, then we got on the queue that had formed in front of the execs. A moment later (and not without trepidation) I was again shaking the strong, slim hand of Steven Venator.

"Merry Christmas," he said heartily.

"Merry Christmas," I said with equal enthusiasm.

We passed down the line without incident.

"Told you," said Shopper Jim.

"Well . . . okay. There's a lot of people. . . ."

"Doesn't matter. They don't see us. We could even . . ." I saw the grin take shape. "We could even do it again."

"Oh, man . . ."

"I'm telling you. No risk."

I was scared but knew there was no alternative. The gauntlet had been flung. We waited another few minutes, circled the lab so we approached from a different direction, then got on the queue behind Medieval Man. I narrowed my eyes and pulled down the right corner of my mouth in a primitive effort at disguise as the line slowly advanced.

"They don't see you . . ." whispered Shopper Jim, distinctive-looking in his Hell's Angels' beard and imitation snakeskin motorcycle boots. It was inconceivable that at least he would not be recognized for the disrespectful miscreant he was.

"Merry Christmas," said Jim heartily as he shook hands with Venator.

"Merry Christmas," said Venator with equal enthusiasm.

"Merry Christmas," I said to Venator for the third time.

"Merry Christmas," he said back for the third time, as I passed on to the others.

I had the impression the loose-chinned guy might've caught on, he kind of looked after me when we'd concluded the handshake, but the others had been as cheery and hearty and genuinely enthusiastically oblivious as ever.

"You're right," I acknowledged to Jim afterward.

He nodded sagely. "All you are is a serial number in some list marked 'labor,' " he said. "No more than a lathe in some list marked 'shop equipment,' or a toilet in some list marked 'lavatory fixtures.' And when the company needs to cut costs, it's as easy for them to X out a number from one list as it is from another. You should remember that."

I have.

Six days later, the night of December 30, a Saturday, I flew into Detroit Metropolitan Airport and met my dad at the Northwest baggage area. My father, Ronald Zaremba, is a tall bespectacled man with thinning hair and slightly stooped shoulders; he is what I will become in thirty years, at least as far as appearance.

We shook hands as I came off the escalator. (I'd seen certain fathers of twentyish sons kiss their offspring on arrivals and departures, but my own dad didn't fall into that group.)

"Good flight?"

"Yeah, not bad."

"You got luggage?"

I held up my duffel bag. "This is it."

"Great. Let's go. I'm parked real close." He led the way through the sliding doors, out across the rent-a-car and hotel pickup strips, and, after a short trek, into the parking lot. Moments later we reached his Town Car and slid into the leather seats.

Presently, we were on I-94, gliding west toward Ann Arbor.

"So how's work?"

"Good."

Outside, it was clear, frigid, and beautiful. Snow-covered landscape, moon-silvered against the black sky, flashed by at seventy miles per hour.

"Like the job?"

"Yeah."

"Like living in New York?"

"Yeah, it's okay."

"You know Reagan's the one responsible for all that aerospace work."

"Uh-huh."

"Lotta people didn't give him credit for that."

"Mmm."

A dentist, his expression is benign and kindly, although in actuality he is neither. Not that he's mean or brutal or anything like that, it's just that his interest level in other people, including my mom and myself, is simply not very high.

"You catch the State game?"

He meant the University of Michigan/Michigan State football contest.

"No, it wasn't on in New York."

"Really? That's incredible."

Talk to him football or Pistons basketball or the deficiencies of the '88 Mercedes, or why Jim Blanchard can't hold a candle to George Romney, he's all ears. But tell him you have a stomachache, you made the tennis team, you're going out with your friends, you're not coming home, you are coming home—it's polite nods, shrugs, one-sentence comments, vacant smiles. He was amazed the college football game was not broadcast in New York. He lives for Michigan State, his alma mater, and was deeply, inconsolably disappointed when I chose to attend the University of Michigan.

"Well, you know, neither school's records were that great, so the game really didn't go national." (Actually, it was State that was ranked sixteenth nationally—Michigan was up at seven—but I spared him the point.)

He shook his head. "Yeah, but still . . . the State game. . . ."

We came to Route 23, headed north, exited at Geddes Road. Five minutes later I was staring up at a medium-sized Colonial house, white-vinyl-sided, well-landscaped—the place I grew up in over twenty-one years. The roof and lawn were coated with a couple of inches of fresh snow; my footsteps crunched softly as I stepped across the grass. Suddenly the front door was flung open and a rectangle of cozy yellow light framed my mother, who immediately plunged into the freezing night air to hug me and shower me with kisses. The three of us went inside, my dad trailing.

"How are you?" asked my mom in the foyer, helping me remove my coat. "How was your flight? How's the job? How's your apartment? How's your roommate?"

"Well . . ."

"You look skinny. I'll bet you don't eat." To my father: "Ron, doesn't he look like he's lost weight?"

My father stared blankly; he'd never observed me closely enough to have any basis for comparison.

"Tell me," said my mother urgently. "I wanna know, do you eat?"

"Ma, I eat."

"Junk food, I bet."

"All kinds."

"How's your clothing situation? You have enough clothes?"

"Yup."

"What about suits?"

"I don't wear suits."

"What about when you meet people?"

"I don't meet anybody."

My mother had the illusion that engineers somehow were involved in high-level conferences; she pictured huge mahogany UN-style tables at which suited techies engaged in profound discourse with moguls of government and industry.

"I know you can't talk about your work," she said. "Come, I made you a snack." She ushered my father and me into the kitchen. "I know you're involved with national security. Did you get your clearance yet?"

In a phone call four months earlier I'd mentioned that the company had applied for a Secret clearance for me.

"Oh, yeah, it came." We sat down at the table. "But it's really irrelevant. For the job I'm on, the frequency isn't classified, and that's all I need to know right now."

She nodded, as she removed the covers from a half dozen Tupperware containers. Spread out in front of me were six freshly sliced bagels, a half pound each of Nova lox, Boar's Head Swiss cheese, chopped tuna, chopped egg, and ham.

Boneless fried chicken fillets peeked out from a plate covered with transparent plastic.

"It's all right," she said. "I know you can't talk about what really goes on." From the refrigerator she produced a container of baked salmon and another with macaroni and cheese.

"Ma," I said, "who is this for?"

"Your mother thinks you're starving to death," said my dad.

I could see his eyes sneaking over to that day's *Free Press*, nestled on one of the chairs. I knew he desperately wanted to read.

My mother sat down on the paper. "It's for you," she said brightly, nudging the salmon in my direction. "Now, tell us everything."

———
°

They were opposites, but why they ever attracted is beyond me. My mother was overprotective, gullible, warm, lacking in self-confidence. She worked as a clerk in an insurance office. She was obsessively concerned with, and wanted to be involved in, every area of my life—which made me quite unhappy and uncomfortable.

My father was aloof, calculating, self-absorbed, quietly arrogant. He was a successful and well-off periodontist. He had little interest in any area of my life—which made me quite unhappy and uncomfortable.

I watched television with them for a while, an *L.A. Law* rerun, and then the news—my father absorbed and commenting cynically on the Noriega and financial stuff, my mother attracted mainly by the human interest errata (people displaced by floods, lost children, treed cats)—and then, after a glass of chocolate milk and a black-and-white fresh from Silverman's Bakery, I lied about being tired and excused myself to go up to sleep.

I did not question the fact that my room was intact and

waiting for me, even as it had been since high school and four years at college. I had lived in Mosher-Jordan Hall at U of M, come home perhaps three times during a school year, but when I had, my room was always ready. Clean starched white sheets hugging comfy full bed, matching walnut chest and desk, laminated high school and (now) college diplomas on the walls, wallpaper with the blue hockey player outlines, half dozen shelves with bowling trophies, sensible nylon carpeting, Michelle Pfeiffer tear-out taped to the headboard. I swung my duffel bag alongside the bed. The room seemed somehow tiny, much smaller than I'd remembered it; I felt, when I visited Kushner, that I was in a doll's house.

"Good night," my mother whispered just before I closed the door. She extended a hand to touch my cheek. "It's nice to have you home scaled for pygmies."

I left at four P.M. on New Year's Day. I'd stayed out till early morning with two fraternity brothers I knew at school, made small talk and danced with one of their girl cousins and a female friend (who they later told me was gay), drank a fair number of gin-and-tonics. My mother hugged me at the door to the car, asked if I'd let her examine my luggage [No], wrote down my flight number and scheduled arrival time, requested I call her when I actually did arrive. "I'll call," I said, violating my policy of not giving in to her compulsive concerns, but wanting just to get away.

"Why do you need him to call?" said my dad. "If anything happens, we'll hear on the news."

"Godfabid," intoned my mom.

I looked again at the house. Despite its warm coziness, it seemed somehow no longer my own but an earlier version's embracing sanctuary, a home in a story that was read to me as a child, a story I'd outgrown.

My father drove me dutifully to the airport. At the gate, with extreme awkwardness, and completely out of character, he leaned forward to give me a quick kiss just as I turned to enter the terminal. It caught me mostly on the side of the jaw and all I could think to do was reach out and pat his head in return.

———
o

On the third day back, Kushner asked me for a favor. He had appealed his FTMP rating to Marv, who, quite naturally, had turned it down, and now Kushner had just returned from a further protest to Meissner.

"What happened?" I asked.

"No good," said Kushner, fidgeting with his tie as he stood alongside my desk. "I made a fool out of myself."

"Hey, look, you tried and—"

"No! No. . . ." I was surprised at his intensity. "I want to take this to Ingrassia. And I'd like you to help me."

"Well . . . okay, but are you sure it's really a good idea to go over Meissner's head?" I couldn't stop myself from picturing a pole-vaulting Warren soaring over the top of our Leader.

"They're not being fair to me. I have no choice."

I nodded skeptically. "So you want me to help you figure out what to say. . . ."

"I want you to say it for me. I want you to represent me."

"*Represent?* War, I'm not a lawyer. Besides, you speak very well yourself."

"Only when not stressed, or when I have lots of time to think of a response, neither of which will be the case with Ingrassia." His shoulders slumped. "Look, the fact is I'm not spontaneous, that's one of the reasons I can't talk to women. I get panicky, tongue-tied." He looked at me with those bovine, pleading eyes.

I drew a breath noisily (theatrically) through my nose . . . and nodded. "Just tell me when."

---
o

At seven P.M. that evening I got a call at home from Jerry
Zigfried, president of the Shoreview Soccer Club.

"We're asking all the team parents to come down and give
their inputs on the situation before the board reviews it."

"I'm sorry, what situation?"

"Well . . . yours."

"Mine? I don't think I have a situation."

"You don't feel a vote to dismiss you as coach qualifies?"

I stiffened. "I never heard anything like that."

"Wait a minute. They didn't tell you? Didn't anybody give
you a call? Manny Rosenbloom was supposed to call you."

Manny Rosenbloom was the league vice president of opera-
tions, or some title like that. "He never spoke to me."

"Oh, Jesus . . ." A pause. "Look, mainly it's about the forfeit. A number of the parents complained and, technically,
you did violate the league rules, and also . . . look, quite
frankly a lotta these people are fanatics . . . but, you know, the
fact that your team hasn't won a game and lost a lot by huge
margins . . ."

"So they wanna get rid of me?"

"There's a petition they gave in to the board. Of the seventeen kids on your team, we got ten parents' signatures. That's
quite a few."

I couldn't believe what I was hearing. "Is that ten parents of
different kids, different last names, or are there husband-and-
wife pairs in there?"

"I donno. I think they're mostly different kids, but there
might've been one or two pairs. Look, I'm sorry about this,
but our constitutional bylaws say that when we receive a petition signed—"

"Do these people understand that I'm a volunteer? That I

don't even have a kid on the team? That I'm . . ." I became aware I was shaking.

"Look, Zack, I'm not the one you need to convince. The board will make a judgment. Come down to Kennedy High School Thursday night at eight and tell your side. Really, the board will listen. It's not a lynching."

"No . . . actually it sounds more like a court-martial."

I could hear his exhalation. "Come to the meeting, Zack. Defend yourself."

"I don't think I want to," I said. And hung up.

―――
o

Wednesday, lunchtime, I saw Boulot on my way to the cafeteria. "Going for your walk?" I asked, as he tilted his beret to just the right angle and tucked his wool scarf into the collar of his brown leather jacket.

"Yes, you want to come?" he asked graciously.

Surprised, I agreed, and ten minutes later we were striding through the II parking lot. "There's mine," I said, pointing at my gray Ford Tempo.

"Very American," said Boulot.

A few moments later, near the fence, he indicated a small, rusted, vaguely greenish Peugeot.

"There's mine," he said.

"Very French," I noted. "And from its position I'd guess its owner was very late this morning."

Boulot laughed, a deep, rumbling, very French laugh. "Eets owner is incorrigible. Eets owner 'as a cheep on 'is shouldair."

"A chip on your shoulder . . ."

"More like a bouldair. Eet is not good, but what can I do?"

We headed out onto the sidewalk of Deer Woods Road, a four-lane boulevard that was home to neither deer nor woods, but rather to a mélange of furniture and fixture stores, discount outlets, third-rate diners, muffler and radiator repair shops, and sundry light industries—machine shops, platers, plastics houses, circuit board assemblers—most of which were International Instrument subcontractors. Boulot's pace was brisk.

"Lunchtime, I 'ave to get out to clear my head. Ozzerwise I am trapped in zat building like all ze rest of ze laboratory mice."

"Doesn't seem like you have much respect for your colleagues."

"My colleagues? Look, anyone who 'as been in engineering more than five years is either a lackey, a flunkey, or a zombie."

I turned up my collar against the chill January wind. "That sounds like something Shopper Jim would say. One of his rules."

"Yes, Shoppair Zhim. 'Ee is crazy, zat one. I sink, one of zese days, 'ee explodes, brings in a gun, kill everyone."

"Jim? Naw! Jim is calm. Cynical, but calm."

"Only on zee outside."

I shrugged. After a mile, he began talking about his daughter. "I don't know what to do wiz her, I am a very bad parent. Wiz her muzzer she used to play, they would sew together, cook somesing, put on, Idonno, hats, shoes . . . and all ze time she would laugh, smile. Wiz me, I try, I read to her, we play board games, cards, but I see, she plays because she sinks *I* want to. She sinks *I* need to be amused. But herself, I don't sink she 'as much interest. And she never laughs."

"What, uh, did your wife die of?"

He shook his head. "Stomach. All zee time she 'ad, how-you-say, dizzy stomachs—"

"Stomachaches."

"Yes. She thought it was nussing. Then one day she visits a doctor, 'ee takes tests. Cancer, 'ee says, but you 'ave a good chance to recover. Three months later Monique was dead."

"I'm . . . sorry. It must have been . . ."

"Thirty-two years old." We walked for a while in silence. At a corner pizzeria, Boulot announced, "I usually turn around 'ere," and we did so. "I was not a very good 'usband to her," he continued, as if the conversation had been continuous. "I was away four nights a week, going—" He stopped, and a step later I did too. "You can keep a secret, Zack?"

"Yes. Sure."

"I tell ziss to no one else. I am going to law school, I 'ave two more years. I stopped for a semester after Monique passed, but ziss year I start again."

"Law school . . ."

"Yes. I am getting out! You sink I want to spend my life under ze dirty little thumbs of people like Meissner, filling out all zeir stupeed forms, obeying zeir stupeed rules, doing zeir backward designs that make no sense. *Non!* I am going where ze power is. I am going to use ze great American legal system to bring people to zeir knees." He laughed. "Or maybe to my knees." He raised his eyebrows. "You sink I am crazy?"

I shrugged. "You have big plans."

In the distance, we could see the roof of International Instruments. "Probably not realistic. . . ."

At the edge of the parking lot I mentioned, "You know, Frenchman, if ever on a Sunday you have nothing to do and you want to bring your daughter—"

"Elise."

"—Elise to a soccer game, I coach in the Shoreview League and I'd let her warm up with the team—they're all boys around her age—"

"She is only seven, but already she loves the boys. I am going to send her to a convent in Normandy."

"—and, after, we could hang out someplace."

Boulot patted me on the back. "Sank you, Zack. We see. You are a nice boy."

And we reentered the building.

———
o

Kushner was hyperventilating. We were standing just outside the door to the Chief Engineer's office just prior to our ten A.M. appointment.

"Kush, relax, I'm gonna talk for you, it'll be okay."

"If I die, tell my mother I'm sorry. And you can have my chess set." His eyes were wide.

"You're not gonna die."

I opened the door and we stepped inside. A severe, short-haired blond secretary greeted us. "You're Mr. Ingrassia's ten o'clock?"

"Kushner and Zaremba," I said.

She motioned to an open office. "He's expecting you, go right in."

Kushner was quivering noticeably as we entered the inner sanctum. It was not as large as I'd imagined, and was furnished mundanely: two walnut bookcases, horizontal suspension file cabinet, shag carpet, two diplomas on the wall, half-dead potted plant in a corner. At his desk—wood, green blotter, metal-framed photograph of a thin brunette, calendar, Rolodex— Vincent Ingrassia was reading documents in a folder. He declined to look up as we entered, a sure sign, I thought, of a dick. Finally, after nearly twenty seconds, he lifted his gaze.

"Which one of you is Kushner?"

Kushner managed to lift a shaky index finger.

Ingrassia turned to me. "And you're the spokesman?"

"Yes."

Back to Kushner. "You can't talk for yourself?"

"I . . . I can, but I tend to get excited, flustered, and . . . and I lose my trend of thought."

Ingrassia's giant Adam's apple strained against his shirt collar. His stare had a detached hawklike intensity. "I don't know what there is to discuss." He held aloft the folder on his desk. "Your immediate supervisor reviewed it and concurred." He gave a challenging what-more-could-you-want? shrug.

"It wasn't fair," croaked Kushner.

Ingrassia crinkled his forehead. "How could it not be fair? *Why* would it not be fair? Does"—he glanced at the folder— "Marvin Sklar have some sort of grudge against you? Is that what you're saying?"

"I—I—" On Shopper Jim's red chart, Kushner's cheeks had risen to about a #18. "I . . . I don't . . . I . . ."

"Warren really doesn't want to make this a personality issue," I interjected.

"Ah," said Ingrassia. "The spokesman speaks."

"He simply feels that Mr. Sklar has been so busy with . . . various interests . . ." I caught the flicker of his grin before he could fix it. He *knew*. The sonofabitch *knew*. ". . . that he really hasn't been able—through no fault of his own—to give Warren's case the attention it deserves."

Ingrassia leaned back, ran a hand through his wavy, iron-gray hair.

"If you read Warren's essay," I continued, "you can see how dedicated and conscientious he is."

"Dedicated and conscientious don't necessarily make a good manager," said Ingrassia. "I read your essay too."

I noticed Kushner had severed himself from the conversation, was staring at a spot on the wall, zoned out.

"You were selected despite what you wrote," continued Ingrassia.

"Life is perverse," I said, then quickly looked at my shoes. *Diffident but aware.*

"So what do you propose I do?" said Ingrassia. "If you're telling me to disqualify Marv, and if all Meissner could go on was Marv's judgment, how could I do any better?"

Kushner was playing with his feet, trying to turn them 180 degrees apart, like Charlie Chaplin.

An idea entered my head. "Let him do another essay. Judge him on that."

I looked up slowly to meet Ingrassia's gaze. For nearly a minute there was dead silence. Kushner was swaying slightly, distinctly unstable in the front-to-back plane.

"All right," said Ingrassia, to my utter amazement. "You got a deal." He pointed at Kushner. "You write me another paper and I'll take a look."

Kushner seemed to deflate, a bloated Thanksgiving float punctured by a light pole. I nudged him toward the exit.

"But I'm warning you," called Ingrassia, freezing us both like trapped squirrels, "you'll be sorry if you waste my time."

○

The Kennedy High School cafeteria was a large vinyl-tiled room with a lunch counter and twenty rectangular tables that accommodated eight chairs each. The place was two-thirds full by the time I got there. I noticed several people flick their eyes in my direction as I made my way to the back and occupied one of the empty seats. The four men at my table ignored me (or pretended to). The audience was predominantly adults, although I did spot several kids from my team, and waved at one, Alan Gunderson, when he waved first.

At 8:05, Jerry Zigfried, seated at a table in a little clearing near the entrance, stood up and addressed the buzzing crowd.

"Ladies and gentlemen, if we can all quiet down and get started . . . we have a lot to do tonight."

The buzzing diminished slightly in volume.

Judy Levinson read the minutes of the previous meeting.

Two men I didn't know presented a report on negotiations with Town of Oyster Bay officials on the possible use of some vacant land for a soccer field.

A middle-aged, high-cheekboned woman went over details of an upcoming girls' indoor tournament in Farmingdale and asked for volunteer coaches to see her after the meeting.

Dennis McGrath, league treasurer, reported on bids received from three competing uniform vendors and selection of the winner.

And then they got to the main event.

"The next subject," announced Zigfried, reading from some notes, "concerns a petition we've received from parents of the Queens County Savings Bank Pee-Wee boys' team." He held up a sheet of paper. "The petition asks for removal of the coach, Zachary Zaremba. The reasons given are—and I'm quoting now—'his sole responsibility for the unnecessary, demoralizing, and totally illegal forfeit of the November twenty-seventh game with Jack In The Box, and his general complete lack of knowledge about, and unfamiliarity with, the game of soccer.' " He put down the paper. "In cases like this—and we've had them—what we do is, we throw open the floor for any comments or discussion, and then we immediately take an open vote of the board. But I want to make a few things very clear right at the outset. The people who coach our teams are unpaid volunteers. They give of their own time so all our kids can have an enjoyable experience. Although they cannot and should not be held to the standards of professional coaches, we nevertheless expect them to offer some reasonable level of instruction and guidance and, in general, to adhere to the policies and bylaws of the club.

"I'd like to remind you all that this is not a courtroom here, and so the person we are being asked to pass judgment on is not being afforded certain basic rights. Comments will be made that are pure opinion or hearsay or even prejudice. What I do expect is that everyone who speaks does so with respect and consideration for those who have different views. Those who can't or won't do that, I promise you, I'm gonna throw right the hell out." A pause. "Okay, floor's open."

Michael's father went first. "As, whatayacallit, instigator of the petition, I suppose I'm the one should say why we did it. Well, it wasn't something we were happy about. And even though a lot of us felt the coach really had no knowledge at all of the sport and, further, really couldn't handle a bunch of kids this age—which I'm not sayin' is easy—and even though we'd lost all our games—still, we were willing to let things ride . . . until the forfeit. When that happened, my son was devastated. He don't even wanna play anymore. I mean, we were *ahead* for the first time all year, there's only a few minutes left, a few minutes, and the coach, he just throws that completely away. Everything the kids worked for.

"Okay, so it was raining. Rain never killed anyone. The kids were already wet, they weren't getting any wetter, and the other team was wet too. *They* didn't forfeit. The referee, an experienced league ref, *he* didn't think the game should be stopped. It's *my* kid, *I* didn't want the game stopped. In fact, not one parent, *not one*, went over to the coach and asked him to take their kid out. But totally on his own, in clear violation of all the league rules, this coach pulls the team. You should've seen how many kids were cryin' because of that." He looked around belligerently. "Frankly, I want my enrollment money back. My kid hasn't learned anything the whole year. This coach stays, I want my money back. And I don't mind saying I will take legal action to get it."

He sat down. I saw a few people near him, including Cory's father, and Eric Nowicki's mother, pat him on the back. His reasoning had sounded good to me. I was clearly a criminal.

Julia Hibbert, Lee's mom, spoke next. "You know, most of us like the coach," she began, then proceeded to echo the previous argument, though in somewhat softer terms.

Barry Gunderson, Alan's dad, did the same.

Carmen Bilenko, Peter's mom, did the same.

A parent from another team told a story about a baseball coach in Smithtown who'd pulled his team off the field in protest over a balk call.

Don Shea, the Pee-Wee Boys' Division head, made some remarks about the stresses coaches were under.

Linda Nowicki noted how it was necessary for coaches to control their egos.

And then, suddenly, there were no more hands. "Is that it?" asked Zigfried, seeming reluctant to resume control.

Silence.

"Okay. Well, in that event . . ." His eyes swept the crowd. "Is Coach Zaremba here? I think he deserves the right of final response"—I heard "right" as "rite"—"if he wants. . . ."

I'd known the moment would come, had known it all along, and had been torn as to whether to defend and rebut—rationally, clearly, logically—or to simply make some kind of gesture—dramatic, emotional, symbolic. As the proceedings went on, the gesture was proving overwhelmingly appealing. It was so attractive to be hurt, wronged—hell, *martyred*. The Coaching Martyr of Shoreview. I would be legend. I could phone it in to *Newsday*.

I half rose, preparing to utter a single statement along the lines of, *Forgive them, for they know not what they do*—when suddenly a hand shot into the air and a woman stood up. It was Lilah Li.

I had seen her only twice since the infamous game, once in the II cafeteria, once in the hall outside the CREDIT UNION. Both times we had greeted each other cordially, politely . . . and with an imposed distance. After the postgame "appreciation," I had felt myself drawn in, weakened, over my head in a body of water I wasn't ready to enter. Though she was only three years older than me, it might've been ten, twenty. She seemed mature. She had a child. I'd felt the immense power of her attraction . . . and shied away. I'd restrained myself from contacting her and been relieved when, for whatever reasons, she too had declined to follow up. Regardless of what that kiss in the parking lot had meant, I wasn't ready.

She began speaking before I could utter a word. "Is there . . ." She looked around, for an instant caught my gaze. "Is there not one of you who would say something kind about this coach? Not one of you who might mention how devoted he is to the children, to *our* children? Not one of you who might note that, *unlike every other coach in this club,* he does not have a child on the team? That he coaches purely out of the goodness of his heart?"

(And because the Phantom told me I needed an activity.) The audience had hushed and was giving her total, concentrated attention.

"Is there not one of you who would note how much the children like him? How considerate he is of their feelings, how nice he is to them? How he never ever yells at them? How *fair* he is? How he gives everyone a chance, even the kids who aren't so good, who aren't hot shots and goal scorers, who on some other team would be relegated to playing half the game and in the back line—how he gives them a shot at playing up front? And how he does it at any cost, at the cost of losing and incurring the wrath of the win-whatever-the-price parents who can't distinguish six-year-olds from professionals? Is there no one else who would even mention that?"

I could see Kevin in the seat next to her, as mesmerized as everyone else.

"Is there no one who has seen this man minister to our children when they are hurt? Bandage them when they bleed, apply ice packs when they've been bruised, comfort them when they're distraught?" Even at a distance, I could see she was trembling. "Is there no parent here, on this team, who can admit that maybe, just maybe, on that day of pouring icy windblown rain, this coach was a better parent to our children than we were? That he could see more clearly what was important, that he was not so intimidated by the prospect of peer disapproval that instead of blindly acquiescing to league rules written ten years ago by men seated around a table in a comfortable room—he did what was *right,* instead of easy? What was sensible and reasonable and mature. What we should all have done had we only had the guts."

She gestured in my direction. "How dare you subject him to this? How dare you treat him like this, when everything he's done, given of himself, has been for us?" She pointed at Michael's father. "You want legal action, you disgusting, overbearing bully, I'll give you legal action." Head whirl. "I'll give you all legal action. If this coach gets dismissed, I'll sue the whole damn bloated bunch of you. I'll have you in court for a thousand years." She extended a hand to Kevin, who rose obediently. "Come," she said, and then, with him trailing, strode through an opening between tables and out the door.

It took nearly two minutes for the after-murmur to subside. Once again, Zigfried, looking now a bit shaken at Lilah's intensity, gestured toward me. "Coach?"

I stood up. "I think, uh, she pretty much covered it."
And threaded my way to the door and left the room.

———
○

In the corridor, Alan Gunderson emerged from a boys' room
and called to me just before I got to the exit. "Hey, Coach, you
know what snow is?"

I grinned. "Okay, what?"

"God's dandruff."

I nodded. "Very good, Alan." He seemed completely oblivious that his father had just argued for my dismissal. Which
was exactly what I'd always liked about kids. No grudges, no
agendas.

I pushed through the outer doors. God's dandruff was
coming down by the truckload, one of those intense, swirling,
foggy snows that bit into every exposed part of your body. I saw
Lilah and Kevin about twenty yards away at the edge of the
curb. She had paused to adjust the hood on his winter coat.

"Lilah," I called, and trudged toward her.

Kevin's face was just a nose and eyes peeking out of a
quilted porthole when I got there. Lilah, in contrast, had not
covered up at all; her long black hair whipped in the wind.

"We always seem to meet in parking lots," I said.

She didn't answer, bent to adjust one of Kevin's gloves. I
became aware of a freezing wetness at my neck and chest. I'd
forgotten to button my coat, but felt somehow powerless to
correct it. Caught in an icy dream, I waited until Lilah rose.

"I . . . I want to thank you." I simply could not form another
thought. "I want to thank you. . . ." I could not stop staring at
her. My breathing was as rapid as if I'd just run five miles.
Standing there in the snow, locking eyes with her, locking
more than eyes, I felt myself begin to shake from something
having nothing whatsoever to do with the weather.

I pulled her toward me and kissed her on the mouth. I had a brief thought that it was inappropriate in front of Kevin and that she might object . . . and then she opened her lips and our tongues intertwined and our salivas mingled and every bit of blood in my brain and body ran down toward my penis and I just about blacked out. Minutes later, when somehow, some way, we managed to disengage, I said to her, "I love you," and thought I heard her say the same before we dove into each other again, and stayed there like a living mandrel for the snow to surround and encase.

---
o

"No good," said Meissner, cheeks at *Cardinal-carmine.* "No good, no good, no good, no good!" He pounded his palm on the table of Conference Room F.

"Situation's not any good," echo-croaked Whispering Bill.

"CDR in six weeks," continued Meissner, "and we don't have a design. We don't . . . have . . . a . . . fucking . . . design. We have no design."

CDR was Critical Design Review. The real testicles-to-the-tree scrutiny. Bullshit's end.

Meissner's head swiveled from Marv to Boulot. Laser eyes on Marv—"Not only have we *not* reduced the current required for the transmitter output stage"—hot coal stare at Boulot—"but now you're telling me the current we do draw exceeds the rating of the power supply transistor."

"The present transistor, yes," agreed Boulot. His tie and belt were still on backward.

"And a new one—"

"Motorola has one zat can take ze current, but zey cannot deliver it before three months."

"And you've been to Purchasing to see if they can pull some kind of national defense priority shit?"

"Zey cannot," said Boulot. "Zey pull, but nussing comes out." He laughed.

Meissner's face went to Titian-scarlet. "Well, try them again, you hear. Try them again!"

"Gotta give 'em another try," elucidated Whispering Bill.

Meissner ratcheted back to Marv. "And you . . ."

"We are working the problem," said Marv smoothly. It wasn't the first time I'd heard that locution, and always found the missing "on" very annoying. It sounded to me like they were massaging the problem or kneading it, providing the problem with calming strength instead of solving it.

"Who's 'we'?" asked Meissner, jaw thrust forward. "You?"

"I'm furnishing the guidance, yes," said Marv, "but I'm spending most of my time on the oscillator-multiplier chain and the pre-amp stages. As you know, the transmitter output stage operates Class-C, and Class-C microwave amplifiers are an exceedingly narrow and deep specialty."

Meissner's eyes bulged; his head tilted at forty-five degrees. "So . . . who . . . is . . . 'we'?"

" 'We' is Warren Kushner and, of course, any technician assistance he may require."

Meissner swung slowly around to Kushner. "And . . ."

Kushner had a cold. He was sniffling and blowing his nose almost continuously. His lips were chapped, red, and puffy. Something yellowish was leaking from the corner of his left eye. "I'm trying," he croaked.

Meissner nodded slowly. "How *hard* are you trying?"

"He worked ninety-four hours last week," said Marv brightly.

"And how many did you work?" asked Meissner.

Marv fumbled through some papers. "Uh, it was quite a few, I don't have the exact figures in front of me."

Meissner to Kushner: "Is it theoretically possible to reduce the current?"

Electronic amplifiers use steady power in the form of direct current (such as might be supplied by a battery) to increase the amplitude of an alternating signal, in this case a high-frequency radio wave that would be beamed out an antenna. Unlike so-called Class-A or Class-B amplifiers that draw power supply current all the time or half the time respectively, the Class-C amplifier consumes current only during the fraction of a cycle it is on. Thus, it is very efficient . . . but also tricky to get working, particularly at microwave frequencies.

"Well . . ." said Kushner, then sneezed twice, blew into a shredded tissue, and wiped. "The problem is that the basic Class-C mechanism is augmented . . . or sometimes it can be—what's the opposite of 'augmented'—I donno—"

"De-mented," suggested Wonderboy.

"Excremented," suggested Boulot.

"—decremented," continued Kushner, "by . . . by"—three more machine-gun sneezes into virtually dissolved tissue, blow, wipe—"by a parametric mechanism that I believe involves the collector-base capacitance, and this mechanism, although quite variable from transistor to transistor, because the manufacturers don't—"

"Ahhhhhhhhhhhh!" Meissner had blown off the color chart. Was that actual blood oozing from his facial pores? "No. No. No no no no no no no. No. No."

Whispering Bill shook his head gravely.

"Don't . . . want . . . to . . . hear . . . it," said Meissner, holding up a palm. "Do not . . . do not . . . want to hear it."

He had lapsed into baby talk. I could see Shopper Jim tuck his head into the crook of his elbow in a desperate attempt to prevent an outburst of cackling laughter.

Meissner redirected at Marv. "Have you asked"—a blank pause—"for help?"

"I went to Him," said Marv. "He said He was too busy."

Meissner pursed his lips, shook his crimson head. "Well, it better get done. We're gonna look like fools otherwise. I am telling you, gentlemen"—this directed now at all of us—"I don't care how, but this just goddamned better get done."

8

Q3 AND Q7

Parkinson's Law: Work expands to fill the time
allotted for it.
SHOPPER JIM'S COMMENTARY:
INCORRECT. WORK EXPANDS *BEYOND* THE TIME
ALLOTTED FOR IT.

They didn't kick me out. I arrived home from work the day
after the soccer meeting to find a message on my machine
from Jerry Zigfried. The board had voted 5–2 to let me keep
coaching.

I had dinner that night with Lilah at a Chinese restaurant
and thanked her for "saving my job," although she steadfastly
refused any credit. "They simply came to their senses," she
said, as I watched steamy morsels of Three Flavor Shrimp disappear into the wet little tangerine-lipsticked *O* of her mouth
to get flicked between the perfect snow-white teeth by the
darting pink-pearl tongue.

"Cooler heads prevailed," I said.

"Decided not to start something they might not be able to
finish." Closed smile, still chewing.

"Unlike tonight. . . ."

"Unlike tonight."

133

I tried not to look at her as we drove back to my apartment. I was already so inflamed with lust that the mere inadvertent sight of a breast or thigh might lead to an embarrassment beyond words. I was practically gasping as we got out of the car.

I was not experienced with women. I'd had a girlfriend, Anne-Marie, in the spring semester of my junior year in college, and we'd slept together over several months, but she dumped me after the summer (she'd met a pharmacist from Flint) and I'd spent my senior year searching unsuccessfully for a replacement.

Sex with Anne-Marie had been good—physically almost as satisfying as my hand and with somewhat more emotional rapport—but two things had always bothered me a little. One was the sounds she made, periodic, forced *hnnnnn*'s, as if something were being squeezed out of her, more like turds than orgasms, or the expulsions of weightlifters as they strain to press a heavy barbell. The second was her references to God, seen even in blue-lettered GOD PROTECTS US signs in her dorm room, or her "Oh, God, ohh God, ohmagod," when I'd slide my hand up her thigh. Not that these objections would have even come close to making me give her up, but of course the sonofabitch Flint pill-pusher had taken the decision out of my hands, leaving me depressed and horny. A few dates in my senior year, some preliminary kissing and groping, one under-the-bra episode that regrettably never went further—and there was the extent of my sex life. The sexual revolution may have been in full gushing flow—if you believe all that ultra-trendy *Esquire-Cosmo-Playboy* bullshit—but yours truly was out on the banks of the stream.

I unlocked my apartment door.

"So," said Lilah playfully, "you gettin' much lately?"

We stepped inside.

"Sleep? Yeah. Quite a bit."

She nodded. "Good. That's good. Glad to hear it." She put her arms around my neck, flicked off her shoes, and, still wearing her tight leather jacket, stepped onto my feet. I began to shuffle backward.

Somehow, we ended up in the bedroom of my ex-roommate. "Why are you glad to hear that I sleep?" I asked.

She thrust her chest forward as she removed the jacket. "Because . . . I don't think you'll be getting a lot tonight."

She let me look. I lay on the Phantom's bed, steel-bar erection poking painfully at my Fruit of the Loom briefs, while she slowly opened her frilled white blouse and then zipped down and stepped out of her short black skirt. Standing there in stockings, panties, white garter belt, and bra, she let me devour her with my eyes. Anne-Marie, a bit on the fleshy side, had always insisted on being in the dark.

"Okay?" she asked after several moments.

"Uh . . ." I nodded. I had lost the power to move my jaw. My penis was the size of a golf club (okay, a *toy* golf club), and just as rigid. I pushed down my briefs, reached over to the end table, and extracted the Trojan Enz packet from where it had been ossifying in my wallet. A few fumbling moments later, I was officially vulcanized.

She came toward me, sat on the edge of the bed, reached around, and removed her bra. Her mouth had fallen open slightly and she, like I, had begun to breathe rapidly. Her nipples, as I brushed them lightly with my palms, were hard as gemstones.

I slid one hand between her thighs, felt the soft warmth, moved my fingers upward to the apex. It took a moment to realize the wetness was not perspiration, that it was seeping out of her like milk from a leaky container. I thought I heard myself moan as she undid the garters.

"I—I don't think I'm gonna be able to last very long," I gasped.

She slid off her panties. "It's okay," she whispered. "Me neither."

And then she took a long look at me. My face, my eyes, my chest with its feeble sprout of hairs just filling in at the center, my torso with the sit-up-rippled abs, my groin with its tight scrotal sac and huge swollen and veined *thing*, that aching shaft of blood-engorged muscle, encased in its latex shrink-wrap. I felt a tingling in each area of my body swept by her gaze; it was as if she were warming me by convection, her eyes like the heat guns we used in the lab to temperature-stress components.

"I—I really . . ." She couldn't speak.

She straddled me, her knees resting on the bed alongside my hips. Raising herself slightly so I could see the salmon-colored opening inside the black pubic triangle, she gently wrapped her hand around my member and guided it between her thighs. As the warm and sopping internal flesh dilated and collapsed around its turgid intruder, I heard a small involuntary sound escape from one of us, or maybe both. I was quite unable to tell.

She lay forward on top of me, and we opened our mouths and mingled our saliva and tongues. Six or seven thrusts was all it took—on my part it was quite involuntary by now—a molten rising magma, irresistible, and then the massive full-body spasms, the total *letting go*, the spurts jerking upward and out, one after the other in rushing waves of twitching release.

She was still moving, pistoning her body against mine, quickly—*one, two, three, four, one, two.* . . . A sound ripped from her throat, "Uhhhhhhhhhhhhhhnnnnnnnnnnnnnnnn," and kept going on, ululating for many seconds, perhaps fifteen, perhaps thirty, then halting briefly, then starting again, more choppy, her body still pumping ferociously, and I matching it with my own. I have no idea how long it was before the sound, and the thrusting, stopped.

She lay against me, her hair wet with perspiration, film of sweat bridging and blending the flesh of our bare torsos. After several moments, she lifted her head. "Not bad . . . for a first try."

"No, not bad."

We clung together awhile without speaking. I felt the tip of her tongue probe my right earlobe. "So, how you feeling?"

"Like my insides came out."

"Mmm." The tongue dipped into the shell of the ear. "You?"

"Good. Very good." A hesitation. "Good enough to want to go—"

"Again?"

A movement of the hips. The golf club, more like a banana now, began to stir. "Can you give me a minute?"

"Absolutely. Relax. I'll just explore."

She sat up, dropped one hand behind and beneath her— and onto my baby ass, whose cheeks she began to fondle. After another minute or two, her breathing picked up again and I felt the hand move toward my scrotum. Eyes shut, she continued the massage, breasts rising and falling, nipples all engorged and red, as large as cherry tomatoes. I reached out for her waist, twisted, and rolled us both over, coming loose from her in the process.

She lay before me now, brown eyes large and liquid, expectant hungry thighs spread wide at 180 degrees, glistening pink sheath open and ready. And my own plunger was once again curved steel.

"I believe I'm set to resume," I offered.

The mouth opened. "Then resume away. Please."

In the next several hours I managed to resume twice more, while Lilah claimed to have done so "at least six times."

"*Six* times?" I tilted my head incredulously. "Come on."

"You're skeptical." She stood, naked. I was still stretched out.

"Well . . . yes."

"You were there. There was, after all, certain evidence, although perhaps not conclusive."

I exhaled. "No, no, I believe you, it's just . . ."

She shrugged, then knelt to retrieve various items of scattered clothing. "It's been a long time, a *long* time."

I glanced at the Mickey Mouse clock on the wall, a Phantom artifact he'd neglected to take with him on his headlong flight to L.A. It was 1:15 A.M.

"Jesus," I said, "is everything okay with your sitter?"

"It's fine," she said. "I told her I might not be back till two."

I watched as she put on her bra backward—cups under her shoulder blades—fastened the hooks in front, rotated it into normal orientation, then stretched it outward as she tucked her breasts in and under. The garter belt went on next, but panties and stockings were neatly folded and placed in her handbag. Skirt pulled up, blouse tucked in, a wriggle into her shoes. The whole procedure—women dressing—was as fascinating and erotic as its reverse. I rose from the bed to find myself aroused. "How come you're not wearing your panties?"

She wrinkled her nose. "Too yucky."

I reached out to touch her face, moved to kiss her on the mouth. "You know the craziest thing? I could actually resume again."

She kissed back, gave me a flick of tongue, then pulled away. "Let's save some for later in the week."

I followed her out of the room, helped her on with her jacket, lingered with her at the front door. "You know, the stuff

I manufacture, I make it fairly quickly down there, and in large quantities. We don't really have to save it."

She kissed me this time on the nose, then opened the door. "It was . . . wonderful. I'll see you at work."

And she was gone, leaving me alone with my subsiding erection. Already, I was starting to picture her, to replay the evening, every second of it, a rerun in every hypersensory dimension—sight, sound, smell, touch, taste—in slow motion and stop action, with images from other times and places blended in. I was crazy flat-out in love with her, drowning in her, mind and body exploded in a million fragments and dispersed in every cell of her.

I slept in the Phantom's bed that night, identity lost, awash in the flood of Lilah Li.

○

"You went over my head. That was very disappointing."

Meissner had called me into his office after lunch.

"It wasn't meant in any way to be disrespectful, sir. Warren just felt that since you really didn't have any basis to overrule Mr. Sklar's judgment he wanted to try Mr. Ingrassia."

"So you're saying it was Kushner's fault. . . ."

"Well . . . no, not his fault, it's just that he asked me to be there."

"It was the wrong thing to do, you know that, don't you?"

I didn't answer.

"Don't you?" He leaned forward over his desk.

I remained silent and he kept staring. Fuck him, I wasn't going to cave.

After about thirty seconds of clench-jawed immobility and a final, theatrically loud inhale and exhale, he said, "Okay, we'll move on. The fact remains that Kushner needs help, and least of all on the FTMP. I want you to spend at least half your time working for Marv, assisting your friend in the modulator part of the design and with ECNs and measuring Q7s."

The output transistor, designated Q7, was the last element in the transmitter chain, the one that blasted out the high-power microwave signal.

"The measurements aren't easy," he continued, "and they need to be precise. Is that something you think you can handle?"

"Yes, I believe so. Same job charge?"

Momentary lip-tightening, then deep breath. "Right, 2301-4, the transmitter."

I backed toward the door, then ventured a final question. "If I have some problems, can I ask . . . Him?"

"Who?"

"Uh . . . the guy Marv referred to at the last meeting."

"Who's that?"

"Well, you seemed to know. *Him.*"

A look of disgust contorted Meissner's features. "*He* won't help you. Now get out of here."

I opened the door to find myself face-to-face with Boulot.

"One leaves, one enters," he said, squeezing by me into the office. "Conservation of cannon fodder." He closed the door behind him.

When I saw him later, I asked what had gone on.

"Oh, ze usual, 'ee screams at me for ten minutes, zen asks me to do somesing completely stupid."

"Like . . ."

" 'Ee looked up ze current rating on Q3, and 'ee says we can exceed eet, because eet would be only by ten percent."

Q3 was the twenty-eight-volt power supply transistor that provided current to the transmitter. "Did you tell him that if the manufacturer thought the part could take ten percent more, they would have increased the rating?"

"You know what zey say about a leetle knowledge," said Boulot. "It ees a dangerous theeng. 'Ee 'as *very* leetle knowledge, and so 'ee is very dangerous."

"So what exactly—"

" 'Ee says it would be only temporary, until ze transmitter group reduces ze current draw."

"And you said . . ."

Boulot shrugged, popped two Chiclets in his mouth. "No, of course."

——
○

Later that day, I reported to Marv, who was on the phone as I stood by his desk. He held up a palm to keep me at bay while he finished his conversation.

". . . so you'll ship on the twenty-third? Yes. Yes. No, *I* need them to satisfy *my* customer. Right. No, bill MES Technology directly. Right. Same as my home." A pause. "Same here. Hey, I'm counting on you." He hung up.

I reiterated what Meissner had told me.

"Well, good," Sklar said pleasantly. "Warren is right in there." He pointed to a doorway. "I think it's best to start on the ECNs."

"Okay," I said.

The phone rang and Marv snatched it up. "Marvin Sklar speaking." A moment of delay. "No, no, this is MES Technology. . . ."

I sidled away and entered the doorway, which opened into another small lab. Inside, I saw Kushner working at a benchful of equipment. "War?"

He looked up.

"Guess who's been assigned to give you some assistance?"

He peered at me dully, his eyes swollen rheumy slits, nose a peeling onion. "You wanna make it easier on me?" His voice was a hoarse bleat, scarcely different from Whispering Bill's.

"That's why I'm here."

"Then help me rewrite my Goals and Aspirations essay."

"Well . . . sure . . . whatever. But in the meantime—"

"In the meantime I got six ECNs I need to get out."

"Hey, just talk me through 'em, I'll get the prints, mark up the FROM-TOs, and do all the rest."

He nodded wearily.

Four hours later, having successfully used Shopper Jim's technique on Renee in Repro to extract copies of three drawings, I was bent over the last schematic when I noticed a notation near a component connected to Q7, the transmitter output transistor. "Hey, what's this?" I asked Kushner, who was recording oscilloscope settings in a notebook.

"What?"

I showed him the handwritten *OMIT B.*

"Beats me. I guess somebody wanted that inductor left out."

"But what does the *B* mean?"

Kushner rolled his head around. "It's probably some kind of rev letter."

As designs were altered, drawings retained their numbers but were given successive rev, or revision, letters each time there was an ECN.

"But then it should be on the drawing number, not on a note."

"Zack, I got work to do. Just make the changes."

"Which reminds me, I notice you're taking all your own readings. Shouldn't you be working on design? This is technician stuff. Where's Gung Ho?"

Kushner's head extended forward, like a chicken's. "Where's Gung Ho? Where's Gung Ho? Gung Ho is working on oscillators for MES Technology. Okay?"

I shrugged. "Just thought I'd ask."

I took the completed ECNs to Tim Mee. There was now an

array of six trailers in the fenced-off rear parking area; Mee's office was in the largest, Yu's in the smallest.

"How come they separated you?" I asked Mee. A small radio on his desk was tuned to 103.1; Little Anthony was singing "Tears on My Pillow."

"We tell too many joke," said Mee. "Boss afraid we not work enough."

I motioned out the window. "It looks like your work is expanding exponentially. Are these trailers all for AIR?"

"All AIR."

"How many ECNs are you up to?"

"Oh, maybe two-fifty, three hundred."

"Three *hundred* ECNs. . . ."

"No, three hundred *a week.*"

I rolled my eyes. "Wow."

"They building another building," said Mee, gesturing through a different window. A group of hardhats labored on the steel frame of a small two-story structure. "Just for ECNs."

"Amazing." I handed him my own ECRs. "Well, here's three more."

He reached in his desk, gave me a sheaf of ECR approval forms. "You gonna be one busy fella."

"I'm sure he already is," I said, grinning as I left.

---
o

I called Lilah while I sat in the Reliability Department. "I've been thinking about you all day," I said quietly. A dozen feet away, one of the Reliability guys was slowly poring through a huge black loose-leaf binder in an effort to find a component comparable to the one in the TO column of my ECR.

"I've been thinking about you," said Lilah.

"I'm ready to resume," I said.

"Me too."

"Right now I'm about to zoom, but tonight I'll be ready to rezoom."

"Are you . . . like . . . right now, are you . . . excited?"

"I'm sitting down, but I'm covering my lap with ECRs."

"So that's yes. . . ."

"Yes."

"Oh, God. That really . . . I wish we could do it right now."

"You're . . . excited too."

"Oh, am I."

"Jesus." I felt it engorging down my left thigh. "Are you . . . you know . . . wet?"

"Dripping."

"This is gonna kill me. I gotta hang up."

I clicked off. The Reliability guys occupied six desks. They were all overweight, heavy-breathing, perspiring men in their mid-fifties/early sixties who gave off an air not of energy or cleverness, but rather of stolid unimaginative competence, of . . . well . . . reliability. Somehow they brought to mind an article I'd once read in my father's office about Japanese pines, that one of their attributes was stability in high winds. These men might not invent the laser, but neither would they blow away in monsoon season. The guy I'd approached beckoned me over, and I was glad I'd hung up on Lilah when I had.

"Found a part here"—he indicated a page in one of the books—"says it's a 'beryllia substrate.' That what you're goin' to?"

Reliability was a service department; they were really not familiar technically with new components.

"We're going to a *resistor* on beryllia," I said. Beryllia was a ceramic that conducted heat extremely well and permitted higher power dissipations than older devices.

The Reliability guy nodded and thumbed through a dozen more pages. "Used a resistor on alumina in 1983, C-Com job."

"That's not it."

He closed the book. "You'll need to get me the vendor's data sheet on this."

"Okay," I said slowly. "Then what?"

"Then, after I call him, I can put it in the book."

"Okay. Then what?"

"Then I can sign off your ECR."

"Oh. Can't do it without that?"

He looked at me as if I'd just suggested he shove a cantaloupe up his butt.

I nodded. "I'll get you the specs."

———
o

Lilah was licking my nipples, her black hair sweeping across everything from my chin to my abdomen.

"Li, I can't anymore. I'm . . . done."

She looked up. "You did it to me."

"That was two resumes ago."

"So? Now it's payback time." She grinned. "Tit for tat."

I inhaled. "Li, I cannot have another orgasm tonight. There's nothing left."

She pouted theatrically, then raised herself up. "You know a woman's idea of a perfect lover?"

"Is this a joke?"

"A guy with an eight-inch tongue who can breathe through his ears."

I rolled my eyes.

"Rhonda Montalione told it to me yesterday. Now let's get back to resuscitating you." She licked her lips salaciously.

"Li—"

"Kidding. Kidding." She leaned down and kissed me softly on the lips. "I'm gonna go. Same time tomorrow?"

I reached out and caressed her cheek. "I love you, Li."

She took my hand and kissed the fingers. "I love you too."

---

o

We were in the lunchroom, helping Kushner with his Goals and Aspirations essay.

"The first thing you need to understand," said Jim, "is that what you write should have nothing to do with your goals and aspirations."

Kushner popped in three sunflower seeds from the bag he was working on. "But—"

"Rule Six: To gain management's favor, tell them what they want to hear, which is always different from the truth. In this case, the truth is you want to get into the Fast Track Management Program to shore up your own self-esteem and please your mother—both horribly misguided, if not clinically pathological, but nevertheless your real motives."

"So what does he write in his essay?" I asked, chewing on my plain-hamburger-nothing-on-it.

Shopper Jim shrugged. "He tells management that he wants to be like them."

Kushner scoffed. "But that is so transparently fawning and phony—they'll never believe that."

Jim raised his eyebrows. "Oh, but they will. What you're failing to perceive is management's almost limitless capacity for self-delusion. These are people who *want* to believe. And I offer as prima facie evidence how they conduct the programs they're in charge of. All they want to know is that the job is ahead of schedule, under budget, and meeting or exceeding technical goals. Now, talk about your load of shit, did you ever hear of anything ever that ran that way? But we are continually browbeat to say that our projects do. When you report the opposite, they refuse to acknowledge it's even possible, force you to work day and night to make it un-so." He pursed his lips. "You wanna get in the FTMP? Pick a hotshot manager and say you wanna be just like *him,* and then say why."

Kushner licked his lips. "Think he's right?" he asked, addressing me.

"Well . . . it's possible. Your last approach certainly didn't work." Kushner's first essay had been a kind of extended existential missionary statement. He wanted to be in management purely for the reward of doing something well—he'd cited Ivan Denisovitch caring about how he laid bricks on the Siberian tundra.

"So who should I pick?"

"Well . . . what manager do you admire?"

"No one! Are you crazy? They're all dicks."

I looked at Jim. "Warren feels there's a dearth of suitable candidates."

"Who's gonna read your essay?" asked Jim.

"Ingrassia," said Kushner.

"Pick him," said Jim.

o

Friday night, I left the lab at six-thirty. "You stayin'?" I called to Kushner.

He nodded, then sneezed three times.

"You coming in tomorrow?"

"Whadda you think? You?" He wiped his nose across his sleeve.

"Yeah. Okay." I watched him lean over to squint at a meter. "You getting anywhere?"

"Some," he said. "You put in twenty-two amps, you get two

hundred watts out. Stand on your head—stand on your dick—
that's what you get."

"I left the six hot ones over there," I said, referring to the
few specially responsive transistors I'd culled from a much
larger batch.

"Great," said Kushner. He looked up. "Thanks."

"Uh, you, uh, do any work on your essay?"

"Almost done," he said.

"You researched Ingrassia?" Kushner had been going
around the company asking people about the Chief Engineer.

"Best I could. You'll read it?"

"Sure. Absolutely. Anytime."

He nodded, and I left.

Seven hours later, I was lying in bed with Lilah in my apartment. Kevin was sleeping over Cory's house; Kevin's mom and
I had the entire night and most of Saturday morning.

"You know," I said, stroking her hair, "this still won't get you
preferential treatment."

"No? God, what's a person have to do these days?"

She was in a mint-green silk robe, I in undershirt and
briefs. We were talking about selections for my indoor soccer
team. In the winter months, a cut-down group of nine players
was chosen for the six-on-a-side indoor tournament. The picks
were strictly up to the coach.

"Well, there might be something. . . ."

"Believe me, anything that gets Kevin on the team. Any
twisted, disgusting sexual perversion you want, all you need is
to ask."

"We've already done eighty percent of 'em, but . . ." I
inhaled her scent, a delicate flowery perfume of some kind,
lilacs plus something else. "Actually, there is one particular
act, although a lot of women consider this over the line."

She shrank back ever so slightly. "I'll try anything . . . almost."

I'd been staring into her hair; now I turned to face her. "Move in with me."

I saw the eyes widen, the rosebud lips part.

"Look, it makes perfect sense. You said yourself you can't stay where you are, the basement is bad for Kevin's asthma. So now with the Phantom's room vacant, he could have that. It lets us get to see each other every night without you having to get a sitter and worrying about getting home, and . . . and . . . best of all . . . you would chip in toward the rent so I'd have to pay less."

The jaw stretched. "Ah, so now the true motive emerges."

I leaned forward to kiss her neck. "You can't deny it's the only reasonable course of action."

"I can't?" Her eyes closed, the long black lashes grazing the high cheeks.

"Can you?" More kissing; her breathing grew faster. I loosened the robe, kissed down below the clavicles. "Can you?" The robe was off. The legs went around my torso. "Can . . . you?"

The abdomen began a slow grind against my own. I felt her hands tug downward on the waistband of my briefs.

"Can you?"

"No," she whispered.

---
o

We were sitting up in bed, watching *Cool Hand Luke* on channel nine.

"I saw you started a new project this week," she said during one of the interminable commercials.

"You saw? Whaddayamean, '*saw*'?"

"I pulled you up on my terminal. Your name."

"You did? Why?"

"I do it all the time. I just . . . I like to have it in front of me. It makes me feel, I donno, like I'm with you."

"My time charges make you feel like you're with me?"

She grinned sheepishly, endearingly. "It's a girl thing."

I shrugged. "I suppose so."

"So how do you like the new job?"

"Well, it's not really new, it's just a different part of the same one I was working on, the Advanced Interrogator/Receiver."

"No, it's not."

"Yes. Now I'm working on the transmitter; before I was working on the power supply."

"Job 6208?"

"Nnn . . . no. I think it's 2301-4. Something like that. Who remembers?"

"Job 6208 is the E2C upgrade. That's what you charged."

"Doesn't sound right."

"Yup, it is."

"You sure?"

"As sure as I am that twenty minutes ago someone's penis was in me." She grinned.

"You could have imagined it."

No answer.

"You could have dreamed it."

Luke, at last, was resuming.

I put my arm around her. "Well, Ms. Li, thank you for pointing out the possible error in my job charge. I'll check it out."

"I'd appreciate it," she said. "We in the Accounting Services Group of the Software Engineering Department like to think we're a hundred percent accurate."

"Uh-huh. Well, I like to think I look like Tom Cruise, but that doesn't make it so."

Luke was in the process of eating fifty eggs when the phone rang. "I'm not gonna answer it," I said. "It's probably a crank. Who calls at two-thirty in the morning?"

"No, no, it might be Kevin. Maybe he's sick or something, some emergency."

I rolled over and snatched up the receiver. A familiar voice intoned my name at the other end. I listened for several moments, then said, "Hold on," then covered the mouthpiece. "It's Warren," I whispered. "He finished his FTMP essay."

"Okay . . ."

"He wants me to read it."

"Okay . . ."

"Now. He wants to bring it over."

She nodded. "You were right about the crank call."

"Should I let him? He's, you know, quite loony about this."

She shrugged. "Okay by me."

"You can bring it," I said into the phone.

"Great," said Warren. "You're an unbelievably terrific friend." He hung up. I turned to Lilah. "He wanted me to look at it so he'd have time over the weekend to make any revisions."

Lilah patted my cheek. "Anything that makes you happy."

───
o

It was four pages long. Warren sat on a kitchen chair while Lilah and I took turns reading it on the couch. Lilah was still in her robe, I had put on jeans and T-shirt. Warren had declined an offered cup of coffee when he arrived; he fidgeted now as I glanced up from the last page.

"Almost done," I said.

"Take your time."

It was 3:15 A.M. The essay read like a condensed version of his first one, except Ingrassia was featured throughout as prominent idol. References were made to his "managerial style," his flexibility, his demeanor, his sensitivity to people, his technician-to-Chief Engineer rise through the company. *I see the FTMP as my start along the same hallowed path,* read the last sentence.

I looked up. "I think maybe you should take out the 'hallowed.' "

"Uh-huh, uh-huh," said Warren. "Okay. But how is it otherwise?"

I glanced at Lilah.

"It, uh, it really does suck up quite a bit," she said.

"That's by design," I interjected quickly. "Shopper Jim said management will buy any amount of that."

"I still agree 'hallowed' crosses, Idonno, some border."

"How about 'sacred'?" said Warren.

Lilah and I exchanged glances. "I don't think so," I said.

" 'Honored.' "

"It's a path. You don't really have an honored path."

" 'Fateful.' "

"I don't think that's exactly—"

" 'Exalted.' "

I puffed my lips.

"Damn!" said Warren. "I need a word, give me a goddamn word!"

There was a moment of silence, then Lilah said, "Dildo."

"That reads well," I said, " 'Along the same dildo path.' "

Even Warren laughed.

" 'Challenging,' " said Lilah. "How about that? Management always talks about challenges, as if anything easy is automatically no good."

"I like it," I said.

"I like it too," Warren agreed.

We made a few more grammatic and stylistic changes and then, at four-thirty A.M., Warren finally left.

"I feel sorry for him," said Lilah. "He's quite disturbed. I hope they let him into the program."

"It'll be a challenge," I observed.

9

SEVEN UP AND DOWN

Peter Principle: In a hierarchy, people are promoted until they reach their level of incompetence.
SHOPPER JIM'S COMMENTARY: THIS APPLIES ONLY TO MANAGERIAL PERSONNEL. A COMPETENT ENGINEER IS SO VALUABLE THAT HE'S KEPT AT HIS POSITION UNTIL HE'S LAID OFF.

The library had no books on the indoor game. It was played with six on a side, three forwards, three fullbacks, with small netted goals at each end of the gym. The tournament took place in one day; the games were divided into four six-minute periods.

I had invited everyone on my outdoor team to try out, dreading the idea that I'd have to make choices, not knowing how I would explain it to the kids, determined to evaluate them only on skill, not whether I liked them, not whether their father had petitioned to remove me, not even whether I was fucking their mother as fast and as often as I could. Fortunately, providence spared me: Only nine kids showed up—three were sick, two away with parents on vacation, three had decided not to return to the team—and so I was able to take everyone who attended.

Ed Nowicki had not returned as assistant coach and I'd impressed Lilah into the position.

153

"But I don't know anything," she'd protested.

"Me neither," I'd said. "I wouldn't worry about it." (Actually, I did worry about it quite a bit.)

I discovered, after we'd lost our first game and tied the second, that unlike in the outdoor version, lanky kids with open field speed tended to do less well than low-to-the-ground chunky kids who could churn their legs. Also unlike the outdoor game, the goalies couldn't nap between the other team's attempts. The heavy rat-a-tat thuds of missed-shot rebounds off the walls behind them were better awakeners than any of my shouted admonitions. As always, I kept my own focus on fundamentals (since I didn't know anything beyond them): "Trap the ball, first, Eugene, before you try to kick it! Side of the foot, Lee, *side*, not toe! Kevin, stay even with Cory! When he moves up, you move up." Et cetera. Lilah, while calling out encouragement, helped me with time management, making sure our substitutions let everyone get about the same playing minutes.

Between games we went into the corridor, where we practiced headers in a circle. I embarrassed Lilah into participating, reminding her, as I did the kids, to keep her mouth closed and teeth together. Everyone seemed to enjoy trying to keep the ball in the air with only heads; in some ways it was more fun than an actual game. When we rested ten minutes before the next contest, I saw Cory and Eugene in excited discussions. Finally, Cory turned to me.

"Coach, who runs the school, the principal or the custodians?"

"Well . . . it's the principal, actually."

Cory whipped around to Eugene. "See? I told you."

"I think it's the custodians," said Eugene. "Mah dad is a custodian an' he tol' me he an' his buddies, they run the school."

I considered a moment. "I see. Did he maybe say something like, 'If not for us, the school couldn't run'?"

"Tha's it."

"So," said Lilah, "in a way, he does run the school."

Cory looked upset.

"We'll talk about it after the game," I temporized, shooting Lilah an evil look.

As it turned out, we won our next three games and finished second in the tournament. I took the kids, and whichever parents wanted to tag along, to a nearby place for pizza. When we were there about a half hour, Alan Gunderson (whose parents *hadn't* attended) came up to me, holding a half-eaten slice of Sicilian.

"Coach, if God made people from nothing, where did he get the stuff to use?"

I glanced quickly at Lilah across the table; she shrugged.

"Alan," I said, "I'm just a soccer coach. I'm really not good at answering God questions."

"I am," piped up Lee Hibbert, a tiny kid with a very short crew cut. "All I can tell you is that God is everywhere."

"Great," said Alan skeptically. "So he's in . . . this chair?" He pointed to the back of my seat.

"Yup," said Lee smugly.

"What about the floor? Is he in the floor?"

"Yup."

Alan pointed to his pizza. "How about this? You tellin' me he's in this?"

"Yup."

"So if I ate this, I'd be eating God. . . ."

Lee looked uncertain.

"Alan . . ." I cautioned.

Too late. Alan took a big bite out of the Sicilian, then several more before it disappeared completely. He brushed the crumbs from his hands with great self-satisfied cymbal-clanging motions.

"I just ate God," he declared loudly, repeating it several times as he returned to his chair.

Afterward, on the way out, Lee's mom approached me at the door. I could see she was trembling. "Coach—" she began.

"Zack."

"Zack. I just want to say, I—I'm very embarrassed and ashamed of what went on at that meeting."

"Look, that's in the past, so—"

"No. No. It was wrong. All of us. You know, we're a tight community here, a lot of us have known each other for years, and all it takes is one or two to put some pressure on. . . ." Her appeal seemed as much to Lilah and Kevin, who stood behind me, as to me.

"I appreciate your saying that," I said.

She reached out, gripped my hand (quickly, quite hard), then let go. "You're a good coach."

"Thank you."

She exited to join her son, as Lilah and I and Kevin lingered for a moment, last ones in the restaurant.

"Coach," said Kevin quietly, "did Alan really eat God?"

"Whadda you think?"

Kevin raised his eyebrows. "I don't think so."

"Well . . . I don't either." I looked over at Lilah. "So."

"So."

"Nice day."

"Very nice."

"And now comes the best part."

She tilted her head and scrunched her eyebrows in that five-year-old-girl/I-don't-understand look that I found totally irresistible.

"Going home."

It took an instant, then her face relaxed into a smile of comprehension. I put one arm around Kevin, another around her, and we walked through the door. They had moved into my apartment two days earlier and now we were returning there together.

---

o

The executives dwelt on the second floor, and you could tell you were in a different place. The ceilings had sound-absorbing tiles, two-inch pile carpeting groveled under your feet, potted plants occupied alcoves in the corridors. Kushner, rheumy-eyed, sneezing, flat-footed, trudged alongside me through the nylon. A day earlier Ingrassia had bumped his essay to a higher level in management.

"Recused himself," Shopper Jim had commented.

"What?"

"It's a legal term. Like when a judge feels a particular case presents a conflict of interest or otherwise has an aspect that would lead to his not being impartial."

"So 'recuse' means he doesn't want to do it."

"Right."

According to Kushner, Ingrassia had decided that since the essay was so full of praise for him, it prevented him from judging it fairly.

"Or giving the appearance of fairness. Appearance is very important," said Jim.

"Appearance to *who?*" said Kushner. "He's the only one going to see it."

It made no sense, but nevertheless, Ingrassia had passed the essay onward and upward to Yale Sanders, executive vice president of the Military Systems Division of International Instruments. Kushner and I both had been summoned to see him.

I felt Kushner stumble alongside me, reached out to steady him. "Hey, relax. It's gonna be okay. I'm sure this is just a formality and he's gonna let you in."

"Idonno, I really don't know."

We were approaching Sanders's office.

"He's not gonna invite you all the way up here just to tell you you didn't make it. If that were the case, he'd've sent a memo or had his secretary call."

"You think so?"

I'd just about convinced myself. "Absolutely. Relax. You're in."

Sanders's secretary, one Marla Hastings, had dyed blond hair, pouty cocoa-lipsticked lips, and wore a clinging tan knitted miniskirt ensemble that outlined every lushly curved protuberance of her body.

"If I wasn't so exhausted, frightened, and depressed," whimpered Kushner, after we'd sat for twenty minutes on a couch that faced her desk, "I'd have a boner the size of my arm."

"Two Clydesdales, at least," I agreed, invoking Shopper Jim's rating system. In addition to Ms. Hastings's physical structure, she had a certain indefinable *look*, a certain evil/needy combo that was powerfully seductive. Less exhausted and frightened than Warren, certainly not depressed, I in fact *had* developed an erection, although smaller in size than Kushner's arm. I pictured Ms. Hastings leaning backward atop her desk, legs apart, panties at her knees, talking extremely professionally into the intercom while I grazed between her juicy thighs. I quickly covered myself with a *Microwave Systems News* that I pretended to browse. I had a brief pang about being mentally unfaithful to Lilah, but, hey, fantasies were fantasies. Evanescent, they arrived unbidden and flickered through the consciousness without control.

"Mr. Sanders will see you now," said Marla in an evil/needy voice.

"I'll take this with me," I said, standing up with the magazine, using it to partially shield my groin as I shuffled toward the inner office. "Middle of an article. . . ."

She smiled faintly in an evil/needy way. I was sure she knew.

Sanders's office was as large as my parents' living room in Ann Arbor. Cream-white carpet, rubber plant in one pot, dieffenbachia in another, cherrywood bookcase, Moroccan leather couch, matching tufted leather easy chairs. Sanders himself had the kind of blond-gray hair that makes it impossible to tell where one color ends and the other starts. His features were chiseled: aquiline nose, small flat ears, narrow mouth, square jaw. In short, he looked like Superman (actually, Clark Kent), and, just on appearance alone, I would have immediately hired him to run any company I'd ever own. He wore a light gray perfectly fitted suit, and as he came around from behind his desk, I could see that his gray shoes were a perfect match.

He didn't ask us to sit down. "This is going to be short," he said, his face unsmiling. *Uh-oh.* "I'm going to talk to you"—me—"and then you"—Warren.

Warren sneezed five times. I didn't look, but I knew by then he must be smearing his nose, cheeks, and lips with wet shreds of tissue, a papier-mâché snot-mummy in the making.

Sanders stood directly opposite me. "Christmas, you shook my hand three separate times and thought I didn't notice. I'll remember that."

He didn't wait for a response, not that I could come up with any, before moving to face Warren. (I did become aware, with some residual grudging gratitude, that my erection had completely disappeared.) "I read your essay," he said.

I thought I heard some kind of sound escape Warren, something liquidy that was halfway between a moan and a choke.

"And I've investigated your work here thus far," continued Sanders. "And I will tell you this." His left index finger rose in the air and pointed at my friend. "You are a seven, you will always be a seven, and I will always think of you as a seven. Seven. Seven. That is what you are." He turned and walked back behind his desk.

Warren and I, both stunned into silence, backed toward the door. "Thank you," croaked Warren as we passed through.

○

"He's depressed," I said to Lilah. "He had his heart set on this thing." Warren had gone home "sick" immediately after we'd left Sanders's office and hadn't shown up for the next two days.

"But it's so stupid. I mean, just because somebody, some obvious asshole, calls you a seven doesn't suddenly make you less capable."

"Yes, I know that and you know that, but Warren doesn't think that way."

"So what're you supposed to do?"

"I don't know. The only thing I can imagine that might make him feel better is . . ." I averted my eyes. "Idonno, if he could get some kind of . . . date."

"Zack—"

"I mean, you must know somebody, she doesn't even have to be pretty, you know, *anything*, as long as it has a crack between its—"

She looked at me sharply.

"Sorry. Look, the guy just needs some female companionship. He's lonesome and he's horny and—"

"Needy is a turnoff," said Lilah.

I thought of Sanders's secretary. *Not necessarily.* "Well, okay, so we'll coach him to act more cool. Come on, isn't there anyone . . . ?"

She chewed her lip. "Idonno, let me think. It's possible.

There's this girl who delivers the interoffice mail, Rhonda. . . ."

I raised my eyebrows. "Is this the Rhonda who told you a woman's idea of a perfect lover?"

She nodded.

"She sounds about right."

"Oh, so one dirty joke tells you all you need to know about a woman's character?"

"Well . . . it tells me she has a sense of humor, that she's not a prude, and—hey, it's something."

She nodded glumly. "I'll see what I can do. But you need to do two things in return."

"Sexual favors, perhaps . . . ?"

"Coach Warren so he doesn't appear desperate when he calls her."

"Okay. And . . . ?"

She pursed her lips and swayed a little. "Something's going on with job charges. I want you to find out more about it." I'd already checked for her that my own charge was 2301-4, as I'd thought, and confirmed with Meissner that that was correct. "I'd like to know who else among the engineers is actually working on AIR but charging E2C."

"It's not E2C."

"It *is* E2C. Somehow, some way, your charge—every week—is showing up as 6208."

"What's the difference? So they're playing a little game, balancing out some costs, what's it to you?"

"It's illegal."

"So . . ."

She shrugged. "They shouldn't be doing it."

"Li . . ."

"I want to know."

"And what will you do with the information?"

Her eyes widened and for the first time I saw something there I hadn't encountered before, something defiant, challenging . . . and resentful. "I'll take it to my supervisor."

I decided not to push it further. "Okay. I'll see what I can find out."

"Good."

With a '*Good*' delivered in that tone, I wasn't eager to find out what a '*No good*' would sound like.

Three evenings later I was playing chess with Kevin when the phone rang. "I bet it's Uncle Tim," said Kevin. Lilah had two older brothers: Tim, a chemist who worked for Dow Corning; and Alan, a neurologist. She was fairly much estranged from Alan, as she was from her father, but had recently resumed contact with Tim. In general, she was secretive about her relationship with her family and resisted my efforts to get her to talk about them—efforts I'd decided not to press. Still, I could not resist prying just a little.

"Is Uncle Tim married?"

"I think so," Kevin said. "I know he has a son."

"You mean . . . your cousin."

"Yeah." He was studying the chessboard intently. "Cousin Steve. But you don't need to be married to have a kid." He looked up, grinned.

"So I've heard." One more tiny pry. "So when was the last time you saw Cousin Steve?"

"Never."

"Never?"

"Mom doesn't get along with Uncle Tim. The only reason he's calling is because Mom owes him money." He pushed a pawn up one square, opening a path for his bishop, which now threatened my queen. A pretty sophisticated maneuver for a seven-year-old.

"Nice move, Kevin." I myself had never progressed beyond

plodder as a chess player; in another year, I imagined Kevin would be beating me.

"Mom owes a lot of people money," continued Kevin matter-of-factly.

Suddenly I wanted to change the subject. Not only was I violating a certain implicit trust, but he was telling me things I wasn't sure I cared to hear.

"The reason is Grandpa didn't give her any when she was going to college and she ran into a lot of deb."

"You mean *debt?*"

"I don't know how to pronounce it. Is that it? I read it in a letter she once wrote Grandpa. I thought the 't' was silent, like, did you ever hear of silent letters?"

"Sure."

He looked at me slyly. "Did you ever hear of noisy letters?"

I nodded slowly. "Very good, Kevin."

"I was gonna ask that to Mrs. Formentate when she taught us about silent letters, but I chickened out."

"Probably a wise decision, Kevin." I moved a knight to block his bishop's path to my queen and he shook his fists in a theatrical gesture of frustration. I really liked Kevin; in the past week I'd begun kissing him good night. He slept in the Phantom's bed and seemed fascinated with the detritus of the latter's musicianship: a worm gear from the neck of some guitar, a plastic pick on the floor of the closet, a torn magazine page featuring ads for four-track mixers. In the back of my mind, I was planning to buy Kev a starter guitar of his own. I looked up to see Lilah standing in the doorway.

"That was Rhonda," she said. It was Wednesday; we were planning to double date Friday night. I had told Warren that he needed to call Rhonda before the date so they'd each feel more comfortable when they met in person. Lilah would set it all up so Rhonda would be expecting it.

"It's *not* a cold call," I'd told him. We were talking over the phone; Warren still hadn't shown up at work, claimed "some kind of bronchial thing" was keeping him immobilized. "She's already agreed to go out with you."

"But you know how I get . . ."

"Warren, you just talk to her like you would to a guy."

"I can't talk to men either."

"You just say whatever comes into your head."

"But nothing ever does."

"Ask her about herself. She's a mail girl."

"Has she ever seen me?"

"Probably. Probably has."

"So she won't be disappointed."

"No. No, absolutely not."

"Have I ever seen her?"

"I don't know. Maybe. Lilah said she has curly hair, wears cutoffs."

Silence. "I'll never be able to talk to her. She'll hang up on me."

"She won't hang up." Silence. I decided to appeal to his horniness. "Lilah says she's, you know, a hot babe."

"You mean hot as in *pretty*?"

"I mean hot as in strongly craving male companionship. Hot as in, 'Insert tube into slot and push.' " I wasn't above being crude if it would accomplish the objective.

"If she's hot and willing to go out with me, she must be ugly."

The old Groucho paraphrase: I wouldn't go out with any girl desperate enough to date me. "Warren, you *have* to call her. Just shut your eyes, dial, and do it. It'll be over in ten minutes and then you can look forward to a nice date."

Silence.

"Warren, nookie. Real live hot girl flesh. Much better than

pictures. Lips, breasts, nipples, tushie, *thighs,* Warren. Mmmmm. Warm wet thighs . . . panties . . ." I was getting *myself* excited. "And the head talks too, says nice things, whispers to you, says she likes you, *listens.* Warren, come on, you'll call?"

Silence, then a long sigh. "I'll try."

"Nipples, Warren. Good boy."

Lilah was shaking her head now. "It's off."

I shut my eyes. "Why?"

"I donno, he—"

"Did he call?"

"He did but she said, Idonno, she couldn't describe it, his conversation wasn't right. Something . . ."

"Whaddaya mean, *'wasn't right'?"*

"Like, she'd say something and he'd say something back, but it was as if he wasn't talking to her, he was having another conversation. Like he would just hear a word or a phrase, and then say something related to it. She asked me if he was autistic."

"He's not autistic. How could she think that?"

"Well, she just said she couldn't talk to him. Also, he took very long to respond after she said something. And he'd sneeze a lot, maybe five, six times every other sentence."

"The guy has a cold. He's had it for two months. Lots of guys have colds." Seize on the non-issue.

Lilah shook her head. "She tried the best she could."

"You told her he was shy?"

"Yes, she knew that."

Poor crazy Warren. "So how'd they leave it?"

"Nowhere. She's not going out with him."

०

Boulot showed me the technical memo he'd written. It was addressed to Meissner, with a copy to Whispering Bill and Wonderboy. I scanned it, although I already knew the content.

Boulot, after a personal appeal from Whispering Bill, had relented on his refusal to evaluate Q3, the power supply pass transistor, at currents exceeding the manufacturer's rating. Between him and myself we had tested nearly fifty units. Surprisingly, nearly sixty percent had passed, that is, had functioned adequately over the temperature range, even though reliability would likely be compromised. The problem was with the remaining forty percent. These broke into oscillation, i.e., acted like miniature generators, producing spurious uncontrolled frequencies that completely destroyed their operation in the circuit and that, in a few cases, had actually burned them out. In the memo, Boulot carefully detailed the experimental results and, using nonlinear feedback theory, presented an outline of the explanation. The inevitable conclusion seemed clear: The present Q3 could not reliably be used at a current level greater than that specified by the manufacturer.

I put down the memo and shrugged. "As you thought."

"Of course, a waste of time. Uh, did you read ze addendum?"

I snatched up the pages, flipped through them, found nothing. "No. Where—"

Boulot handed me a ten-power loupe he kept in his front desk drawer. "Left-hand corner. Top."

I stared at the first page, noticed what looked like a very small blurred line in the area he'd indicated. As I positioned the loupe so the spot was magnified, I could see that the line was actually a series of incredibly tiny printed letters.

FUCK YOU ALL, read the minuscule message.

"Very good," I said.

"My personal advice to management," said Boulot. "I do eet all ze time."

I passed the loupe and memo around for the others to read: Jim, Nussbaum the tech, Wonderboy.

"I can write half that size," said Wonderboy.

"Here it comes," said Jim. He turned to Wonderboy. "No, you can't."

"Actually," I said, "I'm pretty good at small-writing myself."

Boulot chuckled. "All right, so we 'ave a contest. Who can write ze smallest. But we need a judge."

"I'll be the judge," said Jim.

"Unacceptable," said Wonderboy.

"On what grounds?"

"On the grounds that you're an asshole."

Before Jim could respond, Nussbaum offered, "If it's okay, I won't enter. That way I can be judge." He looked around; the silence confirmed there were no objections.

"We each get three days to submit samples," said Wonderboy. "Smallest-sized print. Uppercase only. At least ten letters. No mechanical aid other than a handheld pencil. Each letter individually legible, as judged by Nussbaum." He looked around. "Agreed?"

We all agreed.

"This should consume about a hundred grand of U.S. taxpayer defense money," said Jim.

"I contribute howevair I can," said Boulot.

○

Somehow it was not the greatest of surprises when the call came on Sunday night from Warren's mother. Certain possibilities lurk at the boundary between conscious and subconscious, shadow dreads that part of you anticipates but can't bear to really address.

"I gotta go over there," I told Lilah.

"What did—"

"Idonno exactly. She was semi-hysterical. I don't think this is gonna be good."

"I'll come with you. I'll wake Kevin and—"

"No, no. No. Let him sleep. What's the point? I'll take care of it."

I slipped on a jacket and hurried quickly downstairs to my car. Twenty minutes later I was at Warren's front door. I rang the bell several times, but no one answered. I had started to pound the door with my fist (not thinking about why this might be a superior method of rousing the inhabitants than ringing), when I realized the door was, in fact, unlocked. It opened easily as I let myself in.

"Hello? Anybody home?"

Nothing. I advanced into the foyer.

"Warren? Mrs. Kushner?"

Kitchen, living room, den: empty.

Taking two steps at a time, I bounded up the staircase, poked my head into Warren's room. "War?"

Empty.

I had turned and was about to descend to the ground floor when my eye caught something that made me pause. I slowly pivoted again and this time entered the room.

The wall opposite the foot of Warren's bed: Taped to it, ceiling to floor, were at least thirty sheets of loose-leaf paper. I moved closer and saw that the pages were covered with pencil-drawn boxes in the form of a computer program flowchart—rectangles for direct actions, diamonds for IF-THEN-ELSE decisions, circles where various logical paths branched or combined. I began reading the topmost page on the left.

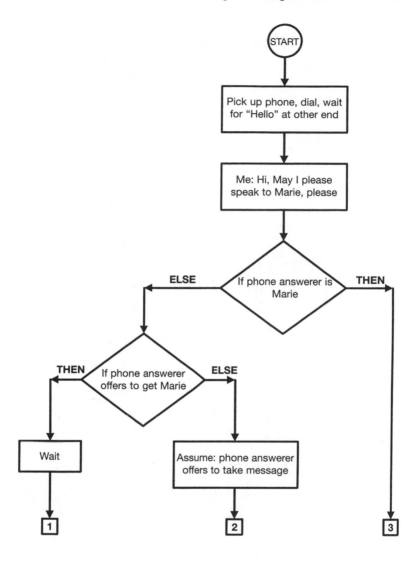

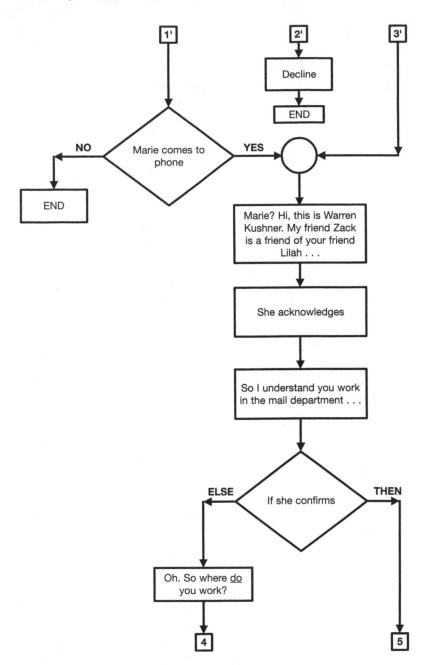

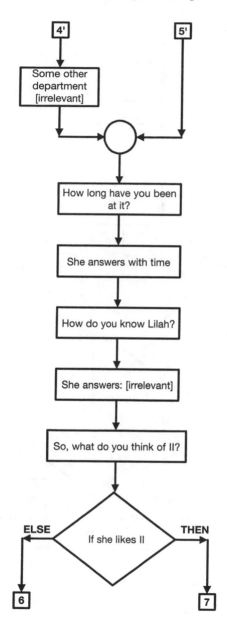

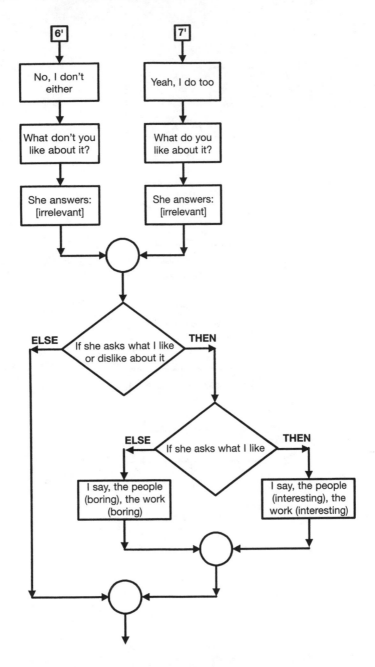

Reading, I felt the horrible guilty fascination one gets with access to another's intimate privacy. The evident aberration only made it worse. About the only experience I could compare it to was when, at age eleven, I found a pornographic magazine in my father's toolbox.

Glancing at the bedroom door (afraid to be caught?), I noticed a reddish flickering out a hallway window that opened on the backyard. I left the room and approached the window. Below, two figures stood next to a burning object.

I raced down the stairs and out the front door. Slowing in the pitch-blackness, I threaded my way around the side of the house to the rear concrete patio. I saw Warren's mom first.

"Mrs. Kushner?"

She had been saying something to Warren, who stood ten feet away overlooking the flames, but she stopped as soon as she recognized me. "Oh, Zack." She extended her arms. "Oh, Zack, thank God you're here! Thank God."

I moved to her side; Warren, motionless, staring, did not acknowledge me. "What, uh, what's going on?"

She was crying. "Something's happened to him."

"I'm not sure I—"

"He's not right. He's not right."

"What, uh, seemed to trigger this?"

"The toilet. All I told him was that it wasn't working."

"Something was wrong with the toilet. . . ."

"Yes."

"And?"

"I asked him if he could fix it, otherwise I'd call a plumber."

"What was wrong exactly?"

"It backed up, as if something was stuck." She sniffled, daubed at her eyes with a tissue.

"And did Warren try to fix it?"

"He got a wire hanger, tried to fish up whatever was in there."

"But it didn't work. . . ."

"No."

"So he . . ."

"Went down to the hardware store and bought a snake, but that didn't work either. So he went back and got some kind of a special snake, specially made for toilets."

"And that still didn't do the job."

"No."

"And was that when he removed the bowl from the floor? Unscrewed the bolts?"

She shook her head yes. Warren remained immobile, trans-fixed, watching the reddish smoke curl into the night sky. At least part of the reason I was talking so long to his mom was to postpone talking directly to him. I continued the questioning.

"After he removed the bowl, he tried to snake it out from the bottom side, the side that normally goes on the floor?"

A sob choked its way past her lips. "He couldn't do it. No matter how he tried, he couldn't do it. He began to scream. I never heard that from him before. 'I can't do anything! I can't do anything! I can't do anything!' over and over, over and over."

"And that's when he came back here. . . ."

"He got kerosene from the garage."

I squeezed her arm, then walked over to Warren. He was as rigid as a phone pole.

"Hi."

No answer, straight-ahead stare.

I put my hands in my pockets, rocked to and fro in feigned down-homey casualness. "Nice night to light up a toilet bowl in your backyard. I finished doing mine, so I thought I'd come over and keep you company."

No acknowledgment. The toilet lay on its side, marble charring and cracking in the heat.

"Burning. One of the better methods for clearing obstructions. Did it work?"

No answer.

"You could take a garden hose, see if the water runs through now."

No response.

"Amazing that whatever was in there wouldn't come out, even with snaking from the back side. Sounds impossible, actually."

No response.

I moved closer. "War? Listen, come on, how about going inside now, whaddaya say?"

Nothing.

"You know, your mom's getting really scared. Come on, come back in and let's talk. I know you've been down lately, maybe we can figure some things to do."

Silence.

"You won't even give me a chance? War, come on. . . ."

I tried for another five minutes, then gave up and returned to Warren's mom. The flames were dying, the fire almost out.

"I don't know what to do," she said. "I don't know who to call."

Who *did* you call in that situation? Man burning toilet in backyard. It was a dilemma. Eventually, we decided on the police; a blue-and-orange-striped Nassau County patrol car showed up fifteen minutes later and two cops, one who looked my age, one older, marched into the backyard, flashlights blazing.

"This the guy?" they asked, indicating the still-catatonic Warren. The fire had died right after we called.

I shook my head yes, then babbled a recital of the evening's events as best I could.

The younger cop attempted to rouse Warren with a few "Ayy, buddy" greetings, but of course met no success.

"Call the paramedics," the older one told him, and the young one returned out front to the patrol car.

Some time after the cops had completed their paperwork, an ambulance came, no siren, just the flashing lights, and two uniformed paramedics joined the party. Warren wasn't going to move very much, but the paramedics flanked him and wedged their shoulders under his armpits and seemingly without all that much effort managed to get him around the house and into the ambulance without a gurney.

They were taking him to North Shore Hospital. His mom and I rode with him in back, his eyes all glazed and vacant, his mom softly cooing his name all the way. But no matter how many times she patted his wrist between sniffles, how lovingly she stroked his forearm, how she begged and pleaded for the slightest, smallest sign of recognition or acknowledgment, my friend Warren said not one single word.

10

GRACEFUL DEGRADATION

ENGINEERING JOKE:
During a lunchtime stroll, two engineers and an engineering manager meet a genie, who grants them each one wish—which can't be money- or health-related. The genie turns to the first engineer, who says, "I'd like to travel to Egypt and see the pyramids and cruise down the Nile." The genie nods, then turns to the second engineer. "I'd like to go to Sweden," says the second engineer, "and frolic in the sauna with voluptuous Swedish women." Finally, the genie addresses the engineering manager. "All right, it's your turn, what is your wish?" The manager thinks a moment, then says: "Can you just make sure those two are back by three P.M.?"

Marv will provide guidance, but you've got to do it. I'm assigning you the responsibility."

I was in Meissner's office, under his direct glare. Kushner's mom had phoned in: Warren had been admitted to the psychiatric ward and would be out of work for an indefinite time. Medical diagnosis: severe clinical depression. Colloquial description: a nervous breakdown.

"But I don't know anything about RF power amps."

"Zack, CDR is in two weeks. This is it. You do it. Marv will assist as much as he can and Nussbaum will be your full-time tech. Good man, very experienced."

"Nussbaum's here twenty-nine years," amplified Whispering

Bill. He'd been absent for a week, had returned only a day earlier.

"And what happens if I can't do it, if no matter what I or Marv come up with we can't reduce the current?"

Meissner's lips tightened; small muscles high in his jaw began to fibrillate. "They will allow operation with the present current."

"But . . . Q3 breaks into oscillation with the present current."

"Not all of them."

"Forty percent of them!"

"The Air Force doesn't know that."

"We're not gonna tell 'em?"

"If you reduce Q7's current draw, we won't need to."

"And if I don't?"

"That's Boulot's problem."

"Not your problem," said Whispering Bill.

I could scarcely believe what I was hearing. "Isn't it all our problem?"

"Look," said Meissner, "Mr. Ingrassia and I had a long talk with Marv and he feels a solution is very possible. There've been other Class C transmitters built right in this company that have achieved exactly the efficiency we're looking for. We didn't just pull these specs out of our ass."

PIDOOMA denied. "These other amplifiers: same frequency, same temp range, same pulse width, same duty cycle, same bandwidth?"

"Close," said Meissner.

"And we have the designs?"

"Sure."

"Did Warren have the designs?"

Meissner glanced at Whispering Bill, then back to me. "Yes." He leaned forward. "Zack, we're not throwing you to the wolves here. Marv is a very experienced box engineer, very capable, and he said he thinks this is something that can be done. He's been tied up personally on the oscillator chain and some other things, but he's assured me that starting next week, he's all yours. Avail yourself of his help."

"Pick his brain," said Whispering Bill.

Over whose? I wondered.

Both men rose from their chairs, a signal the meeting was over.

"Think of this as an opportunity," said Meissner, when I was at the door. "This has high visibility to management. Do well and you'll be noticed."

"Do bad and you'll also be noticed," joked Whispering Bill.

Outside the office, as we walked back to the cubicle, I asked him how he felt. Word was he'd been ill, and he did seem bent over even more than usual.

"Nothing serious," he said. Then, leaning closer to my chest, "Had a testicle removed. But heck, I've got two more." He nudged me, grinning. "They did find some polyps up my ass, though. Gotta watch those."

"You mean in the colon?"

"Idonno, way up there."

We came to the W5 cubicle. "Speaking of assholes," I said, "is there anything I should know about working with Marv?"

Bill looked up at me. "Marv told Meissner your friend Warren was incompetent, that it was his fault Q7 wasn't putting out. That's what he told him."

I nodded and entered the cubicle.

———
o

When the spring soccer season began, I asked Lilah if she would again be my assistant coach.

"That way, it guarantees Kevin's on my team," I added. (New teams were assembled for each season.)

"Why assistant?"

"Wha'?"

"I mean, why not co-coach? You said yourself you got all your knowledge of the game from the library. I could do the same."

Lilah, I'd learned, enjoyed being confrontational. I wasn't sure if it was some kind of intellectual game, a form of teasing, or something else entirely, but often the consequence of disagreement was distance, and I didn't want that. "Hey, you wanna co-coach, that's fine."

"Why would you think I'd not want an equal position?"

"I don't know why I think what I think, I just think. Obviously, this time the thought was incorrect."

"Obviously." Arched brow, faint smile.

The kids were as interesting and funny as ever. At our first practice, Evan Dortch told me he could not remove his hat to practice headers because he had a dry scallop. At our second practice, Richard Napolitano claimed his kicks were weak because his hind legs were cold. When it became overcast at the end of the session, Brian Burnett said that the sky had a stuffy nose.

At my invitation, Boulot and his daughter Elise came to our first game. It was on a Saturday at noon; I had been to work that morning and would return to work afterward. CDR was ten days away. It was the second week in May; at the edges of the field, on the properties of adjoining houses, extravagant sprays of yellow forsythia pushed through the interstices of the chain-link fence. We—*we* now being Hotcha Stationery—won the game 3–2.

"So what'd you think?" I asked Elise, when she and her dad joined Lilah, Kevin, and myself at the end of the game. She was a small girl with a thin face and hair done up in a cascade of brown ringlets. Her longish beige coat and precise speech lent her the air of a miniature adult rather than a child.

"It was good," she answered shyly.

"You don't have to say that," I advised. "I mean, unless you really thought it." I'd sensed she was an obedient type, sensitized to what adults expected and eager to please. I leaned closer to her. "So, is that what you really thought?"

She looked up at Boulot.

"You can tell him," said the Frenchman.

"I thought it was boring," said Elise.

"O-kay!" I said. " 'Atta way."

"But it was boring only because I wasn't playing," she added. "If I was playing, it would be fun."

"Ahhh," I said, turning to Boulot. "Well, there you are. You should enroll her in soccer. They have a soccer club in Huntington. We played one of their teams in the indoor tournament."

"They do, but I 'ave not ze time to bring her to ze practices and ze games and ze meetings. I am at work, I 'ave not ze chance." He shook his head.

"Can't ask a neighbor? A friend?"

The head-shaking continued. "I 'ave no American friends."

I thought a moment. "Well, if you'd like, I could make a couple calls. Maybe someone in the Shoreview club knows someone in Huntington. . . . Would that be okay?" I turned to Elise. "Would that be okay?"

She nodded.

"You're sure? I don't wanna railroad you into something."

"What's 'railroad'?"

"Force you into it," explained Lilah.

"No, I'd like to do it," said Elise. Then, turning to Boulot, "Can I?"

"I theenk about it," said Boulot.

"Lemme know if you decide," I said. I turned to Kevin. "Kev, in the meantime, till we leave, how 'bout showing Elise some of the drills?" I flipped him one of the balls, and he and Elise ran out onto the field, while Lilah and I began gathering up the net, stakes, warm-up cones, and extra balls.

"A beautiful day," said Boulot, lifting his face to the sunshine.

"Perfect," I said.

"Too bad you 'ave to go back to work," he said.

"You don't?"

He shrugged. "Zere is nussing more I can do. I give myself ze day off."

"Aren't you two on the same job?" asked Lilah.

"Absolutely," said Boulot.

"That's AIR, right? Advanced Interrogator/Receiver?"

"Yes, a very hot job," said Boulot. "The place is full of hot AIR."

"What job number do you charge?" asked Lilah.

"Job numbair?"

"Lilah claims I'm charging the wrong job," I interjected.

"You're *charging* correctly," she corrected. "What's showing up in the computer is incorrect."

Boulot shrugged. "I charge 2301."

"You remember that?" I asked.

"I remember only the pathological and the trivial. The normal and essential, I dismiss immediately."

———
o

The moment of judgment had arrived, that key, cusp time when an engineer's accomplishment and ability was exposed for the world to see: We had all produced our samples for the small-writing contest.

The location was in the Transmitter Lab, where Nussbaum could peer through Gung Ho's one-hundred-power binocular microscope with the calibrated graticule and measure our submissions. Boulot's was first, taken from his memo.

" 'FUCK YOU ALL,' " read Nussbaum aloud, tweaking the focus knob. "And the size is—are we talking average size, or what?"

"Size of the largest letter," said Jim. He looked around. "All agreed?"

There were general mumbles of assent. Our assemblage had attracted a small ancillary crowd of engineers, technicians, and precision assemblers (no supervisors, of course). Even Lilah had come over from Software Engineering after she'd seen me preparing for the event and I'd mentioned the time of the judging.

"The largest letter is the *Y*," said Nussbaum, "and that measures eighteen mils."

A murmur went through the crowd. Eighteen mils was eighteen-thousandths of an inch. The thickness of an average human hair was four-thousandths of an inch.

Shopper Jim's submission was next, written on the back of an envelope.

"And the printing reads," said Nussbaum, adjusting the focus, " 'WONDERBOY DICKHEAD.' "

Jim had exceeded the ten-letter minimum in favor of making the message more pungent.

"Largest letter is . . . *W* and *K* are the same size . . . both at . . . mmm . . . fifteen mils."

"Not bad," I said to Jim, who was standing next to me.

"Hey, damn thing took me nearly ten minutes," said Jim.

Actually, I was pretty confident of my own efforts, which had taken nearly an hour (of, I might add, International Instruments' time). Working with a ten-power loupe held solely by eyebrow muscle tension in my right eye socket, I had used a draftsman's pencil with insertable leads for my first strokes. After some experimentation I settled on a Number 6H lead, the very hardest available, finding it necessary to sharpen it using a draftsman's manual sharpener—a device that let you hand-rotate a pencil holder inside an aluminum cylinder lined with a very fine grit sandpaper—literally after each stroke, lest the tip dull and smudge the next segment. Several practice runs later, I was finally satisfied with my fine motor control, plus I'd determined the basic lower limitation on the size of the letters I could produce: the graininess of the paper. After some hunting and further experimentation, I'd finally located a plain cheap white four-by-six-inch pad that had exceptionally smooth sheets. (For some reason, the more expensive the paper, the rougher it seemed. Clearly, the people who prized textured stationery had never tried using it to print microscopic messages.)

Nussbaum had zeroed in on my sample. "And Zack's message reads, 'I DID IT BEST.' "

Jim immediately turned to Lilah. "I'd imagine you'd know if that's true."

Lilah smacked his arm.

"Largest letter is *B*," continued Nussbaum, "and the size is . . . twelve mils."

There were a series of whoas and wows from the group.

"Looks like he *is* the best," said Lilah.

"One more entry," chimed in Wonderboy. "Let's not be premature here." And out of his pocket he withdrew a polished alumina disk.

"Wait a minute," said Jim, as Nussbaum slid it onto the microscope stage. Alumina, aluminum oxide, was an exceedingly hard ceramic (so hard it was actually used on old phased-array antennas to shield them from—it was feared—atomic blasts). One of its properties was that its surface could be polished to extreme smoothness.

Nussbaum adjusted the focus to accommodate the alumina's one-inch thickness. "The message is, 'LLLLLLLLLL.' Largest letter is, mmm, looks like . . . they're all close . . . maybe third *L* from the end. And the size is . . . ten mils."

"You used alumina!" sputtered Jim.

"Yes," said Wonderboy agreeably.

"But . . ."

I finished Jim's thought. "You can make that a lot smoother than paper. And the graininess of the paper is—"

"All within the rules," said Wonderboy.

"The rules specified no mechanical aids," said Jim.

"To the *writing*. Doesn't apply to the medium."

"Who said?"

"If you were going to apply it to other things, we couldn't use a loupe to even see the letters. Did you not use a loupe?"

"The loupe is not involved in the writing."

"Really? How could you write what you couldn't see?"

"And what kind of message is 'LLLLLLLLLL'? That has no meaning."

"Doesn't have to. I chose *L* because it's the simplest letter to form."

Jim shook his head. "Wonderdick, is there any human activity that you do not degrade and besmirch by your participation? This was meant to be a simple contest of skill. There aren't even any stakes here."

The taunting smile on Wonderboy's face was almost too much to bear; I had a brief vision of the entire group suddenly attacking him like a pack of jackals and tearing him to shreds.

"You're just jealous," he said, "that you failed to examine the rules with sufficient thoroughness. That I did, and then took creative opportunities to maximize certain advantages, is a direct testament to my superior intellect." He walked toward the doorway. "*Au revoir,* gentlemen."

I had to admit: His exit had a certain flair. I saw Lilah con-
verse with him briefly as he left and then the group began to
disperse.

"What can you do," I said to Jim.

"I once read somewhere that the only way to educate certain people is to kill them. I think he's a candidate."

I noticed Lilah talking to virtually everyone who left the lab
and making notes on a sheet of paper. Just before my own
departure I asked what she was doing.

"First, finding out if they're working on AIR, then getting
the job number they're charging."

"Li, I said I'd check that for you."

She leaned over to quickly kiss my forehead. "Saved you the
trouble."

———
o

For the next week, I put in fourteen-hour days, learning all I
could about Class-C microwave amplifiers, trying various
experiments with Nussbaum to see if we could improve the
efficiency, i.e., get the same radio frequency power out with
less DC current in. The AIR transmitter amplifier operated at
a frequency of 1030 MHz, 1.03 billion cycles per second. It
consisted of a twelve-by-six-inch aluminum-backed printed circuit board that included a dozen transistors, four each for the
low-power pre-amps, the medium power feeder stages, and
the high-power output stages. The arrangement allowed for
"graceful degradation": The set would work, albeit less well,
even if some of the transistors were to fail.

From a design viewpoint, the thing was complex. The Class-
C amplifier is a pulsed device that produces RF current during
only a small portion of a cycle. It uses capacitors to store up
energy over the time it's not outputting, then rapidly draws

electric charge out of those capacitors during the intervals it produces its pulses.

So its efficiency depends on the energy-storing capacitors.

And on the proportion of power from the feeder stage that gets into it as opposed to being reflected from it.

And on temperature.

And on three or four other things.

Marv gave me Warren's notebooks to study, along with two textbooks and about twenty technical papers on the subject. The latter ranged from nuts-and-bolts articles taken from industry trade pubs *Microwaves and RF* and *Microwave Journal* to arcane, math-crammed treatises out of the International Electrical and Electronics Engineers (IEEE) *Microwave Theory and Techniques* monthly, invariably authored by multiple foreign-born college professors. Unfortunately, the trade stuff was always too particular, the *MTT* material too general (besides being incomprehensible).

I outlined to Marv several experiments I wanted to try, certain avenues that seemed worth pursuing.

"Sounds good," he said genially, adding, "Let me know how I can help," before he returned to his phone conversation.

At the bench, Nussbaum and I sat before the setup—an array of power supplies, ammeters, voltmeters, microwave signal sources, RF power meters, directional couplers, spectrum analyzers, network analyzers, etc.—and performed various tests. We sat on stools and I could see every bump on his brown bald head as he adjusted dials and took readings.

"Three more years," he said. "If I can make it through three more, I can retire."

"How long you been working?" I asked.

"Thirty-five after I got out of the Navy. I was twenty-four."

"Jesus, that's a long time."

He looked back and grinned. "That's what you got to look forward to," he said.

We accumulated pages and pages of data. "You're doing all the right tests," said Marv when I reviewed it with him after the first week. "Let me know how I can help."

I pored through Warren's notebooks, trying to follow the sequence of his experiments, to re-create his thought process. He, after all, had lived with this for months; he was a bright guy, his work had a lot of value.

"I think . . . Jesus, I'd really like to visit him," I told Lilah one night.

"Well . . . sure," she said. "I'll go with you."

"The only thing is, I'd like to ask him some technical stuff, I mean, what he did."

"Mmm."

"You think that would be . . . Idonno . . . crass? Gauche?"

"Well, yes, I suppose."

"Insensitive."

"Yes."

"Callous." I should mention we were in bed and I was kissing her around the neck at this time, working my way slowly downward.

"Yes. Mmm, yes."

"Quite possibly even dangerous. After all, work stuff is what set him off."

"It might cause him a setback."

"I could call his mom and ask her."

"You could. Mmm . . . uhhhhh . . . mmm . . . you could."

Her nipples were the size of Tootsie Rolls; I swirled a foam of saliva over them with my tongue, then suddenly, on crazy impulse, popped my head up. "Do you think all we have together is sex?"

She looked down at me in languid amused concupiscence, Amerasian eyes lust-filled and narrowed. "Even if that were true, would that be so bad?"

"Well . . . no. I suppose."

"Could we just get back to what you were doing?"

"The word is 'resume.' "

"Yes."

"Our word."

She ran a hand through my hair. "Our word."

We visited Warren. The psychiatric ward at North Shore was a small complex of semi-private rooms and a patients' lounge; the entrance was a glass-windowed locked door watched over by a fat guard at a wooden desk. I had told Warren's mom what I wanted to do and, after a check with the doctor, she'd told me it would be fine.

"He needs company," she said. "It'll be good for him. Actually, he's doing very well. Doctor said in two weeks he might even be released. And the work talk will be fine. Make him feel needed."

"You know," Warren said, "it's really not that bad in here." We sat in the lounge. He wore a blue terrycloth bathrobe over light blue pajamas. "They give you meals, you can read the paper, watch TV, and . . . no one expects anything from you."

"Sounds excellent," I said.

"The only thing . . ." He leaned close. "Some of them"—he nodded in the direction of a teenage girl on the opposite couch—"you know, scream. Scream for no reason. A ping-pong ball goes off the table, these people scream."

"Do they scream worse than Meissner?"

"Well . . . no, actually. That's right. He'd be right at home here."

He told us that they'd considered shock treatment for

him—"electroconvulsive therapy," as he termed it—but had opted instead for drugs. "And they tell me I'm responding quite well," he added. "I feel good, but of course, since I'm crazy, I'm hardly a judge." He turned to Lilah. "So, uh, how's Rhonda?"

"Oh. Well, she's fine."

"Did you tell her about me?"

"I just mentioned you were sick."

"Oh. But did you tell her with what?"

"No, no. Nothing specific."

"And did she say anything?"

"Well, she just asked me to give you her regards and to say she hopes you feel better."

"Really? She wanted me to feel better?"

"Yes. Oh, sure."

Warren smiled. "That's very nice. Maybe after I get out of here, I can call her."

I thought about the flow chart on the wall of his room.

"Sure, why not?" said Lilah.

I had brought one of his engineering notebooks with me and I asked him a few questions, mostly having to do with his handwriting. I noticed, in the days just before his breakdown, it had become increasingly illegible, scrawled and extremely tiny. I wondered how he would have fared in the small-writing contest.

He answered the questions easily and completely, even elaborating occasionally, telling me what he'd been trying to accomplish, what his reasoning was, what he didn't understand, and what he did.

"... so what I realized was that, if the driver stage goes into saturation, the pulse delay becomes a lot less temperature-sensitive. That's where I was heading before ... before I got ... sick."

After a half hour, Lilah and I, exchanging glances, realized we ought to leave.

"It was great of you to come," said Warren. "Really, I really appreciate it."

"We'll come again," I said, "or else we'll see you when you're out. Have you, you know, I mean, have you given any thought at all to coming back to II when—"

"I have," he said, as we neared the exit, "and what I decided was, I think . . . I think I'm gonna go to law school."

"Really . . ."

"Well, my mom said she would help me financially and I just feel, for me, maybe that would be a better career path."

"Sounds good," I said. "Lotta smart people seem to be doing it, lotta engineers in particular."

"Great to see you," he said.

We each gave him a hug before signaling to the guard. Outside, in a warm late spring evening drizzle, I asked Lilah if Rhonda had actually sent Warren her regards.

"Not really," she said.

"Well, what did she say?"

"Nothing. I didn't tell her."

"You didn't tell her Warren was sick?"

"No, what for? It's not as if they had some kind of relationship."

"But you told Warren—"

"A kindness. It's not like he's in the real world." Pause. Evanescent grin. "Sometimes I wonder if any of the guys on AIR are."

"Meaning . . ."

"Of twenty engineers and techs, fourteen are listed in the computer as charging E2C when they're actually working on AIR."

"Really?"

We were approaching my car. "Eee-yup."

"So, uh, what're you gonna do about it?"

"Tell Mr. Softy."

"That should be interesting."

"Ee-yup."

I unlocked the door. "Strange," I said. "A year ago, when we all started at II, who'd've thought Warren would be in a psychiatric ward the next spring?"

"Strange and sad," she said, entering the car. "And stranger and sadder still that you'd be coming to him for technical advice."

---

o

Meissner had the four of us in his office: Marvin, Boulot, Whispering Bill, and me. It was two days before CDR.

We sat on folding chairs arranged in front of his desk. For the first time I noticed a picture next to his phone: a homely thick-legged woman, sullen teenage boy, glum nine- to ten-year-old girl, and a stiff, unsmiling Meissner. None of them looked like they wanted to be anywhere near the others. Outside, through the office window that only high-level managers could command, I saw people on their breaks, lounging one story below at the umbrellaed, white-filigreed metal tables that dotted the interior courtyard. Potted plants basked in brightly colored glory in patches of brilliant sunlight.

"Our job now," Meissner said, "is to put things in the best perspective." His facial color was off the chart; indigo veins pulsated like directional signals under the thin skin at his temples. He turned toward Boulot. "Some of the Q3s handle the heavier current, yes?"

A momentary silence. Boulot adjusted the tiger-striped tie knot at the back of his neck. "Yes."

"So in that sense, we've found a solution."

"It's not really a solution."

"If they take the current, it's a solution."

"It's not a solution."

"It's a partial solution," rasped Whispering Bill.

"It's not a solution," said Boulot.

"We could select those transistors that withstood the current," said Meissner.

"It's an unstable condition," said Boulot. "You are operating them above the manufacturer's rating. Forty percent of them fail."

"So you don't talk about the forty percent. What you talk about is the sixty percent."

"I talk about one hundred percent," said Boulot. "I tell ze Air Force everysing."

"No. No, you don't. A good designer finds a way to solve the problem. We solve this one by selection. The Air Force doesn't have to know that. That's our proprietary approach."

"It ees not proprietary because I am telling zem."

"You are not telling them."

"I am. I will not lie."

"I'm not asking you to lie! For God sakes, man, make a distinction! I'm simply asking you not to point out the forty percent of Q3s that we are not going to use anyway. The purpose of CDR is not to talk about all those things we won't do, don't do, or can't do, it's to review what we *are* doing. Any good engineer would recognize that difference. Are you not a good engineer?"

Boulot's head, in a chickenlike maneuver, receded backward on his neck. "Me? No." (The last, very nasal.)

"You're not a good engineer. . . ."

"No."

"Do you not *want* to be a good engineer?"

Boulot stood up. "If this is your idea of a good engineer, I want to be a bad one. I want to be a terrible one! I want to be the worst engineer I can be!"

Meissner rose as well. "Get out. You're not speaking at CDR."

Boulot shrugged, smiled, and stepped through the door. "Fine wiz me. Get someone else to tell your lies." And left.

The laser refocused . . . on Marvin. "How much over are we?"

Marvin glanced at me, then down at the floor. "We're at 21.8 amps, peak pulse draw, I believe."

"And we need to get down to . . ."

"Twenty even. At a one percent duty cycle, that would meet the two hundred milliamp steady-state goal."

"You've done a lot of these, Marv."

"This is something of a toughie. Who bid this one?"

"This is not the time to be asking that!" Shouted. One-minute silent recovery period. (I thought: Meissner is like a Class-C amplifier: Charges up, outputs pulse of intense venom, recovers.) *"If"*—he began again—*"if* you were to get some additional time to work on this, what would be your probability of success?"

"Well, it's hard to say, there are a lot of factors. We've seen some promising avenues, but to put a numerical value on ”

"Fifty percent?"

"I'm not—"

"BETTER THAN FIFTY?"

"Well . . ."

"Yes, or no, *better than fifty*?"

"It could be better, yes."

"He thinks it might be more than fifty," said Whispering Bill.

"Sixty?"

"Anton, I simply don't know. I can't promise you what I'm not sure of."

"I want . . . I want your best . . . YOUR BEST . . . estimate. You've been in the business twenty-six years?"

"Yes . . ."

"Then you tell me, if you and him [me] spend twenty-four hours a day in that lab—I'm talking cots, sleeping here, seven days a week—is your chance of knocking 1.8 amps off Q7's peak current draw greater than fifty percent?"

Marvin worked his lips, rubbed a spot on his forehead as if a brain-genie would emerge and give him the answer. "I would say yes."

"You would say yes."

"Yes."

"And how much total time would this require?"

"Anton . . ."

Meissner opened his mouth so wide, I thought a bird might fly out. "HOW MUCH?"

"I . . ." Marvin's head began to oscillate.

"A month?"

"I don't know. *I don't know.*"

"Six weeks? Six full weeks?"

"Well . . . maybe six weeks."

"Okay. So let me restate: *If,* after CDR, I could somehow get you and him [me] an additional six weeks, it is your opinion, your considered opinion, that you would have better than a fifty percent chance of solving the problem. Is that correct?"

Marvin glanced quickly around the room, the familiar bright-eyed, trapped-animal visual survey. "I guess . . . that's correct."

"You *guess?*"

"It's correct, I think we'd have a fair shot at doing it."

Meissner nodded, inhaled, and exhaled deeply. "Okay. Okay. So we've established that." He balled his fists. "I think . . . I think there may be a chance I could negotiate that with the Air Force. If after the CDR there aren't too many action items, this particular one might fly." He began to nod with excitement. "Okay. Okay. So we have a shot."

"We have a shot," echoed Whispering Bill.

"We got a shot," said I. (Who wanted to be the only one in the room not affirming our chances?)

"At this point in time," said Meissner, "I think that's all we could ask."

"It's all we could ask," said Bill. "We got a shot."

"Actually," said Marv, "we *would* have a shot except for one thing."

Slowly, the three other heads swiveled in his direction.

It took him nearly a minute to say what he was going to. "See, I was intending to discuss this with you later"—to Meissner—"but I think now, in view of what's been said . . ."

"For Christ's sake, Marvin—"

"I'm, uh, gonna be leaving in one week. I'm starting my own business."

Three sets of jaw muscles suddenly lost their tension.

"I really hope this can be on good terms."

o

Later that day I got a call from Lilah. "Can you come over here?"

"Yeah, but—"

"Please. Now."

"Okay, but—"

"Now." She hung up.

I walked through the corridors for miles it seemed until I came to the double doors marked Software Engineering, and entered. The realm of the Softheads was darkened; all that was visible were row after row of young geeks, sitting at their computer terminals, typing away, callow glabrous faces ghostly in the light of fifteen-inch screens. As I walked through the aisles I heard an occasional, "Cool!"—this being, I knew from minor experience, a Softhead's favorite English word. If you told one, "I just murdered your parents and raped your sister," his most likely response would be, "Cool!" in that special supercilious tone that was congratulatory without being admiring, awestruck without being impressed. The overall sensation, as I advanced and my vision adjusted, was of walking through an aviary, where the denizens perched at terminals instead of on branches and chirped or squawked, "*Cool!*" as the intruder passed.

At the head of the room was Mr. Softy's office. Venetian blinds covered a windowed door. I knocked and entered, saw Lilah in a chair, Mr. Softy behind a steel desk. Mr. Softy had a fat round head full of white-white hair and a pipe stuck into one corner of his mouth. He reminded me of a snowman.

"Tell him," said Lilah. Her face was drawn, serious. She seemed about to cry.

"I'm sorry, I—"

"She means about the job charge," said Softy. "You Zaremba?"

"Ya."

"She says you've been working on the Advanced Interrogator/Receiver."

"That's right."

"It *is* right . . ."

"Yes."

"See?" said Lilah, brightening.

"But your charges have been showing up on E2C."

"Oh. Uh-huh."

"Plus some of your colleagues' . . . Lilah claims."

"Uh-huh."

Softy shrugged, looked at Lilah. "Sounds like someone's been sloppy about keying in the time-sheet data."

"Sloppy?" said Lilah. "No. Sorry. This is more than sloppy. This is a lot of people over a long period."

"A *lot* of people? You've brought me one. Maybe the others *are* working on E2C."

"They're not. I asked them."

"Lilah, exactly what are you saying? Are you accusing me of something?"

"No, I—"

"I have no axe to grind here."

"I know that, I just . . . I felt it was something that should be brought to your attention."

Softy stood up, chewed on the pipe. "Thank you. I appreciate that. And if there are further data entry errors that have been made, I will see to it that the culprit is dealt with appropriately."

"But what if it's not data entry, if—"

"Thank you, Lilah." He was practically shooing her out the door. "You too, Zaremba."

We left, made our way through the aviary, out into the corridor.

"Did you see?" exploded Lilah. "He's patronizing me."

"Well, I guess he just doesn't think it's a big deal."

"Well, I disagree. I think it might be."

"Okay."

"And I'm going to do something about it."

"So, unlike him, you have an axe to grind."

"Yes."

I couldn't resist. "Cool!"

o

It didn't take long. Meissner called me in again at five P.M. This time we were alone. He came right to the points. "Number one, I'm appointing you Box Engineer for the AIR transmitter. Just for your information, I believe that makes you the youngest Cognizant Engineer in II history. Number two, Ingrassia wants to fire Boulot if he doesn't do a presentation at CDR. The only way I could convince him not to do so was to tell him that you would speak in his place." Pause. "Zack, I am truly sorry to have to put this kind of pressure on someone so young, but trust me, if there were another way, I would take it. Incidentally, along with that Box Engineer position goes an eight-thousand-dollar raise, effective June thirtieth."

I nodded, trying to shake the new information down into my head. "So the only way the Frenchman won't be fired is if I do the power supply presentation at CDR. . . ."

"Yes. You know I'm a yeller and a screamer and my bark is worse than my bite, but Ingrassia . . . Ingrassia is a hard guy. Boulot is not fulfilling his responsibilities."

"And I would."

"Yes."

I met his gaze. "And I would have to not mention about the Q3s . . . the ones that don't take the current."

"The ones that will be selected out."

"Leaving those that are still marginal, that could go bad over time or temperature or vibration or—"

"It's called being reasonable. Finding a reasonable solution. At any instant, all the air molecules in this room might just collect up in one corner and we'd both suffocate, but that isn't likely to happen, is it? It's not reasonable."

"What about Reliability? How'll they ever approve this?" That's it! I thought. The stolid sweaty men with the Japanese pine stability would be my saviors.

"They're pencil pushers," said Meissner, "priests of statistical bullshit. We'll just tell 'em to justify it, and believe me, it'll get done. We have this all the time."

"Well then what about QA?" My last bastion. Quality Assurance was the final gatekeeper of company integrity and responsibility. The head of QA, Phil Porter, reported directly to the division VP, Yale Sanders.

"We will meet all contractual quality requirements. Screening, burn-in, the works. We have to."

"But—"

"You're worried they'll fail later, out in the field?"

"*And* fail in QA."

"Neither of which is your concern. Your supervisor—me—is telling you that all you need to do is produce units that pass the engineering inspection tests. QA, field maintenance, those are whole other bailiwicks. You know, at II, the design engineers are kings."

"We're kings . . ."

"Absolutely. What you say, goes."

"It goes."

"Goes." He raised his eyebrows. "So, as far as CDR . . ."

I gnawed a flake of skin that was detaching from my lower lip. "I need to think about it."

"Of course. If you elect not to do it, I'll have to—I'd give the presentation myself, but then of course Boulot would be out."

"I'll consider it."

"Good."

11

BEING
REASONABLE

"You're worried about your career? You *have* no career, you're an engineer."
—SHOPPER JIM

They're bluffing."

"I don't think so."

"But it doesn't even make sense. Why, just because *you speak*, will they not fire Boulot?"

"They need somebody to do it, that's all. They don't care who. The Boulot thing is simply a lever, an additional way to pressure me."

"Why you? Why not Bent-Over-Bill or Meissner himself?"

"Bent-Over-Bill was taken to the hospital this afternoon. Slammed a car door on his hand lunchtime, broke it, staggered backward from the pain, fell, broke his coccyx, tore a knee ligament. As for Meissner, he'd have to do it if I refuse. But it's much more credible, way more, if you have an engineer who's actually worked on the stuff. The Air Force guys place a lot more credence in the working engineers than they do in the managers. They know the design engineers . . . have no axes to grind."

Her look would have withered a steel safe.

We were preparing to go out and I was watching her get ready. As previously noted, I found the process of female self-assembly—that's how I referred to the dressing and grooming process—absolutely hypnotic. Oh, no question it was wonderful to watch them take their clothes *off* or do it for them, but somehow the excitement and arousal that engendered interfered with the pure aesthetic appreciation of the procedure itself. To me, observing the languid care they exercised in assembly, the intimate sensuous detail of the process, was like watching Monet live in his studio as he crafted a painting.

She had taken a shower, emerged naked and dripping, dried herself all over with a fluffy white towel (I erected when she patted it between her legs), then used a second towel to dry her hair. This latter was then interwoven with the thick bundles of black strands in some kind of intricate knotted turban, as arcane and mysterious as the structure of a gene.

"Shopper Jim says the whole thing is like some kind of Japanese Noh play. It's just ritual. Everyone paints their faces with very serious expressions. The II engineers say very serious square-mouthed incomprehensible things and the Air Force says serious incomprehensible square-mouthed things back. We give them stuff to find wrong so they can look diligent, they find it and order us to fix it. We all go back to our bosses, who make various wise serious pronouncements, and then we all write very official serious reports with multiple subparagraphs summarizing the whole business. End of play. Which, by the way, is a comedy."

Lilah was sitting on the edge of the tub, using a pink razor to plow a path through a field of shaving cream on her left shin. "And is it your intent to participate in this comedy?"

"I don't think I have a choice."

"There's always a choice."

"Look, I don't wanna see Boulot get fired."

She toweled off the residual shaving cream, then stepped into a pair of white cotton panties, which she slid up the length of her legs. "And you don't mind sacrificing your integrity. . . ."

"It's not my integrity."

"It certainly is, as long as you don't feel what they're doing is right and you're withholding information about it. Do you feel it's right?" She withdrew a makeup kit from the linen closet, leaned over the sink to stare into the mirror.

"No, it's not right."

She shrugged.

"Li, I've got someone's job in my hands."

She began using a small brush, something like one of those old-fashioned shaving cream lather brushes, to lightly feather a coral-colored powder across her forehead. "But he himself wasn't that worried about it. He stood up for what he believed. He put it on the line."

"Boulot is a crazy person."

"Oh, so now it's crazy to do the morally right thing."

"It's crazy to be insanely rigid. This is not that big a deal."

She dusted the powder along her right jawline. "Oh. Okay."

My turn to sit at the edge of the tub. To study her as she leaned forward, still braless, see the small pink-tipped breasts, the seven tiny freckles I called the Pleiades below her left shoulder blade, the lone pearl of water that nestled in the dimpled cleft just above her buttocks.

"Does Boulot know what Meissner asked you to do?" This while she worked from the *kit,* a plastic box filled with special pencils, and brushes, and a palette of colored circles. It *was* like watching Monet as she daubed a line of rosy hue along her right cheekbone.

"I'm gonna speak to him before the CDR."

"He's not going to ask you to lie."

"I know that."

Another ten minutes of voyeur heaven, seeing the eyebrow pencil go on, the lid liner, the spider-slick mascara, the blush, the blue-purple eye shadow whose exotic sluttiness gave me yet another inexplicable boner, the #14-on-Jim's-chart red lipstick with the phallic applicator and that final side-to-side pressing motion that transferred pigment from one lip to the other, the lip gloss that captured the wet color essence the way polyurethane sealed a wood floor.

"Can you?"

A request for me to fasten her bra. I could not resist leaning forward to inhale her hair, the soap-fresh cleanness of it. Her pantied behind pressed against my groin—I was sprouting hard-ons like dandelions.

And then at last she was done, standing before me in the living room in a flowered sundress, holding a white leather handbag. "Lilah, I . . . I . . ." The artist's completed work. And it resided with me.

She reached out to touch my cheek. "I know."

"I loved watching you dress. Thank you."

She nodded. "I believe in you, Zack. I think our hearts are in the same place. I know you won't disappoint me."

I nodded. Later, I remembered my father telling me the same thing just before I selected Michigan over Michigan State.

○

Just before the CDR I talked to Boulot in a small alcove opposite an ice-cream-bar vending machine that stole all your money and never gave anything in return. An embossed metal sign on the machine read, "In event of problem or difficulty, please write to Foremost Foods, Inc., P.O. Box 1498, Modesto, CA." Top II management had changed its refund policy, you were now supposed to contact the vendor to recover your seventy-five cents, an event as likely as a parakeet deriving Maxwell's equations.

"You 'ave to do what your conscience tells," said Boulot. "I doubt zey would actually fire me. I can make plenty of trouble for zem."

"But they may not care. They got a whole staff of lawyers."

He shrugged. "Soon I will be one too. I fight zem."

I nodded without much conviction. "Oh, by the way, I called Don Hilbert at the Huntington Soccer Club. He says, if Elise wants to play, they have a summer league. I told him where you live and he says it's no problem to get someone to pick her up for practices, there's a bunch of kids right in the area who play."

Boulot patted my shoulder. "Sank you, Zack. You are my friend. And don't worry, whatever you do in zere"—he indicated toward the corridor where the CDR was convening— "I'm sure it will be ze right sing."

I myself was equally certain of the opposite.

———
ₒ

In the men's room, I saw the black Air Force colonel I'd noticed at the PDR. He was at a urinal, one hand on his dick, staring up at the ceiling. As I took a position two urinals away, he glanced at me before averting his gaze.

"How you doin'?"

"Good," I said. "You?"

"Good."

I finished my business and walked to the sink, leaving him there. Delayed Responder, I thought as I exited the room, the colonel still glued against the porcelain. I'd expected someone in his position to be a No-Hander or Usurper, and the fact that he was neither made me feel a little sorry for him.

The CDR was held in the same location as the PDR, Conference Room G. The same cast of characters was there as well: the for-this-performance-only black people; Meissner and Ingrassia; A Boy Named Hsu, Mr. Softy, Medieval Man, Wonderboy, Shopper Jim, and myself; the Delayed Responder colonel and a bevy of other white-uniformed Air Force people, including one pretty, cropped-haired blond female lieutenant (with whom I immediately pictured a crisply starched military sex act); and, to Jim's surprise, the proprietor of MES Technology.

"You told me he quit," he whispered. We sat, of course, in the back row.

"He did, but they persuaded him to stay just to give the transmitter talk. They thought it would look bad if I spoke about both the transmitter and the power supply."

"Mmm. So, you nervous?"

"Oh, yeah."

"Figure out what you're gonna do?" I'd discussed the Boulot thing with him previously. Jim's recommendation was simple and consistent—Rule Six: Tell them what they want to hear, which is invariably different from the truth. Make them happy, save Boulot, live to fight (if that's what you wanted) another day. All the rest—integrity, science, concern for the user—was an apparition. The system might never get built, might be drastically changed, might *be* built and never deployed, might be deployed and never used, etc. In fact, at least one of these outcomes was *likely*, way way more so than the system being built, left unchanged, deployed, used, and failing. Be *reasonable*, Jim had counseled, echoing Meissner. Wild men ended up dead, in prison, insane, or unemployed, sometimes all four.

"Not yet," I answered.

"Just remember, it's not a matter of life or death."

"It could be."

"Anything *could* be. You step on a spider that might have eaten the fly that caused an armed robber to flinch when he fired what was meant to be a warning shot at the Dairy Barn attendant and which instead killed him. Does that mean you don't step on spiders?"

"I don't. I read *Charlotte's Web.*"

"We're talking about low-probability events."

"I know," I said glumly.

The CDR proceeded pretty much like the PDR, Meissner beginning with a smoothly delivered forty-five-minute program overview, Wonderboy coming on next with the system design approaches. "We'd expected an overall noise figure for the chain of about 1.3 dB, but now it looks like we'll be up around 1.5, still well within the spec of 1.7."

"They're actually at 1.9," whispered Jim. "And that's with hand tuning in the lab. Production will never break 2.1."

"Why doesn't A Boy Named Hsu present the Receiver section?" I whispered back. "He's Cog Engineer."

Jim wrinkled his nose. "He spoke on the B1 four years ago, but did a horrible job. Embarrassed everyone, so they never let him talk again."

"Really. What'd he do?"

Jim grinned. "Told the truth."

A young Air Force guy stood up; he looked perhaps two or three years older than me. "Excuse me, but at the PDR you said you expected an overall noise figure of 1.1 dB, not 1.3. Now you're saying 1.5 What happened?"

There was a sudden tension in the room, hard to define: perhaps a reduction in whispered conversations, a leaning forward in the seats, a subtle tightening of certain muscles.

Wonderboy nodded slowly, pursed his lips. "Our front-end LNA [Low Noise Amplifier] came in about .2 high—we think it's in the transistor—and we're down another .2 between our cable and the connector. We believe our alternate vendor will come through with the lower noise device, and in any event, as I pointed out, we still expect to be well under spec, so there's no issue."

"Thank you," said the Air Force guy, sitting down crisply.

"Thank you for lying like a rug," whispered Shopper Jim.

"There's no issue," I echoed.

"Not unless you want the thing to have the range it was supposed to. Then there's an issue."

Medieval Man was next up and—wens, blebs, bubos, and tumors pulsating madly on his forehead and cheeks, mossy teeth and gentian-violet lips spraying moist brown and green particulate matter on the lectern—delivered a clear and complete hour-long exposition on the digital processor. Retching, the group was adjourned for a twenty-minute coffee and donut break.

"You'll go on second in the afternoon," Meissner told me as I wolfed down my third chocolate cream. (Shopper Jim was on his fourth, his beard covered with crumbs.) "My suggestion is don't eat a very heavy lunch, you'll want to keep your head clear."

"Too late for that," said Jim, but Meissner did not smile.

Back in the conference room, Marvin began his presentation, a polished-as-a-zircon discussion of the oscillator-transmitter chain. He was not quite candid when it came to discussing Q7.

". . . and so we feel that, although we're currently about eight percent over our internal peak current draw spec, a relatively minor additional effort will bring us below our goal."

The Air Force really didn't care much about the current drawn by each of our boxes. They were interested only in the aggregate, the total they'd need to supply. From our point of view, however, we'd already cut the current consumed by each of our other boxes to the absolute minimum. The transmitter was the only place left that could possibly make a difference.

"See?" Jim said. "He thinks it'll take only a relatively minor additional effort."

"Minor because it's not his."

"Of course."

At the lunch break we went to the cafeteria. (The Air Force people and the II management contingent adjourned to a private dining room.) I ordered two slices of pizza, Jim ordered three and a small salad.

"So you think that little salad is gonna negate the effects of all that pizza?"

"No, but you *not* having salad, never having any, is even worse."

"Bet you die at a younger age than me."

"Okay. Natural causes only, right? Auto accidents, gunshot wounds, animal attacks don't count."

"Right."

Jim nodded. "And what's the stakes?"

"Winner buys the loser a drink in hell."

"Okay. And who's the judge?"

"Wonderboy."

Jim laughed. After lunch, against my better judgment (and even the latter, admittedly, was not very good), Jim persuaded me to go out and play some Wiffle ball against the side of the building. "Come on, you're tight as a drum, it'll loosen you up."

I'd worn my one suit because of my upcoming talk, and I left the neatly folded jacket on the concrete a few feet away from where we played. He was right about the salutary effects: Five minutes into the game, gripping the narrow yellow bat, sensing the muscles in my hands and forearms, concentrating on the impossibly curving white plastic ball, feeling the sharp solid contact at the bat's sweet spot, I had put the CDR totally out of my mind. Sun on my face, imaginary men on first and second, I was twelve years old again, and life was simple.

It didn't last. The one o'clock siren was a shrill reminder that the lunchtime was over. I picked up my suit jacket, brushed it off, and slung it over my shoulder as Jim and I headed back inside the building.

Mr. Softy was at the podium, slide of a particular subroutine projected on a bright screen at the front of the darkened room. His pointer moved methodically down the progression of rectangles, parallelograms, and linking circles that diagramed the program.

"Lights," he snapped as he came to the bottom.

Perspiration stains mottled the beige shirt he wore under the wrinkled white cotton suit. A hundred tiny droplets scuttled down his florid forehead from under the white-white hair.

"And from here we return to the calling routine, and then back to the main module." A roll of tongue under the balloon lips. "Thank you. Any questions?"

The blond Air Force lieutenant rose to her feet. "The interrupts in the warm-up sequence—I noticed they weren't in structured format."

At the podium, the lips worked back and forth. "You'll never structure interrupts, that's just the way it is."

"You mean you can't, or it's impossible?"

"Look, I have no axe to grind on this. I'm just telling you you'll never structure interrupts."

"Thank you." She sat down.

Wimped out, I thought. Not like Lilah. Lilah would've kept challenging him. A few more easy questions, mostly dismissed out of hand by Mr. Softy, and he strode from the podium. Meissner replaced him momentarily.

"Our next speaker is Zachary Zaremba, who'll cover the power supply module."

I rose to my feet.

"Remember," said Jim, "Rules One and Six."

Heart throbbing like the Phantom's E string just before it broke, I made my way to the platform.

Meissner handed me a plastic cylinder from which a cord stretched to something under the lectern. Atop the cylinder were two buttons. "Red to advance, blue to go back. Good luck."

I pulled my notes out of my inside jacket pocket, set them on the podium, leaned toward the mike. "The AIR power supply comprises five separate DC-to-DC converters with the following output voltages: +28, +15, −15, +5, and −5. I'm briefly going to review the requirements of each, including current draw, regulation, ripple, and stability with frequency, and describe the design approaches we've taken to meet those requirements. I'm also going to cover the Special Test Equipment we've constructed and update you on the status of various custom connectors." I scanned the first two rows, saw mainly blank faces. Logy with lunch, I thought, blood rushing from their brains to cope with the Chicken Kiev, concentration would be a challenge. "Lights!" I called, pressing the red button on the plastic cylinder. The room darkened. Three minutes, they'd be comatose, and I could say anything.

The first slide came into focus. Days earlier, along with form 2219, Request to Generate Transparencies, I'd submitted sketches to the drafting department, now metamorphosed into professionally drawn images on screen. "The +5 is a linear supply with Q14 used as the pass transistor," I began.

Halfway through, the nervousness was completely gone. To my own surprise, I actually knew the stuff reasonably well, could explain at least on an elementary level how each circuit functioned and why certain choices were made. My voice, to my own ears, sounded, well, not quite Marv smooth, but certainly not wavering.

A phase- and gain-margin plot came up on the screen. Then a photograph of a six-foot-tall rack-mounted STE. Another circuit, this one of the +28 volt supply. Diagrams of five different connectors. And then, finally, "Lights, please," and it was done.

"Thank you, and I'd be happy to answer any questions."

I stuffed my notes back in my jacket, looked out at the audience, tried to find Shopper Jim, couldn't, noticed only a semisneering Wonderboy in the sixth row. "Thank—"

The Delayed Responder colonel stood up. "I have a question on the +28 supply."

"Sure."

"I noticed that your phase- and gain-margin curves were taken at a current of twenty milliamps."

Uh-oh. I tried desperately to keep my face impassive.

"Yes."

"But you said the actual output is about twelve hundred milliamps."

"Yes."

"Well, might not those curves change for the higher output current?"

"Uh . . . yes. They do." Sonofabitch slow-pissing bastard! I felt it now . . . again . . . that sudden audience alertness, antennas up, postures stiffening.

"Well, have you taken stability data at the highest current?"

"Uh, yes. We have."

"And were the phase- and gain-margins still the same?"

"They were . . . less."

"Less . . ."

Shit. Shit! Why me? Everyone else got Mickey Mouse questions or none, but I, I get quizzed on the one point, the one single sensitive issue—

"How much less? Were they still in a region you'd consider safe?"

The room was now absolutely still. Everyone in the first ten rows seemed pitched forward at forty-five degrees. My heart felt like a live thing hammering at the inside of my chest.

"I—"

"As a matter of fact, that current draw seems like an awful lot for that transistor. Is that within the manufacturer's ratings at eighty-five degrees centigrade?"

I wanted very much to zone out, to faint, actually, to withdraw and wake up twenty years later. I wanted to be out playing Wiffle ball, out on a soccer field, out with the kids, seeing them run, running with them, laughing, kicking. . . . I pictured Elise at the game, standing on the sideline, holding Boulot's hand, him leaning down and mumbling something in French, her high-pitched giggle.

"The transistors are individually tested for stability under conditions of actual current draw in the circuit. Every one used passes the test."

"But are they within the manufacturer's ratings?"

End of the road. He was staring at me intently now, and I was certain he knew the answer.

"Yes," I said.

Another moment of withering focus, the room all but gone, and then, "Thank you," and he sat down.

He'd sat down! It was over. I'd done a bad thing, but it was over and now all I needed was—

"Actually, that's not quite correct."

A voice from the first row. Meissner! Meissner was standing and speaking.

"Actually, Colonel, we feel at this time that this design is marginal. The facts are that the present current draw does exceed spec for the transistor and we have seen a number of them oscillate at various temperatures in the operating range."

What was he doing? What was happening here? I was being—

"Mr. Zaremba was assigned to this project only a few days ago, so he is unfamiliar with some of the more subtle problems we've been having. The fact is this is a fundamentally flawed design, we know it, we're working to fix it, and the employee responsible for it has been dismissed."

I moved to the edge of the lectern, held on to it for support. I felt light-headed, shivery.

"I'd like, if I may, to describe our approach." He turned to face the audience, then swiveled briefly to me. "Thank you, Zack."

I managed to get myself off the platform—"slunk," I think is the operative word—while Meissner delivered a prepared discourse on how the transmitter "group" was confident they could improve the efficiency of Q7 and reduce current draw back into the approved range of Q3. *Prepared.*

He had known this was going to happen.

And the employee responsible for it had been dismissed.

I opened the door to the hallway and went out. I leaned for a time against the wall, stared at it, then gradually, somehow, got myself into a crablike motion along its length. I came to a large picture: A photograph of the B1B on a runway. Under it were the words, *BELOW COST, AHEAD OF SCHEDULE, EXCEEDING ALL SPECIFICATIONS.*

Lies. The B1 had overrun even the wildest estimates of expense, was years late, and had failed dozens of major and minor requirements. I felt sick, nauseated. I made my way to the men's room, pushed open the door, and went immediately to the sink with the OUT OF ORDER sign. I splashed water on my eyes and cheeks, stared at myself for some time in the mirror, saw my face grow hard and cold, and became aware, at last, of just how infuriated I was.

———
o

"You set me up! *You set me up.*" I couldn't believe it, *I* was shouting at Meissner. "I lied, I did exactly what you asked, and you fired him anyway."

We were in his office. Meissner had his back to me. He was staring out his stupid precious window into the stupid interior courtyard that, except for the round metal tables and potted plants, might have been the exercise area of a prison.

"Someone had to go."

"But we had a deal."

"We had a deal. If it was up to me, this wouldn't have happened, but someone at a higher level made a decision."

"Who, Ingrassia?"

"Ingrassia gave me the order, but for all I know it came from even higher."

"Who higher? God?"

He turned. "Zack, I know you're upset."

"Yes. I am. I've been double-crossed, and the guy who taught me everything about the job is kicked out on the street. Yes, I'm upset."

"Boulot brought it on himself. We have fourteen hundred people here working on this job and someone had to go to preserve their employment. Major mistakes were made."

"Yes, but not his!"

"He had a choice. Had he made it correctly, he'd still be here. You saw how he's been acting the last few months, wearing his tie and belt backward, defying me in front of the group, mocking and undermining my authority. I wouldn't have fired him directly, but truthfully, I'm not surprised it came to this. I'm really not surprised."

"You and Ingrassia set me up."

"Ingrassia ordered me to tell the exact letter of the truth if the question came up. What was I supposed to do? It was something they could check! There was no way out." He paused, worked his lips. "Look, we came out of it okay, the Air Force appreciated our candor."

"It's disgusting," I said, just before I left.

———
o

I saw Boulot around four in the afternoon. He was emptying books from his bookcase into a cardboard box.

"Frenchman, I—"

"It ees okay, Zack. I am fine. It ees okay." He reached out to pat my shoulder. He must've seen how upset I was. The box he was loading was full. "I sink I need maybe two more," he said, looking over plaintively at Shopper Jim.

"They screwed you," I said.

"Yes, zey screwed me." He shrugged. "But, I am expecting eet. You cannot be someone like me and not expect eet."

"But I told them what they wanted to hear and they did it anyway."

"Yes, zat is how zey work."

"I'll go get you those cartons," Jim said.

"You are a good friend, Jeem."

"Rule Seven," Jim said to me. "Always keep enough cardboard boxes under your desk to carry out all your stuff." He disappeared out the cubicle door.

" 'Ee 'as great experience in zese matters," said Boulot. "Me, not so much."

"It's just . . . a shame. After all this time—how long you with the company?"

"Seven years." A chuckle. "Seven years of bad luck."

"All that time, and they don't even give you one day's notice? Make you leave immediately?"

"It ees not good for fired employees to stay around. We poison ze minds of ze uzzers."

"Well, mine's already poisoned."

"You are talking, I think, more than you should to Jeem."

"Jim knows everything."

" 'Ee knows too much. Too much knowledge is as dangerous as too little." He began removing folders from a file cabinet. " 'Ee is not a happy man."

I noticed Wonderboy, who'd been sitting at his desk all this time, had said nothing. "Wonderboy, you think this is fair?"

He looked up from whatever he'd been pretending to work on. "Fair has nothing to do with it. A job is a game. The game has certain rules. Frenchman elected not to play within those rules, and they kicked him out of the contest. Case closed."

"It's *not* a game," I said, but he just stared at me a moment and then resumed his make-believe work.

Shopper Jim returned to the cubicle, lugging two large cartons.

"Jeem," said Boulot, "you are amazing. I look all over for zese, I could not get zem. I even go to ze stockroom and 'ee say, 'You need stock requisition form 3128,' and I say, 'But I 'ave no more forms, zey take zem away,' and 'ee say, 'Zen I can do nussing for you.' " He lifted his eyebrows toward Jim. "So you 'ad ze form, Jeem?"

"Form? No. I don't give a femtoshit about some form. I just told the guy if he didn't hand me those fuckin' boxes he'd come out and find his car had four flats."

"He believed you?"

"He did after I identified the make, model, and year." He

turned to me. "It's good to know certain things about certain people."

Boulot began filling up the cartons with more books, file folders, and then stuff from his desk drawers: white lined pads full of calculations, Number 2 pencils, a Reiffler Giant Bow drafting set, four issues of *Microwave Journal,* a pair of scissors, two rolls of Scotch transparent tape, three Pink Pearl erasers, rubber bands, a pad of polar graph paper, a one-inch-thick loose-leaf binder, photocopied reprints of three technical articles . . . and then it was done.

Six boxes.

Seven years.

"We'll help you carry it out," said Jim. "Are you all set? You've been to Personnel?"

"Yes, yes, Mistair Lerner, 'ee told me all my rights, my medical insurance till ze end of ze month, my unemployment, my security debrief, my property pass out ze front door. You 'ave to know a lot to be fired. I tell heem I want to do it right."

Jim smiled. Boulot exchanged a handshake with Wonderboy, who muttered, "Good luck," and then we left the cubicle.

"Best of luck!" called Marie, as the three of us, carrying two boxes each, passed her station and headed out to the corridor.

At the front exit the guard checked Boulot's property pass, did a cursory inspection of the contents of the cartons, then waved us through.

"What, uh, are you gonna tell Elise?" I asked.

Boulot shrugged. "What can I? She is old enough to understand. I tell her ze truth, zey fire me."

"And if she asks why . . . ?"

"I tell her for many things zere is not always a reason."

It was raining out, one of those steady summer downpours, and I hunched forward as we walked, trying to protect the boxes. Boulot's Peugeot, of course, was parked at the very rear of the lot. He opened the trunk when we got there and we managed to fit three of the boxes inside it. The remaining three went on the rear seat. He shook hands with each of us before entering the driver's side and turning the key in the ignition.

"You will keep in touch, won't you?" I said. "I mean, you're not gonna just disappear, right?"

"No, no. We will see each uzzer again, Zack, I promise."

"Soon."

"Yes. Soon." He rolled up the window and pulled slowly away.

Jim and I trudged slowly back toward the building. We were now thoroughly soaked.

"Actually," I said, "considering everything, he didn't take it as badly as I expected."

Jim wiped some droplets from the corners of his eyes, looked at me, and shook his head. "You know, I don't think you have any comprehension of him at all."

12

ROOM WITH
TWO VIEWS

Doing a good job around here is like pissing in a dark suit: You get a warm feeling but no one else notices.
—SIGN IN ENGINEERING CUBICLE

Boulot, it seems, was only one of a drove of people I had failed to understand. I put it directly to the foremost among these after three hours of The Silent Treatment that evening.

"What I'm not getting is why are you so pissed off. This doesn't even have anything to do with you."

No answer. We sat in the living room, I pretending to read *Scientific American,* she a *Sky and Telescope.* Kevin was asleep in the Phantom's bedroom.

"You know, it's really silly. You're going to begin talking to me eventually, so you may as well do it now."

No response.

"Look, how about you just release your anger and that'll be it." I flipped away the magazine, stood up, walked over to her and stood with my legs apart. "Here, kick in my testicles and then let's talk about it."

No eye contact, face resolutely buried.

"Each testicle will chime at a different frequency, so you'll know if you got 'em both."

Silence.

"If you don't talk to me, I'm gonna bring up phlegm."

Nothing.

I began producing a series of deep-throated, thick-liquid bubbling and hocking noises. After a moment she put aside the magazine.

"Everything's a joke to you, isn't it?"

"Most things, yes."

"Everything."

"Not everything. Look, can you just tell me—"

"Because I thought you were someone you obviously aren't!" She shook her head. "I'm more angry at myself, at how easily I misplaced my feelings."

"Lilah, it wasn't that straightforward a decision. I was trying to save a man's job. A friend's job."

"A friend who never asked you to! A friend who, unlike you, maintained his principles and integrity."

"I'm sorry, but it wasn't that simple. Okay, so maybe I compromised a little."

" 'Compromised'? A *little*? You lied. You sold out."

"As I tried to explain to you, my intentions—"

"Are now among those paving the road to hell."

I sat down on the floor in front of her. "Look, right or wrong, like it or not, I did it. I did it and it's over." I shrugged. "Maybe it was a mistake."

"Maybe?"

"All right, it turned out badly, but there was no way I could've anticipated that."

Silence.

I tried a distraction. "Hey, guess who we play this Saturday?"

It was our final soccer game of the season. I knew she wouldn't answer, so I made the question rhetorical. "Bethpage Paneling."

"So?"

"They're coached by Larry Hoffman." Hoffman was Michael's father, the guy who'd instigated the petition.

"So?"

"I'm sure he'll have his kids all revved up. You know, grudge match, that sort of thing."

She stared at me for twenty seconds. "Mr. Softy removed me from my job today."

"What?"

"He said since I was so concerned with data entry, that's what I'd be doing from now on. No more programming."

"Jesus. Sonofabitch."

"He's punishing me."

"White-haired fuckhead."

The bones in her high Eurasian cheeks threatened to split the skin. "I want you to get me copies of signed time cards, yours and as many others as you can from your department."

My turn for silence.

"I want to show that this is not a clerical-error problem. That this practice of charging a job not worked on is pervasive, that at least some of the practitioners knew exactly what they were doing, and that management would need to be deaf, dumb, and blind not to know it was going on."

"I think the 'dumb' is not relevant."

"Will you do it?"

I stood up, began to pace the floor. "When you say you want to 'show' this is not clerical error, show who?"

"Whom."

"Okay."

"I don't know yet. Maybe Sanders. Maybe even Venator."

"Venator? He's the CEO of the whole II, right? He probably

won't even know what you're talking about. Guys at his level are interested only in international mergers and global currency transactions. They don't get involved in diddly-shit like this."

"I said I'm not sure." Delivered very deliberately.

"You know, time cards like those, the wrong people get a hold of them, technically, I mean . . . they could be incriminating. Guys could get in trouble."

"Maybe they *should* get in trouble."

"Including me. . . ."

She rolled her eyes. "Look, no one is interested in an engineer's filling out job charges. The culprits are the supervisors who tell you what number to put in. Those are the guys trying to cover up cost overruns and financial losses on jobs they bid too low."

"So you mean people like Meissner. . . ."

"And Mr. Softy."

"Ingrassia?"

"It's anyone's guess how far up it goes."

"How do you know it doesn't include Sanders?"

She shrugged. "Maybe it does. If I end up bringing it to him, his reaction will be a clue."

I pantomimed a pitching motion, paused on the imaginary rubber to check the imaginary runner on first base. "It's not right that I put my colleagues in jeopardy by getting copies of their time cards."

She considered this a moment, then said, "Suppose I promise not to show them to anybody."

"Then what good would they do?"

"Because if I had them—and I let Sanders know I had them—that would be just as effective. After all, *he* could certainly get them *if*—big if—he wanted to."

"So the purpose would be just to let him know, or Ingrassia know, that you know."

"And have proof. That's the key."

I delivered the pitch. "And you guarantee you won't show them to anybody." Perfect strike.

"Guarantee. If it ever came to where I wanted to, I'd discuss it with you first"—our eyes met—"but you would make the decision."

I knew that what she was asking of me was at least, in part, a kind of penance for lying at the CDR, a penance I felt was unnecessary. And yet, despite this, I wanted very much to redeem myself in her eyes. I nodded slowly. "Okay."

"Okay?"

"Can you throw in a sexual favor?"

She stiffened. "What kind?"

I leaned over and whispered it to her.

She nodded. "So you'll hold up your end of the deal—"

"As long as you hold up your . . . end." Big grin.

"Well, then I agree."

"Good."

"Good."

It wasn't that good.

———
o

I could imagine no other way to accomplish the task than with two linked, frontal questions: Do you keep any copies of past time cards? And if so, can I have them? My own response as to why I needed them would be that Lilah was requesting them for a check on data-entry accuracy—an explanation that was almost true and yet totally evasive.

Shopper Jim kept copies for a month back—he phoned in his weekly hours to his Job Shop—and never asked why I wanted them.

Wonderboy would not answer if he kept copies and inquired why, if Lilah wanted them, she didn't ask for them herself.

"What's the difference?" I said. "Because then I could tease her before saying no, and she's a lot better looking than you." "Oh. So you do have copies?" Wonderboy shrugged. "Can't say."

"Why would I keep copies?" asked Nussbaum. "Who gives a shit what I worked on?"

A Boy Named Hsu was dismissive: "Last week, I worked ninety-four hours, you think I'm gonna take time out to make you copies? You tell Meissner he wants copies, he should come make them himself." "But it's not for Meissner." "Oh . . . right," he said, rolling his eyes, then walking past me.

When I asked Whispering Bill—back three days now from the hospital—he motioned to both ears, which were stuffed with cotton. I repeated the question at higher volume. "Infection," said Bill, again indicating the ears and signaling that he still hadn't heard. It wasn't till I wrote down the request that he nodded, fished around in his desk awhile, then handed me a stack of photocopied time cards. I glanced at the most recent week:

MON.	TUES.	WED.	THURS.	FRI.	SAT.	SUN.
Sick	Sick	Sick	Sick	Sick	Sick	Sick

I flipped through the rest, saw they were all the same. "That's okay, Bill," I said, handing them back. "Thanks."

And then it dawned on me.

At 12:03 P.M., lunch hour, I returned from the Transmitter Lab and walked to Marie's desk. Marie, I knew, would be in the cafeteria now, spooning up strawberry Dannon Light, sitting with Joanna-who-wore-men's-shoes from PRODUCTION CONTROL, and Brillo-haired Loraine from PURCHASING. But I still had to be extremely stealthy: Just across the aisle was Meissner's office, with Meissner inside, feet on desk, knocking back his can of Slim Fast and reading the *Wall Street Journal.*

I walked around behind Marie's chair, leaned down, and began opening drawers. I found it easily on the bottom left, a Pendaflex folder labeled TIME CARDS. A *big* folder with maybe two hundred xeroxed sheets. I removed it, thumbed through it, saw it was exactly what I—well, Lilah—was after.

I walked through the halls trying to think where I could copy this thing with no one asking any questions, no one pacing impatiently behind me while I ran my covert material, someplace where processing voluminous meaningless documents was routine. . . .

"Hey, how you do?" asked Tim Mee.

I looked around, even as the high-speed automatic Kodak copier churned away at my pile of time card sheets. "I'm sure he's doing fine," I said.

"You never get tired that joke," said Mee.

"Never."

"You are easily amused."

"Well . . . I know I'll never find another Yu."

We were in the ECN Building, a separate two-story structure that had been erected adjacent to the main II plant.

"So"—he gestured toward the stack I was copying—"looks like you very busy."

"Oh, yeah." I noticed he held his own pile to be copied.

"How job go?"

"You're the one who'd know best. How many AIR ECNs you got?"

"Me? Lots." He held up his papers. "We up to one thousand."

"*One thousand.* Holy shit. And that's per week, right?"

Mee grinned. "That per day."

I walked back to the main building holding my copies. It was inconceivable. I knew AIR was an exceedingly big job and exceedingly FUBARed—Fucked Up Beyond All Recognition—but five thousand ECNs a week was a figure as ungraspable by the human mind as a million light-years. It meant that almost nothing was being done that wasn't immediately being undone.

I entered the rear door and walked through the corridors toward the RF Engineering area, passing occasional clumps of lunchtime strollers. I myself would have little or no time left to eat; at best I'd be able to grab something from the cafeteria to take out and consume at my desk. Fortunately, Engineering still seemed fairly much deserted—I'd had paranoid fantasies of Wonderboy returning early from lunch, catching me with the copies, and turning me in to HUMAN RESOURCES, commenting as he did so, "Case closed."

But the office was empty and I simply placed the stack of copies in a manila folder, which I secreted in my right bottom desk drawer under a *Scientific American* article my father had sent me on new materials to fill teeth. Two minutes later I was bending over Marie's desk, having just restored the originals to their prior location—when suddenly, with a tremendous bang, the door to Meissner's office flew open.

He stood framed there for a full second, his face round and wet and so bursting red it seemed bloody—and I knew I was going to be dead here at II, caught for stealing, or breaking into another employee's desk, or some even worse career-ending disgrace—when it occurred to me that his face *was* bloody, real crimson dripping gore running down his cheeks, and then two hands grasped his collar and yanked him back inside the office.

I could hear a struggle, crashing sounds, truncated epithets, loud thumps, breaking wood, but my mind still could not quite absorb it. The context was all wrong: There weren't physical fights here; this was a domain of the mind, an engineering department, an area of gentility and intellectual investigation. I slowly approached the doorway. We didn't *hit* each other here. Hitting was for brutes, something the non–college graduates did, or perhaps, under *extremes,* the emotionally fragile liberal arts majors. But engineers? Hitting? Impossible. We would have to take courses. . . .

And then, as I entered the office, I understood. Boulot was behind Meissner's desk, bent backward over it, gray sweater imprinted with the rings of the monthly calendar, eyes wide open, mouth making a staccato squawking sound as Meissner's fingers tightened around his throat. As I advanced, Meissner's eyes briefly met my own, a strangely calm, sad look, as in, *See what I have to do to control my staff?* and then suddenly he was propelled backward. For an instant it seemed as if he'd been lassoed by an invisible rope, and then I realized Boulot had managed to get his feet up between himself and Meissner's sternum and had kicked outward.

I think the next things happened simultaneously, the heavy chunking sound of breaking glass, Meissner's backstroke windmill at nothing, his still-calm, *Now look what happened* expression as the window splintered under the impact and his momentum carried him through and out.

I stood rooted, my mind simply rejecting the auditory and visual inputs. He couldn't have actually fallen *out* of the window. Windows don't shatter like that; there must've been something wrong with the glazing or the tempering of the glass or—Because if he *had* fallen out, he'd be—

Boulot was making a kind of *uhhhhh, uhhhhh, uhhhhh,* chuffing noise you hear from aged hospital patients when they're in distress. I finally managed to stagger to the window frame, just as he began to lift himself off the surface of the desk. It was not until I felt the outside air on my face that I finally accepted the situation as real.

I looked down into the sunken courtyard. The drop was

about fifteen feet. I saw Meissner lying on his back, just beyond one of the white circular metal tables. His eyes were open. An irregular stain (chart color #20, *lobster*) amoebaed out on the concrete behind his head. Two men and a woman clustered around him. Another man was running toward the building door.

I felt detached, dizzy, placed my hand on the wall to steady myself. My eyes wandered to the striped umbrella over the table. He could've been impaled, I thought, and the picture came with it, the white metal pole poking up through a glistening ruby hole in Meissner's abdomen. As if the reality—the incredible, impossible reality—weren't bad enough.

" 'Ee is dead?" Boulot had come up behind me.

I turned, saw him massaging his throat. "I don't know."

" 'Ee . . . 'ee went crazy. 'Ee try to keel me." He looked out the window at the scene below.

"*He* tried to kill you?"

"Yes. This is why I defenestrate him."

"De-fen—"

"Eet means when you poosh someone out a window."

"There's a *word* for that?"

"From ze French. The English took eet. I did not mean to murder heem."

There was a crowd of about a dozen people around Meissner now. I thought I had seen a movement in one of his legs. I stepped back from the window frame; several people were looking up, gesticulating. The office floor was littered with broken glass. "Are you okay?" I asked Boulot.

He inhaled, shrugged, and shook his head. "I 'ave done a terrible thing. Terrible." He slumped forward.

I put my arm around his shoulders. "Come. Come back to the cubicle. We'll sit."

I walked him slowly toward W5. It was empty when we got

there—I was thankful that Wonderboy was still out to lunch, wished Jim would've returned. Boulot sat down heavily at the now-vacant desk that had once been his.

"I'll make you some coffee," I offered, removing my "works"—half-empty jar of Maxwell House instant, plastic spoon, styrofoam cafeteria cup, Japanese-made immersion heater.

"I 'ave finished myself," said Boulot.

"Be right back," I said, grabbing the cup.

I filled it slowly at the only functional sink in the Engineering men's room. I had offered the coffee as much to get away as to try and soothe him. I had trouble forming coherent thoughts. Should I call someone? Who? The police? In-plant Security? Ingrassia? 911? No, the last could be ruled out; Meissner clearly had people attending to him. *But what then should I do?*

I returned to the cubicle, plugged in the heater, placed the coil in the cup. Exactly two minutes later the water was boiling; I spooned in some coffee, gave it to Boulot. His hands were trembling.

"I'm sorry," I said, "I don't have any milk or sugar."

"I came only to yell at heem," said Boulot. "But 'ee looked at me and 'ee say, 'I already 'ave told you I am sorry, what more can I do? This is my lunch hour now, I need ze time. You 'ave more problems, go to Personnel.' And 'ee wave his hand like thees." Boulot made a dismissive motion. "And that is when I grab heem, his shirt, I pull ze front and it rips. And then he goes crazy and we fight." He held the cup in two hands, sipped slowly at the steaming liquid.

"Edouard"—I think it was the first time I ever called him by his first name—"this is just . . . I don't know what to say."

"I am going to prison," he said, "maybe worse. What will 'appen to Elise?" He shut his eyes tightly. "Who will take care of her?"

In the outer hall I could hear footsteps, indistinct voices of many people.

Boulot opened his eyes. "I thought one day, when I retire from ze law, one day I would go back to Paris. I 'ave not been for twenty years. But I thought, one day I go back. Maybe I open one of zose tiny book stalls you see on ze banks of ze Seine. Zey don't make any money, but so what? You 'ave ze books."

The voices grew louder, more urgent; I could make out some of the words: "In there, in there!"

"And lunchtime I would go into a *boulangerie*—you know what this ees? a bakery—and I would buy a baguette, one of those long French breads, and maybe a bottle of red wine, nussing expensive, and I would go down and sit along ze Seine. And I would read my book and eat my bread, and I would 'ave a little wine, and I would watch ze *bateaux* on ze water—"

The footsteps were in the Engineering area now. A deep voice said, "Stand back, people. Please stand back."

"—and I would be ze 'appiest man alive. I would be truly 'appy." He looked at me. "Eet's some dream, eh?"

"Yes. Some dream."

"But now eet is gone forevair."

In the doorway stood two uniformed security guards, a tall black one and a squat white one.

Boulot, facing me, had his back to them.

"Edouard," I said softly, "they're here."

But the tall black one strode past him, crossed to my desk, and snatched the immersion coil from where it rested on my blotter. "Got it!" he said, holding it aloft.

The squat white one approached my chair. "Zachary Zaremba?"

"Yes . . ."

"You understand that it is illegal to brew your own coffee or any other beverage under the terms of our contract with Foremost Foods?"

"I . . . What're you talking about?"

The black one said, "Would you come with us, please."

It wasn't a question. "What?"

"Please stand up, sir," said the white one, "and come with us."

Always the good boy, I slowly rose.

"But this ees crazy," said Boulot, as the two guards flanked me. "It ees me 'oo 'as defenestrated ze boss."

"You ready?" said the black one to me.

"Where are you taking me?"

"Just come with us," said the white one. And the two of them led me out the door past the curious, pitying, baleful gaze of Shopper Jim, Whispering Bill, Wonderboy, Marie, Nussbaum, and half a dozen other head-shaking engineers and techs.

13

OMIT B

I want to be the worst engineer I can be!
—EDOUARD BOULOT

I sat in a chair in the HUMAN RESOURCES office, across the room from the two guards, who said little inaudible things to each other that periodically made them snigger. What was audible were the voices of Herman Lerner and Mrs. Leeping, the elderly secretary who'd escorted me in on my very first day at II. Behind a closed door Lerner's voice was escalating in volume as he questioned her.

"You know what we're trying to do here, I explained that, didn't I?"

"Yes, but . . ."

"But *what?*"

"He didn't meet the basic guidelines. He had no ID, no driver's license, not even a Social Security number."

"The guidelines. I see." Pause. "He wasn't a hunchback, was he?"

"No."

"Did he have cancer?"

"Well . . . not as far as I know. . . ."

"Palsy?"

"No."

"Was he blind?"

"No, he wasn't—"

"Dwarf? Midget? Peg-leg?"

"No, none of—"

Shouting now. "Drooling, snaggletoothed, pecker-out-of-the-pants cross-eyed mental defective?"

"Mr. Lerner, I don't think—"

Quietly intense: "Was he black?"

"Yes. He was black."

"*Well, that's the next best thing!* For chrissake, go out there and try to get him back. Find him. Go out to the parking lot!"

"Yes, sir."

The door opened and Mrs. Leeping scurried out past me (or at least scurried as fast as a sixtyish, slightly overweight woman could under the circumstances). Lerner turned his attention to the next case, crooking his finger for me to enter the office. "You! In."

He closed the door behind us, motioned me to a wooden chair in front of his desk. He shook his head. "Tell ya, what I wouldn't give right now for a decent paraplegic. . . ." He held up a folder. "State human rights people, all over us. You miss the quota by one or two minorities, short a couple of cripples, and right away they're up your ass. Had a microcephalic quit in Shipping—imagine! Guy with a two-inch head gets a better offer—and five days later I get a notice in the mail." Tap on the folder. "Five days! Crazy. Just crazy. Now I gotta hire three minorities just to make up for one retard. That's the rule these days. Isn't it absurd?"

I congratulated myself silently for withholding even a slight nod.

Lerner put down the folder and picked up my immersion heater. "And on top of all that, now we got *this.*"

"Mr. Lerner—"

"You probably think this is a joke, don't you?"

"I don't know what it is."

"Were you warned?"

"Look, I don't understand—"

"Were you warned?"

"About what?"

"About not making your own coffee at your desk."

"I—I don't know. Someone may have mentioned it."

"Did Marie Antonucci not advise you on several occasions"— he flipped open another folder—"on July tenth, on September nineteenth, most recently on March twenty-forth, did she not advise you that it was a violation of company policy and a contravention of our contract terms with Foremost Foods?"

"I'm sorry, but I just don't see why it's such a big deal."

"It *is* a big deal!" Shouted. "It's a very big deal. We have arranged with Foremost for them to be our exclusive vendor. Exclusive! Negotiated at an outstanding rate, but with very severe financial penalties for contract violations. They get even a whiff of someone doing their own food preparation, and do you know what kind of restitution II would need to make? What sort of remedies and curatives they could invoke?"

"Remedies and—"

"Lawyer talk for we get fucked!"

"But I wasn't *selling* coffee, I just—"

"Doesn't matter. You can't draw the line. You brew coffee, someone else gets a hot plate and makes popcorn, a third person barbecues weiners, and before long the entire place is one huge stinking-from-beans picnic! The cafeteria may as well close completely."

"I'm sorry."

"You ought to be."

"But isn't it some kind of violation of my basic rights not to be allowed—"

"There is no constitutional right to make coffee at work. The Founding Fathers didn't give a shit about that." He leaned forward. "Look, I am trying to be honest with you. You want the company line? It's a safety issue. Fire hazard. Can't have employees using heat-generating appliances at their desks. That make you feel better?"

"Well . . . yes. Now at least I understand—"

"But I just told you that isn't it! That's a subterfuge. The real reason is . . ." He rolled his eyes. "Ach! Engineers. You know what 'subterfuge' means?"

"Yes."

"All right, end of story. You've been officially warned. Once more and you're out."

I stared at him. "Mr. Lerner, ten minutes ago Anton Meissner was defenestrated in his office."

"Defenestrated? I know he went out a window, but . . . you mean someone also cut off his nuts?"

"I was a partial witness to what went on."

"Oh, yes. We're aware of that. The police are on their way. You'll give them a statement."

I stood up.

"You'll wait outside with our own security people until the cops arrive."

I moved toward the door. "So . . . you know I was a witness, but you brought me in to talk about coffee."

"First things first," said Lerner, closing the door behind me.

○

Two detectives asked me questions for about an hour. I told them everything I had seen, answering objective questions accurately, subjective ones inaccurately. Had I actually witnessed either man strike any blows? No. Was I aware of any previous animosity between them? No. Did Boulot propel Meissner backward using one foot or two? Two. Had Meissner, in the past six months, ever humiliated Boulot in public? Yes. But he humiliated everyone in public, and private. What was I doing outside Meissner's office at that hour? Returning from lunch. (All right, so that one wasn't accurate. What should I have said? Pilfering company-confidential material from his secretary's desk?)

Anyway, they dismissed me, told me to keep myself available for additional questioning, not to leave the state. I asked about Meissner's condition, but they said they didn't know. It was late afternoon when I returned to the cubicle. Shopper Jim and Wonderboy were at their desks, Whispering Bill was at Kushner's, and an unkempt, scraggly bearded black man in filthy Army fatigues was at Boulot's.

"Anyone see what happened to the Frenchman?" I asked.

No answer.

"Did the cops take him?"

No answer.

I stood in the middle of the cubicle, shaking my head. "Is anyone here aware that something horrible and unusual occurred today involving people in this department?"

Wonderboy slowly rotated his head. "You mean the notice about canceling the Labor Day holiday?"

I lingered another instant, then turned and walked out.

○

"Engineers," I said to Lilah as I paced the sideline. "They're like robots. Like horses with blinders on. I think it's a form of attention deficit, like they can concentrate on only one thing at a time, and work comes first."

Lilah, looking wonderful in tight ribbed pants and nipple-outlining wool sweater, turned to follow me. "I can't talk to you if you don't stand still."

"Move up! Fullbacks, move up!" I shouted, then shook my head. We, Hotcha Stationery, were down 5–0 in the third quarter. The kids had forgotten or ignored everything I'd thought they'd learned. A major backslide, and against Beth-page Paneling, the team coached by Larry Hoffman. "They can't do a single thing right," I said to Lilah.

"It's not their fault, that's how they are," she said. "They compartmentalize."

"What?"

"They put each thing into a separate area of the brain."

"The kids?"

"No, the engineers."

"Oh, I—" Back to the field. "It's a direct! It's a direct, line up! Form a line! Barry, get—" Too late. Bethpage Paneling scored its sixth goal on a direct penalty by my former star, Michael Hoffman, against a disorganized, straggling, zombie-looking Hotcha. On the opposite sideline, I thought I saw Larry Hoff-man smirk just before he turned to pat his son on the butt.

It happened late in the fourth quarter, when we were down 8–zip and, admittedly, Bethpage did not have its best players on the field. On my team, Lilah's son and Brian Bur-nett were advancing the ball toward the opposition's goal. Kevin cut toward center, exchanging positions with Brian on the wing, an attack option I'd read about and practiced with the kids—once. Suddenly, as they passed the penalty box, Brian crossed the ball in the air (miracle number two) to the trailing, huffing Kevin—who, to my utter astonishment, *headed* it into the goal.

I raised both arms in flabbergasted triumph. "Did you catch that?" I shouted to Lilah. "Did you—I mean, holy, holy shit!"

The parents were going crazy, cheering, pounding each other. I mean, it was just not something you ever saw seven-year-olds do. Even Hoffman was slowly applauding, while simultaneously shaking his head.

Lilah came over and flung her arms around me.

"Did you see that?" I repeated.

"I saw, I saw."

"Was that unbelievable, or what?"

"Absolutely impossible." I felt her body against me. "I knew you were a great coach."

"But we're losing 8–1."

"Maybe, but no one ever saw a goal like that."

I observed Kevin trotting back to the center of the field, his congratulating teammates clustered around him. He looked over at me and raised a clenched fist, and I raised one back. It was, I understood, the reason why all the unrewarded effort of coaching—all the points taught but not learned, repeated but not mastered, all the practices on chill dank dark winter late afternoons, all the time waiting for parents to just show up and take their kids home, all the political bullshit with the soccer club, the ultra-competitiveness of other coaches, the incessant hectoring by parents—why all of that could in one precious instant be rendered void: the Perfect Play. One true thing.

It was the game's final score. Afterward, I stood at the end of the queue of kids as we slid past the Bethpage line, slapping hands in a show of (at best grudging, in general feigned) sportsmanship.

"Nice game, Michael," I said as I passed my former player.

"Thanks, Coach." (I liked that; he still called me Coach.)

And then, at line's end, his father.

"Good job." Stiff nod.

"You too." Stiff nod.

To Lilah: "Good job."

From Lilah: "Good job."

And then it was done and the team was scattering and Lilah and I and Kevin were lingering behind to gather up the balls and the practice cones and take down the nets. Two days earlier I had given Lilah 213 copies of the time sheets I'd stolen from Marie's desk. She had been grateful. She had been contrite about her recent treatment of me, which she'd acknowledged as "cold." She had expressed the feeling that this would end the strain in our relationship. We'd resumed having sexual congress and engaged in two intense, explosive sessions. And now we'd lost a game together, but it was a beautiful, sun-splashed day in late June and there had been one perfect play involving her son, and I thought that things had turned around. I loved her (again) and she loved me (again) and that was the best, most satisfying feeling in the world.

"Great goal," I said to Kevin as I bent to pick up a ball. "I'm glad at least someone on the team actually absorbed something."

"You wanna know a secret?" said Kevin.

"Sure."

"It was an accident. The ball just banged off my head and went in."

I straightened. "You mean you didn't try to direct it?"

"I was trying to get away from it. It just hit me."

As Lilah giggled, I slowly shook my head, reluctantly erasing the extravagant mental credit I'd so generously self-bestowed and wondering if I'd misinterpreted everything else just as thoroughly.

———
o

The next morning I received a call from Marla Hastings, the sensual/evil/needy/slutty secretary to Yale Sanders. (Actually, I had no idea whether the "evil," "needy," or "slutty" really applied. They were entirely my own fantasies.)

"He wants to see you immediately in his office."

"Sanders," I said to Shopper Jim, munching on his morning cruller. I rose from my chair.

"Did he say, 'Bring all your stuff'?"

"Uh . . . no."

"Good. Then you're still employed."

When I got to the office, Marla, erection-baiting in teeny black miniskirt, quickly ushered me into the inner sanctum. Ingrassia and Lerner were already there, seated in the tufted leather chairs, facing Sanders, who sat on the couch. Sanders motioned me to a third chair, a wooden one obviously brought in for the occasion.

"Zack, please . . . glad you could make it."

(What? Huh?)

"Care for some coffee? Or would you rather make your own?" All the men laughed heartily. "I heard about your little to-do." He winked theatrically in Lerner's direction.

"Oh . . . yeah . . . I—"

"Don't worry about it. I like self-reliance. It may have been technically against the rules, but hey, when did someone who always toed the line ever do anything great?"

"Well, I—"

"Rhetorical question. Now, coffee?"

"Uh, okay. . . ."

"Marlaaaaah!"

Marla scurried in.

"Coffee for Zack." To me: "Decaf or regular?"

"Regular. Extra-caf if you got. Black. No sugar."

He nodded and Marla disappeared. Back to me: "Now: You're wondering why you're here."

I thought of the last time I'd been in his office, when Warren had appealed his seven. "Well, I—"

"Rhetorical statement. I'll tell you why. Meissner. Meissner and Boulot."

"The defenestration."

Ingrassia quickly interjected. "*That* part is a rumor. He *was* thrown out a window, but his testicles were not damaged."

"I see."

"You *did* see. You were the only witness."

"Yes."

"Herman tells me you've already spoken to the police."

"Yes."

There was a soft knock on the door, followed immediately by Marla's entrance with a mug of coffee on a little tray. She bent forward to place it on a black circular end table near my chair. "Thank you," I said.

She mouthed a silent, *You're welcome,* then tiptoed from the room.

When I looked back to Sanders, he was holding out his hands, two inches apart, slightly cupped. So he *did* covet Marla! He was human after all! I wondered: Was he an ass man or a titty man; were those grasping concave palms pantomiming a caress of breasts or buttocks?

"Two employees," he began. "One good, one not so good—one poor, you might say—and the good"—he lifted the right palm slightly—"gets rid of the poor."

All right, so it wasn't about Marla. Furthermore, the statement seemed somewhat short of brilliant recap. Yes, Meissner had canned Boulot.

"The good is a teacher, an innovator, a nonconformist. The

poor is as a giant nattering bird, filling the hallways with his brainless squawking."

Wait a minute . . .

"The good has integrity. The poor cares only for documentation, independent of content. The good is obsessed with a working design. The poor . . ." He looked over at Ingrassia.

Ingrassia said, "He once assigned Whispering Bill to research the use of umlauts, because he thought somebody left one off the second *o* in 'cooperation'."

I couldn't be hearing what I was hearing. "Excuse me," I said, "but is Mr. Meissner still alive? We heard he was in the hospital."

"He's alive," said Lerner. "Fractured skull, two broken legs, busted ribs, ruptured spleen. He'll recover, doctors said, but it'll take at least nine months."

"Terrible," I said.

"The point," continued Sanders, "is that even when he was whole, the man was an impediment to the defense of the United States." He put down his hands. "That is the business of this division, is it not? I mean, this is why we have all these Army and Navy and Air Force contracts, is it not?" He glanced from face to face. "Am I out of line here, fellas, or what? Please. Tell me."

No one spoke.

"For godsakes, this is *not* rhetorical."

"Then no way are you out of line," piped up Ingrassia.

"You're right *in* line," affirmed Lerner.

"Mr. Sanders," I began, "I'm not—"

"Yesterday—imagine how quick these people act—his wife had us served with a lawsuit. Negligence, loss of earning power, the whole works." Index finger pointed at me. "Which is why you figure into this." He glanced down at a paper on his desk. "In the statement you gave the police, you estimated the time that Meissner went out the window as about twenty-five minutes after twelve. How firm are you on that?"

"Why—"

"Just answer."

I sipped at the coffee. "It was an estimate. But I think it's pretty accurate."

"Plus or minus, mmm, three minutes, would you say?"

"Yes."

Lerner clapped his hands and grinned. "We got 'em!"

"I'm sorry, I—"

"If he didn't work past midway through the lunch hour we don't have to pay him for the day! It's in our Human Resources manual." He turned gleefully to Sanders. "So there's no last day's pay and no severance."

"You mean . . ." I struggled to grasp it. "You mean you're firing Meissner?"

Sanders steepled his palms. His silver cuff links shone in the recessed lighting. "You think we should mail the termination notice to his house or directly to the hospital?"

———
o

"They're madmen," I said to Shopper Jim. "All of them, absolute crazy people."

Shopper Jim said, "The American corporate mind thinks short-term. The twenty-million-dollar liability lawsuit will be fifteen years in the courts; a middle manager's salary, even one day's worth, is an immediate subtraction from this quarter's bottom line."

We were in the corridor outside the Transmitter Lab, lined up at the Payroll cart, and I was telling him about the meeting with Sanders three days earlier. I hadn't seen Jim since then; I'd been working nineteen hours a day trying (unsuccessfully) to reduce the transmitter current draw while still maintaining the power output.

"But isn't Meissner . . . wasn't he a salaried employee, paid by the week?"

"So you're thinking that he could've taken it as a vacation day or sick day. . . ." We moved up toward the two uniformed guards. The cart, stuffed with payroll checks and cash, made its appearance every Thursday afternoon.

"Well, yeah. Seems to me if you got thrown out a window that would qualify as sick."

"He probably used up his sick days. Whadda you Directs get, eight, somethin' like that? And a vacation day no doubt requires you notify your supervisor at least seventy-two hours in advance. As Lerner said, check the manual."

"But—"

"Meissner's mistake was failure to anticipate a midday defenestration."

"Zaremba," I said to the guard, as I reached the front of the line. He handed me an envelope.

"Another daring daylight robbery," said a voice behind me. I turned to see a smirking Nussbaum, who handed me a data sheet before taking his own check. "By the way," he added, "amplifier's no good."

I'd discovered that Nussbaum was all doom-and-gloom, a flat-footed, shuffling, perpetually pessimistic harbinger of hopelessness. Whenever I came up with something to try, his comments would run along the lines of a resigned, "Well, I'll do it if you want," without the slightest sign of enthusiasm or energy.

"You don't think this'll work?" I'd ask.

He'd shrug. "Hey, you're the engineer, that's why they pay you the big bucks."

"Well, let's try it."

And off he'd go, shaking his head.

I pored now over the new data sheet as we headed back into the lab. "Shit. Shit fuck shit." I looked up at Shopper Jim. "It's impossible. It really is fuckin' totally, hopelessly impossible. I tune it up to get out the power and it detunes over temperature. I put in a temperature compensating circuit and the goddamn half-frequency parametric comes in. I tune out the parametric and the current draw comes up. It's like a balloon filled with shit. You push it in one place, it bulges out another."

"I told you," said Nussbaum. He seemed about to add something, but I suppose the look on my face shut him up.

"Unlike most other laws," said Jim, "the laws of physics are hard to break."

"I'm at wit's end."

"Short trip," muttered Nussbaum.

"I think it's time you met somebody," said Jim. "Let me make a call and I'll get back to you." He left the lab. Ten minutes later he poked his head in the door. "Ay Zaremba, come follow me."

We walked through the halls, usual route, past the CREDIT UNION office with its single motionless female (robot?) attendant, past the Foremost Foods coffee vending machine that stole your money, past the SECURITY OFFICE, the CAD Lab, the Plating Room, the SHIPPING AND RECEIVING cage, the Electronic Stock Room . . . and then onto the epoxied concrete—leg muscles feeling a tinge of strain now—Assembly Area One, with its chained employees; the block-square Production Machine Shop; SPECIAL ASSEMBLIES, where they put together the STEs; Assembly Area Two, with its tape-and-reel, pick-and-place machines that stuffed printed circuit boards with electronic components; Assembly Area Three, with its vapor-phase soldering ovens that did the actual attachments—must've walked half a mile by now—until at last we came to a blue steel door in a gray brick wall at the very farthest end of the factory. I followed Jim through into the alcove of a staircase.

"Shit, I didn't even know this was here."

"Lots of stuff you don't know," said Jim.

We descended one flight of backless, dusty metal steps, pushed through another door, and entered . . . a basement. A basement! It had never dawned on me! This vast place, this sprawl of an engineering ranch, had an entire equally vast basement. White-painted, brick-walled corridors stretched out before us in three directions.

"What the fuck is this? Looks like a goddamn dungeon." The floors were bare cement.

Jim raised his eyebrows. "This is where they keep the smart guys."

We passed an open doorway labeled ADVANCED MICROWAVE INTEGRATED CIRCUITS, another labeled ADVANCED HYBRIDS. Inside both offices, middle-aged men were hunched over microscopes or writing at desks. A third doorway was labeled CLEAN ROOM D; inside, through a long glass window, we could see a dozen white-gowned, white-capped men and women seated at bonding machines. Doors four through nine appeared to be single-person offices, most containing men, some who looked up at our passage, some who stared vacantly, one who hummed loudly. A tenth door said ADVANCED ADHESIVES. The sign over the eleventh read ADVANCED COATINGS.

"Everything here is 'advanced,' " I said.

"Except us," said Jim.

"Will you tell me where we're going? This place is giving me the creeps."

We turned into another stone corridor. It was really looking medieval now. Even some of the caged overhead lights were out. I imagined pretty soon we'd be wading into sewer water and then the hordes of rats and cockroaches would emerge.

"Ever see on a drawing a note that said, *OMIT B*?" asked Jim.

"Yes! I always wondered—"

"What that meant."

"As a matter of fact . . ."

"It doesn't mean to omit anything."

"Okay . . ." We passed a doorway with a sign ARTIFICIAL DIELECTRICS.

"*OMIT B* stands for Old Man In The Back."

"I'm not following you."

"He wrote those notes."

"A guy?"

"Every high-tech company that's existed for a long time has one."

"What does he do?"

"OMIT B has three major attributes: He's very smart, he was here from the beginning (or close to it), and he knows everything there is to know about his particular field. Everything. Not only the theory, not only the design steps, not only the test methodology, but all the little tricks and details and quirks of processing that never make it to the formal prints. All the history that explains why something that seems irrational really was the best choice at the time."

We made a left turn and passed ADVANCED CONFORMAL ANTENNAS and ADVANCED RECEIVERS.

"You told him I needed help on the transmitter?"

"Yup."

"Why couldn't somebody have referred me to him before?"

"Wouldn't have done any good. He wouldn't have seen you."

"Whaddaya mean, 'seen me'? What is he, a fucking neurosurgeon or something? Meissner could've just ordered him to."

"He doesn't—didn't—report to Meissner."

"Then Ingrassia."

"He doesn't report to Ingrassia."

"All right, then Sanders. Everyone in this division is under Sanders."

"Nominally, yes, but in fact OMIT B is under no one. He does what he wants, what he deems is most needed."

"You mean if Sanders gave him an order and he didn't obey, he wouldn't get fired?"

"No."

"That's impossible."

"Not if ten other jobs depended on his knowledge. But you see, it never comes to that. I doubt if Sanders even knows he exists. OMIT B has been putting in eighteen-hour days seven days a week for thirty-five years. You can't ask him to work *more.* So the way the system functions, the different project leaders and department heads come to him and beg for a little of his time on their particular job. If he's interested and he likes you, he'll do it. If not, then on to something else." Jim grinned. "I don't think he cared much for Meissner or Ingrassia."

"Then how did you—"

"I saw him once in the parking lot at two A.M.—this was before all my evenings were taken up by law school—trying to start his car."

"And you gave him a boost?" I didn't think I'd get a straight answer had I asked what Jim was doing there at that hour.

"He had no gas. Anyway, I took him to a station, we talked, stopped in a diner, and that's how it began. Five times since then I've phoned to ask him stuff. He always returns my call, so I guess I'm one of the favored."

We entered a doorway labeled ADVANCED TRANSMITTERS. There were three offices off a dingy, airless section of stone corridor. We walked to the last one, unmarked, and Jim knocked at the door.

"Come in," said a voice.

We entered. A balding, round-faced man with wire-rimmed

spectacles, no tie, and open-necked striped shirt smiled up at us from behind a ramshackle desk piled high with papers.

"Zack Zaremba," said Jim formally, "I'd like you to meet OMIT B."

"Siddown, please," said the old man, grinning, indicating two wooden chairs fronting a row of horizontal steel file cabinets.

We sat.

"So, Jim tells me you godda problem wid' a Class-C amp."

I nodded. The accent was Italian, but with an overlay of something else.

"You workin' on the AIR job."

"Yes, ten thirty megahertz."

"Class-C's a bitch."

"So it seems, yes."

"Everythin' affect everythin' else."

"That's exactly what I'm finding."

"So tell me aboud your problem, maybe, Idonno, maybe I give you some ideas. Maybe I help you, or maybe I set you back six months." He chuckled. "Either way is equally possible."

I told him about the problem, all of it, everything I'd tried, every bad result, the whole balloon full of shit. When I'd finished I saw he was looking downward and off to the side, his gaze defocused.

"You didn't say what transistor you usin'."

"Oh." I told him.

He raised his eyebrows. "Oh, that one." He slid open his front desk drawer, pulled out a bag of corn chips, tore off the top, proffered the bag to Jim and me.

"Saturated fat's no good for you," said Jim, reaching in and grabbing six or eight. I declined.

OMIT B stuffed five chips in his mouth. "So I die happy," he said. I could hear the crunching from his molars. "I work wid the designer of that transistor, man named Bill Hutchings at Motorola. Maybe back in '78. Or '77. No, I think '78. He wanted me to test it for him. It was a very hot device, produced lots of power."

"You actually helped with the transistor design?" I recalled Jim's words . . . *all the little tricks and details, all the history.*

"I work wid a lot of them. Problem wid that one, it tend to produce parametrics—you know what dose are?"

"Spurious frequencies generated by the modulation of some device parameter."

"Only way out was to build an idler circuit for the half-frequency right into the transistor package. You know what they call the half-frequency? A degenerate parametric." He grinned at Jim. "All my life I been working with degenerates."

"I've hung out with some myself," said Jim.

"Degenerates are interesting."

I asked, "And did the idler solve the problem?"

"Oh, sure. It work beautiful."

I was puzzled. "But . . . the parametric still seems to be there."

"Of course. That's because the device has been *improved.*"

I shook my head to indicate a kind of appreciative non-comprehension.

"See, in 1982, some company, Idonno, maybe ours, we tell Motorola we like to use your transistor, but it would be at a little different frequency. Not a lot different, just a little. And they say, sure, we can do that."

"By adjusting the impedance match and retuning the idler."

"That would be the right way."

"But—"

"Pain in the neck. Impedance match broad band, idler narrow band. Much easier to just take the idler out."

"But—"

"Hey, it almost works. Don't forget, you pushin' it for efficiency."

"But what did Bill Hutchings say about the redesign?"

"Oh, he long gone, he retired, got some kind of duck farm or something, whatever."

"And you knew about this."

"Of course."

"But when they first began the AIR development, how come— Didn't Marv come to see you?"

"Who's Marv?"

"You mean no one ever asked you to help select the output transistor?"

OMIT B glanced at Jim.

"He's involved in a lot of things," said Jim. "You think this job's in bad shape? There are jobs in ten times worse condition."

"The Korean . . ." said OMIT B, and they both laughed. "The Egyptian . . ." and they laughed harder.

"So it's hopeless," I said, when they'd finished. "I mean, what I'm trying to do."

OMIT B narrowed one eye. "Well . . . probably, but . . . maybe there's a slight chance. If you could make an idler right *on* the package, wouldn't be quite as good as inside, but maybe it still work." A white pad appeared from under a wad of papers. He began sketching with a pencil. "Here, maybe something like this. . . ." A loop of wire right up on the ceramic of the case, a tiny capacitor at a ground pad. "Now, let's see how much inductance you can get, what kinda Q you need. . . ." Algebraic symbols began appearing on the pad, tiny numbers, sketches of other views. A moment later, he tore off the page, handed it to me. "Something to try, give it a shot."

"Thank you," I said, practically bowing as I edged backward toward the door. Jim rose as well.

"One more thing," said OMIT B, staring directly at me. "Some advice. This I give you for nothing."

"Okay. . . ." I could see his eyes sparkle behind the round lenses.

"You like your job, like what you doin'?"

I glanced quickly at Jim to see if he was in on what I took to be some kind of joke between the older men—but his face was serious. "I . . . yes, I kind of like it."

OMIT B nodded. "Good," he said. "Because my advice is to take your enjoyment—any little pleasure you can get—take it from the work. The politics, the power games, the titles, they all mean nothing. Even the money. What's the difference whether you ged a four percent raise or a seven percent raise? Not gonna make one iota change how you live. But when you make something *work*"—his face lit up—"*that* is beautiful. You created something. You did something no one else ever did. And in that moment, and it don't last long, that's where you take your pleasure." He shrugged, and resumed eye contact. "*Capische?*"

"Yes."

"Good. Sorry, I don't have more time right now. Lemme know how it works out." He waved. " 'Bye, Jim."

Jim shut the door behind us and we retraced our steps through the dungeon and eventually, gratefully, back into the real, nonadvanced world.

---
o

At five P.M. Ingrassia called me into his office. He explained: That an announcement would be made the next day that he himself would be assuming project leadership of AIR. That he knew the job was in terrible trouble. ("I don't like to criticize the near-dead, but we all know where the responsibility lies.") That after the CDR, the Air Force had still left us a window of opportunity (the one Meissner flew out of?). And that I was now the key technical cog.

"I'm sorry it's come down to this," he said. "I mean, having all this pressure on you after being here only a little more than a year, but there was no way we could've foreseen all the things that happened." He held up some papers. "Three more weeks, that's what they're giving us."

"What if I can't do it?"

"You *can* do it. I have every confidence in you. We'll give you every support you need."

"But what if I still can't?"

His steel-gray eyebrows knitted into snakes. "There'll certainly be penalties, contract could be canceled, people laid off . . . the works. You want disaster, that would be it."

I remembered Shopper Jim's description of the aerospace game. "But aren't they already so far down the road with us, wouldn't so many people on their side look bad, that . . ."

Ingrassia was shaking his head. "Those days are over. You got congressional oversight committees now, the Russians are practically our buddies. . . . The times when even a flawed system was better than none have passed. We gotta perform."

I nodded (not quite so diffident anymore, aware but with no need to show it).

"Now get back to the lab."

○

I arrived home that evening at 10:45 to find a man seated in the living room. He was wearing a gray suit and he rose as I entered and Lilah greeted me at the door.

"This is Special Agent Mathis," Lilah said very self-consciously as I stared at the intruder. "He's with the FBI."

14

WHISTLE-BLOWER

Plus ça change, plus c'est la même chose.
—FRENCH PROVERB

Mathis flashed some kind of credential, then quickly sat back down. He motioned me to sit opposite him, but I remained standing. "Sorry to intrude on you like this, particularly after the workday, but I've been talking with Ms. Li and she tells me you've been strongly involved in the area we're investigating."

I looked from him to Lilah; I was not in a great mood. "What area is that?"

Mathis seemed surprised. "Oh, the, uh—Haven't you two communicated?"

"We have," said Lilah quickly, "only not about FBI involvement." Then, to me, plaintively: "I meant to, but you haven't been home and I just—"

"I still don't know what either of you are talking about," I said coldly.

"Falsified time charges at International Instruments on an

Air Force contract," said Mathis. He pulled a folder out of a maroon attaché case.

I glared at Lilah, then sat down.

Mathis smoothed the pompadour on his black, thinning hair. He was clean-shaven, but you could tell he had a dark beard. My guess was, on days when he had evening appointments, he'd shave twice. "Look," he said, "I understand it's late, so if you'd rather do this another time, say tomorrow or Friday . . ."

"Do *what?*" I said.

"Answer some questions, go over the evidence you provided." He held open the folder.

I recognized the time sheet copies I'd given Lilah. "I think I've done enough," I said, and again shooting her a vicious glance, "and so has she."

Mathis snapped the folder shut. "Mr. Zaremba, you do need to talk to us, so it's just a question of when."

"I'm not talking to anybody."

Abruptly, he closed the attaché case and rose.

"Well, of course, that's your choice. . . . I should point out, however, that you—and others—have signed false time cards on work done for a branch of the U.S. government Armed Forces. That's fraud. So unless you're willing to cooperate, you could be up on a whole heap of charges." He raised his eyebrows to emphasize the point, although it just made it seem like he was gloating.

"Cooperate with who? On what?"

"FBI and DIS, in answer to your first question." As always, my puzzlement must have been apparent. "Defense Investigative Service," he elaborated. "Investigation of II's contractual allocations, in answer to your second question."

I shook my head and exhaled sharply. "So, what, you want me to incriminate myself and all my colleagues? We don't even look at the goddamn charge numbers. We don't give a femtofuck. We just sign what they tell us; we're not into this accounting shit."

Mathis was already near the door. He glanced quickly from Lilah to myself. "Mr. Zaremba, I'm assuming you're aware that, under the Whistle-blower Act, if funds are recovered by the government, the original informant is eligible for a substantial portion. And believe me, no one is interested in prosecuting some engineers who weren't attentive to their time cards." He grinned. "With all due respect, that's not where the money is." He handed me a card, then closed the door behind him.

I looked at Lilah, who seemed about to open her mouth.

"Are there any Elio's left?" I asked. "I'm really starved." Elio's are the world's best frozen pizza. I turned toward the kitchen.

"Zack, I want to explain—"

"That should be interesting." I headed for the refrigerator.

"Please just give me a chance."

"It's called 'betrayal,' Lilah. It means when one person trusts another, places his faith in the word of another, counts on the other's fundamental human decency—and then finds out that all of those things were wrong." I extracted a frozen rectangle of pizza from the freezer, popped it in the toaster oven. "So go ahead, you explain."

She looked genuinely frightened and I could see her eyes become watery, and for a moment I forgot how furious I was.

"I was angry," she said. "Angry and hurt and tired."

"*You* were angry?"

"With Mr. Softy and with losing my job and . . . and with my father."

I sat down at the table. "Your father . . ."

"I told you. After I had Kevin in my freshman year, my father refused any further payments for my college education.

My father is an importer, quite wealthy, and he was very happy to finance my brother Alan's MD degree, eight years, and my brother Tim's master's, five years. But when it came to me— and he never was keen on my going in the first place, girls not having any real reason to get an education—when it came to me, he cut me off. The baby and I—" her voice cracked, "he never called him 'Kevin' or 'my grandson,' just 'the baby'—we could live in his house, but that was it. I'd disgraced him, and he wasn't about to support me for it."

She sat down at the table and, for a full minute, remained silent while her mouth trembled and two tears trailed down her left cheek. "But I'm a stubborn person, I don't give up. So I borrowed the money to stay in school. Begged for it, actually, from my brothers—who weren't anxious to go against my dad, and, besides, kind of agreed with him—and anyone and any-where else I could get it. I worked part-time, and it took me seven years to graduate."

"What about student loans?"

"Last couple years, yes. Before that, my father insisted on claiming us as dependents, and since he was rich, I didn't qualify."

I stood up, taking my pizza out of the oven. "Okay, so you borrowed . . ."

"And ran up a tremendous debt. I had a child, I needed someone to watch him while I went to school and work. As of graduation, a little more than a year ago, I owed over forty-five thousand dollars."

I put the pizza on a plate, sat down at the table, began to eat ferociously without looking at her. "So all this . . ." I flut-tered one hand in the air. "All this bullshit, it's about money. You need money."

"It didn't start that way, but as things went on, got deeper, as I experienced the arrogance—"

"You saw an opportunity."

"Yes, an opportunity."

"And I was part of that."

"You're twisting the words, making it sound like—"

"So what is this Whistle-blower thing? Where did you hear about it?"

"Whistle-blower is just what they call it, the real name is the False Claims Act. There was a story on it on *60 Minutes* last year, an engineer suing Northrop over a guidance system for nuclear missiles, some scheme they had for getting around Pentagon purchasing rules. They said Congress amended the act in 1986, made it easier for average citizens to sue. And if you win, you get anywhere from fifteen to twenty-five percent of the settlement." A pause, a look up. "We could share. . . ."

"How much are you suing for?"

"Well, I'm not—I'm not suing yet. According to Mathis, the Justice Department may want to be involved, and . . . But I estimate, very roughly, the total would be between seven and eight million dollars."

"Of which you would get fifteen to twenty-five percent."

She nodded.

I used a napkin to wipe tomato sauce off the corners of my mouth. "Okay . . . so now I understand." I stared at the tabledtop.

"But you don't, do you?"

"I understand that you used me to rat out my co-workers and didn't trust telling me your plans because you were afraid I wouldn't go along."

"Would you have?"

"No."

There was a long pause, and when I looked up, her lips were quivering, and once again the tears were streaming. "It's

easy for you, isn't it, to sit in judgment? You had your education paid for and you don't have any kids."

I didn't respond. I'm a very bad arguer. I do what all the
psychologists advise you shouldn't—clam up, retreat, go into a
shell. After a moment she left, turned and walked out, and I
heard the door to Kevin's bedroom slam. We would not be
sleeping together this night, nor possibly any other. Slowly, the
sickness at that thought began seeping up through my body, a
chill, creeping poison that gradually permeated my flesh and
turned it to stone. I would have the moral high ground but
not Lilah's warm body, her wet pink mouth, the comforting
touch of her long fingers on my neck, her high-pitched giggle
at my silly jokes, her attention when I expounded on something, the smell of her hair when she stepped out of the
shower. I wondered: Was being absolutely right worth all that?

—o—

I worked for two days in the lab attempting to implement the
advice I'd gotten from OMIT B. A rep from a capacitor company was going to bring me tiny single-layer ceramic chips I
could mount right up against the transistor case. A loop of
wire and a larger chip had definitely killed the degenerate
parametric frequency and had pumped up the efficiency. As it
stood, I was now within three percent of meeting the current-
draw requirement. Almost there . . . at room temperature. Of
course, testing over the full mil-spec operating temperature
range, 40°C to +85°C, remained.

I called my parents the day after I met Mathis, and my
father recommended a lawyer—a friend from his Michigan
State days—in the New York area. I'd half expected my dad to
yell at me for putting down the wrong charge numbers, but he
was completely supportive. "You let Jack deal with those FBI
fuckers," he said. (Jack was the lawyer.) "They get a load of

Jack, they'll shit their pants." "But don't do the mischarging anymore," said my mother. They always got on the phone together when I called; presumably, it was a big event. "He's not gonna keep doing it, Margaret," said my dad. "He's not stupid." "I know he's not stupid, but he said it was a mistake." "It wasn't a mistake, they *gave* him the wrong charge number. How could he have known?" "Well, I don't know, maybe he was supposed to check." "You know, you're really being silly." "Why is that silly, I—" Et cetera, et cetera, et cetera. That was the problem when they were on together they ended up arguing with each other, with me as spectator.

I excused myself a few minutes later, referencing a phantom errand I needed to run to "the auto parts store, before it closes." I'm sure they knew I just wanted to get off, but of course they were too polite to say anything. I contacted Jack the lawyer the next day, calling at lunchtime from an outside pay phone. As it turned out, Jack did only corporate law, contract stuff—hardly the sort of thing to make the FBI "fuckers" shit their pants, whatever that meant on an organizational level. But Jack did refer me to one Greg Libnitz, Esq., whom he assured me was experienced in dealing with "the kind of problem you're presenting."

I tried Libnitz several times over the next few days, finally receiving a call back at home on a Wednesday at nine P.M. He listened patiently as I described the situation. I avoided, of course, giving Lilah's name, referring to her as "a close friend at the company," even as she flitted around the kitchen, pretending to wash a plate or return for a napkin. I turned my back on her so as to muffle my voice when I spoke into the mouthpiece. Ten minutes later Libnitz and I were finished, and I walked into the living room and turned on the TV, a new show called *Northern Exposure*. Lilah was on the couch, reading the September *Astronomy*.

262 o|o Robert Grossbach

"This disturbing you?" I asked, indicating the TV.

"No," she said. The cover of the magazine featured a story on X-ray pulsars.

I watched in silence, assimilating neither plot nor dialogue. She read in equal silence, though I suspected she too was absorbing very little. After a while, she said suddenly, "Was that a lawyer you were talking to?" She put the magazine down.

"As a matter of fact, yes."

She nodded, paused. "Are you his client?"

"Not really. I asked him for advice."

"Oh."

"Wanna know what he said?"

"Okay."

"He said if the FBI questions me I should tell them anything they wanna know. He said they don't have a ghost of any kind of a prosecutable case against any engineer. That all they care about is money, getting it out of the company, and maybe going after a few of the higher-ups."

She nodded. "So none of the people whose time cards you gave me can really be hurt."

"Apparently not. At least in his opinion."

"And did you ask him anything about, you know, participating in the lawsuit?"

"You mean with you and the Justice Department?"

"Yes."

"He asked me."

She waited expectantly, long eyelashes brushing the bottoms of the sockets, mouth dropped in the darling little *O*.

"I told him no. That's when he lost interest in the conversation."

She gave a little snort accompanied by a quick head shake, then buried herself in her magazine.

"I guess he isn't the only one to lose interest."

No response. Thirty-second interlude.

"So how 'bout them pulsars?"

No response.

Fifteen minutes later she rose from the couch, walked to the closet, and slipped on a light jacket. "I'm going out for some Tampax. I'll be back later." She closed the door behind her.

I was into *L.A. Law* when a small voice asked, "Are you and Mommy having an argument?"

Kevin, clad in PJs, stood in the doorway of the Phantom's bedroom.

I walked over to him, patted his head. "Hey, big guy, you're supposed to be asleep."

"Are you?"

"Am *I* asleep? No."

"I mean, are you arguing?"

I nodded slowly. "Yes, we had a disagreement."

"Is it serious?"

I grinned. What did a seven-year-old know of "serious" arguments? How could you explain? "It's . . . somewhat serious."

"Are you gonna break up?"

"Kevin, I—Nothing is decided."

"But you might?"

"It's possible."

He looked up at me. "Don't," he said.

"I'll do my best." I leaned down and kissed his cheek, and he kissed me back. "Now go to sleep, okay?"

"Okay." He retreated back inside his room and I gently closed the door.

I was going to miss him very much.

०

Two days later, when I arrived at work, I found everyone out in the parking lot. All the employees were standing around on the concrete in the morning sun, leaning on their cars or clustering in small groups. I spotted Marie as I walked toward the building.

"What's going on?"

She pointed at two men emerging from the lobby. They were carrying large cardboard boxes and wore blue jackets. "FBI," she said.

Sure enough, one of them turned and I could see the yellow lettering on his back, FBI. And I'd thought that was only on television! That actual FBI guys would never walk around with an identifying logo any spy or criminal could read. I mean, did the Secret Service go around wearing "SS" T-shirts? But there they were, FBI guys, lots of them, maybe twenty or more, coming out of the building now in droves, pushing handcarts loaded with file cabinets, holding folders, lugging drawers, entire *drawers,* ripped from desks.

"We had this three years ago," said Marie, sipping coffee from a Styrofoam cup. "Morning raid. Very annoying. But they let you back in after around an hour."

"But what's it about? Does anyone know?" I wondered what she'd say.

"I'm sure *someone* knows. But believe me, it has nothing to do with us. It's always some financial thing or fraud thing with the managers." She shrugged. "Not our problem."

"Mmm."

At least she was right about when they let us back in the plant—it did take about an hour. In the lab, Nussbaum had a radio and tuned it to WINS. "The FBI today raided the Defense Systems Division of International Instruments in Shoreview, Long Island," announced the anchorman after we'd listened for ten minutes, "just before eight A.M. No information is available regarding the objective of the raid, although agents were seen removing a variety of file storage media from the building. International Instruments, a medium-sized defense contractor, employs about forty-eight hundred people at the Shoreview facility."

"That's us," said Nussbaum.

I shrugged. "Did you get the efficiency data on that last run?"

"Thirty-six-point-six percent, min," he said. "Not bad." Pause. "But a spurious came up at −33°C. Jesus, my knees are killing me."

At that instant, I hated him very much. "Whaddaya mean, what spurious?"

"Idonno. It's around eight hundred megahertz."

"Fuck! Lemme see." I walked to the setup, which was in an oven cooled by liquid nitrogen. The AIR system had to meet its specs down to −40° centigrade; I stared at the screen of the spectrum analyzer, an instrument that displayed the relative magnitude of all output signals. There should have been only a single vertical line at 1030 MHz, the transmitter frequency, but instead, there were two lines; a second, smaller signal had popped up from nowhere. "Shit! Shitfuck! Shit shit fuck fuck! Where did this fuckin' thing come from?" I pounded the bench in frustration, then glared at Nussbaum.

"Didn't come from me," he declared.

○

I had to tell someone, so I told Shopper Jim. I told him everything, how I'd taken and copied the time card records from Marie's files, how Lilah had deceived me and turned them in to the FBI, how I had jeopardized not only the jobs but the very freedom of my colleagues.

Jim regarded me coolly for a moment, then said, "I wouldn't worry about it."

"Sure, *you* wouldn't worry, you're not the one that did it."

"Just keep in mind Rule One."

I rolled my eyes. " 'Don't take it too seriously.' "

Jim smiled. "See? You've learned something."

At three that afternoon I got a call from Ingrassia's secretary, a woman named Emily who kept a Bible on her desk. "Mr. Ingrassia just wanted me to ask if you were making any progress."

"I honestly don't know," I responded. "For every step forward, I take an equal one back. I can give him the details if he wants."

"Oh, I doubt he'll have time. He told me this morning that between the FBI, the DIS, and the Air Force, he'll be tied up continuously for the next two weeks."

"The Air Force . . ."

"Oh, yes, they're here."

"Mmm. Okay. Well, I gotta get back to the—"

"Remember, Zachary, the Lord works in mysterious ways."

"—degenerate parametrics."

"What?"

" 'Bye." I hung up.

———
o

I never was questioned any further by the FBI or anyone else. Ten days after Shopper Jim advised me to keep in mind Rule One, an announcement was made plantwide over the loudspeaker system.

"Attention, all employees. This is Yale Sanders. Please stop work for just a moment so you can listen to what I'm about to say."

I looked up from the microscope under which I'd been adjusting the wire-loop inductor on Q7.

"It is the opinion of every company officer that this morning's panic selling of International Instrument stock [what panic selling?] is completely unjustified. In the first place, the

Defense Division contributes only twenty-two percent of total corporate gross revenues. In the second place, although we are currently under FBI investigation as a result of certain allegations by a very small number of employees, these allegations are absolutely false and erroneous, and we have every confidence the evidence will bear this out."

O-kay . . .

"What *is* true is that, with the complete concurrence of the Air Force, and in the best interests of both parties, we have today made a decision—with great reluctance, I might add—to bring the Advanced Interrogator/Receiver program to a premature termination. The reasons for this are complex, mostly having to do with contractual considerations, but, again, both parties are in agreement that this is the best resolution.

"While there will be some unavoidable effects on our divisional employment levels, I want to assure you that these will be entirely minimal. [Meaning it won't involve him.] There is an abundance of other work in-house to keep us fully staffed, and your management is resolutely determined to minimize any impact on what we at II have always considered our most important resource: our people.

"Thank you for listening, and my door is always open for anyone at any level who'd like to speak to me. Thank you."

There was a final crackle from the speaker before it went dead.

"His door is open," said Nussbaum, "but he won't be in there."

I sat down on a lab stool and cradled my forehead. I had single-handedly closed the job. All that work, all that effort from so many people—I had brought to nothing.

"Well," said Nussbaum, "so much for that. We're all done now. Jesus, my hip is really killing me."

---

o

They called us in groups to the Human Resources office and I found myself in the same room where I'd experienced Herman Lerner's incoming spiel a year and three months earlier, this time awaiting an exit briefing along with Whispering Bill, Nussbaum, five other engineers and techs, and four regular people. I'd been sitting stone-faced for five minutes when I looked up to see Boulot pop through the door. Slack-jawed with surprise, I motioned for him to sit next to me.

He removed his beret and unbuttoned his gray sweater. "Zey ask me to come in so I can be laid," he said, grinning.

"You mean, 'laid *off.*' "

"Yes, of course. You cannot just do it, zere is a lot to know."

"But . . . what about Meissner?"

"Oh. Zey are not charging me. Zey agree it was self-defense."

"Really? Well, that's terrific."

"I feel very bad about what 'appened. I visit 'im in ze hospital, we talk, 'ee say 'ee is not mad at me anymore, only ze company, for firing 'im."

"Well, that's—"

"Zen I get a call from Ingrassia, 'ee wants me to come back. So I say, okay, fine, I am 'appy, but ze very next day zey call again and say I 'ave to come in so zey can lay me." He shook his head. "Even in ziss, zey don't know what zey are doing."

I was about to respond when I looked to my left and there was: "Warren! Holy shit!"

"Yes, the criminal returns to the scene of the crime." We shook hands enthusiastically.

I'd visited him once since his release from the hospital three months ago, had found him distant and uncommunicative, and hadn't—to my embarrassment—made any further efforts to contact him. "You know, I've been meaning to call, I just—"

"Yeah, yeah, yeah. Listen, no apologies. The phone works two ways. I was still pretty depressed there for a while, but now I'm fine."

"Except you're here because—"

"I was on, I donno what they call it, some kind of extended leave of absence, unpaid, of course, but still technically employed. They told me to come in so they could lay me off."

"We are alike!" said Boulot.

"Well, we're alike if you also don't give a nanoshit. I'm enrolled in law school full-time, so I couldn't care less. Only reason I'm here is they said no-shows wouldn't get the two weeks' severance pay."

"But *I* am enrolled in law school," said Boulot. "And I am also 'ere only to be severed . . . so we *are* alike."

"Except," I interjected, "for the fact that Sanders doesn't think of you, Frenchman, at all, whereas he thinks of Warren—forever—as a seven."

Warren's face darkened, then broke into a broad smile. "Well, this particular seven is looking forward to the day when the FBI slips a pair of handcuffs over his Rolex and leads that sick cuff-link-wearing fuck out through the parking lot on his way to a multi-year, rape-filled prison term."

"Could happen," I noted. "Let's be optimistic." Warren was sounding much better. I noticed, up front, that Mrs. Leeping had tottered into the room.

"Well," she began in a surprisingly strong voice, "if I may begin, please sign the attendance sheets"—she held up some papers—"I'm about to pass out."

"She ees about to pass out," whispered Boulot. "We ought to help 'er."

"Today we'll be discussing the following topics related to your employment termination: severance stipend, accrued vacation and/or sick pay, private continuation of medical and dental insurance, procedure to apply for unemployment compensation, security debriefing where relevant, use of company-proprietary knowledge at future jobs, return of company badges, and return of any materials currently on loan from the company library."

"I didn't know the company had a library," said Boulot.

"Me either," I noted.

"Me either," said Kushner.

Boulot looked around. "Almost, ze gang ees all here. Except of course for ze bosses."

"And Shopper Jim. And Wonderboy."

"Shoppair Jeem, 'ee ees a Job Shoppair. 'Ee just goes to ze next place. But Wonderboy, I don't know."

I shrugged. "I haven't seen him for two weeks. I don't think anyone has."

"Maybe he's on vacation," mused Kushner. "Maybe they'll call him back from Hawaii so he can listen to Mrs. Leeping's outpatient lecture."

Mrs. Leeping was droning on, but we ignored her. Boulot looked up once when she began talking about insurance, but Kushner and I kept mumbling and making stupid jokes about the proceedings. Among the myriad subjects young single guys don't give a nanoshit about, insurance ranks near the top.

---
o

It seemed highly appropriate that Lilah's move-out was that night. The next day at II, Friday, was to be my last, and that would about close out the endings. End of job, end of girlfriend, probably end of apartment (I'd try to break my lease), end of life as I knew it.

I watched as she gathered her suitcases—four large ones, two small—near the door. All her possessions, hers and Kevin's, in the world. Not very much. She had told me a week earlier, as all of us were finishing a pizza, that they had decided to leave.

"I want you to know," she said softly, "that whatever you think of me, I never ever meant any hurt to come to you. I only did what I felt I had to . . . and maybe . . . Idonno . . . maybe I was wrong." She looked up and met my gaze as I wiped some tomato sauce off my chin. "And I want you to know too . . . that I still love you." She rubbed the top of Kevin's head. "That we both do."

I wondered why such warm words, such touching, sad words, somehow sounded so calculating.

"If we love him," said Kevin, "then why do we have to leave?"

I awaited her explanation for that one.

"Because sometimes, even when people love each other, they have an argument, and in order to make up, they have to be away from each other for a while."

"A long while?"

She looked at me. "Well . . . it depends."

"Depends on what?"

"I don't know," she said. I could see the teardrops coalescing in the corners of her eyes.

Kevin turned to me. "Sorry," I said, surprised at the hoarseness of my voice. "I don't know either."

Now, outside, we heard the cab honk, and I opened the door to the hallway. They were moving to a tiny furnished apartment Lilah had found in Hicksville. I grabbed three of the large suitcases, Lilah took a large and a small, and Kevin the remaining small, and we schlepped our way outside to the taxi. The autumn night air held the faint chill of distant winter.

I helped load the bags in the trunk (two of them had to go in the back seat) and then lingered at the curb.

"Good-bye, big guy," I said, hoisting Kevin to eye level to give him a kiss. He was crying quietly and didn't say anything back, just kissed me.

"It's gonna be okay," I said inanely, knowing that it wasn't, as I let him down and he crawled into the cab.

For a moment it seemed that Lilah would just climb in after him, but at the last second she turned and stepped quickly into my arms and kissed me on the lips and hugged me very tightly for ten seconds.

"You be good," she whispered as she let go and entered the cab.

Far too late for that, I thought. But I said nothing as the yellow door chunked shut and the taxi pulled away into the blackness.

o

I began saying my good-byes in the midafternoon. Whispering Bill. Yu and Mee. Nussbaum. Rosemary in Repro. Gung Ho. A Boy Named Hsu. Medieval Man. Marie. Emily, Ingrassia's secretary. Ingrassia himself.

"I really am sorry it worked out this way, Zack. Good luck." A firm shake of the hand, a nod from me. No need anymore to be diffident; finally, at last, perfectly aware. Emily wrote me a property pass so I'd be able to leave the building with my possessions without being machine-gunned by the door guard.

Finally, at four P.M., Shopper Jim helped me carry my stuff to the parking lot. It was interesting: On your last day it was apparently traditional to leave a little early; no one said anything. Jim himself was staying behind. They'd switched him to some radar system II was building for the Turkish navy.

A light rain was falling. Perfect. Atmospheric and emotional congruence. The parking lot was full of fiftyish men hauling things to their cars.

As we made our way through the rows, I had a sudden flashback to Michigan, to autumn football games and the walk through the streets of Ann Arbor to the stadium, trickles of people joining to become rivers, then torrents, then oceans, the fraternity houses blaring the fight song from balconies, the fall air fresh and clean in my nostrils . . . all gone now. Another time, another life.

"See?" said Jim. "If only you'd remembered Rule Seven, you wouldn't need my help."

"Which one is Seven?"

"Always keep enough cardboard boxes under your desk to carry out all your stuff."

"I'd like to be in a place where I don't have to know your rules."

He raised his eyebrows. "There is no such place."

We threw my possessions—engineering textbooks, vendor catalogues, some plastic templates—into the trunk along with what I was stealing from II—assorted pads, pencils, pens, staplers, hole-punchers, Scotch tape, staple removers, Magic Markers—and started back toward the building. I'd been unable to carry and had to leave behind five last textbooks. We were just about to enter the lobby when we saw OMIT B emerge.

"Wait a minute," I said, stopping him. "You? It can't be the layoff included *you*. . . ."

A crooked jack-o'-lantern grin split the round face. "Oh, no, I'm not laid off, I quit."

"You quit?"

He indicated Shopper Jim. "Your buddy here and I have been talking. He finally convinced me."

"Convinced you of what?"

"I gonna become a lawyer!" he declared. "I'm enrolling in law school, starting two weeks."

―――
o

The cubicle was completely empty except for the bedraggled black man, who seemed to show up every third or fifth day, usually after eleven A.M. We had nicknamed him "HR1," for Human Resources One. HR1 did no work anyone could discern, responded to questions with monosyllabic or zero-syllabic answers, and never seemed to be intruded on by the managers. " 'Bye," he said to me now. "Hey, you happen to know anything about Legendre polynomials?"

"Sorry," I responded, startled. HR1 obviously had unplumbed depths . . . which I'd never get to know. I retrieved the five textbooks from my desktop.

"Sure you can make it?" asked Jim.

"Oh, yeah."

"Well, I guess I'll stay here, then." He thrust out a hand, looked me directly in the eye. "So?"

I shook the hand. "I'll call you sometime."

"Absolutely."

"Thanks . . . for everything."

"Ayy, you're a good kid."

I let go of the hand. "I just wanna ask you one thing—and please don't take this the wrong way."

"I take everything the wrong way."

"But knowing all you know, having done this for so many years, how . . . I mean, how the hell do you get through the day?"

He grinned, nodded slowly. "Like this: Each morning when I arrive, I imagine a giant hourglass has just been turned over, and its top half is filled with pennies. As the day goes on, every second I hear the sound of each penny tumbling through the neck into the bottom, which contents at the end of the afternoon I take home.

"So A Boy Named Hsu gives me some rude shit, I hear, *kuh-ching*. The guy in Receiving slams the cage shut in my face, *kuh-ching*. Meissner tells me to do two hundred Wire Run Lists. *Kuh-ching*. The stock room guy makes me fill out ten forms to get one resistor. *Kuh-ching, kuh-ching, kuh-ching, kuh-ching*." He nodded. "That's how I do it." Eyebrow raise. "So, you thought about where you goin' for your next job?"

I looked away. "Not really."

"Well, if you decide to give up being a Direct, gimme a buzz. I know all the shops."

"Okay . . ."

"It's not that bad, you know. You're your own man, independent contractor. Don't need to suck up to any particular company."

I waved and left the cubicle.

Kuh-ching.

---
o

I was in the corridor when it hit me, I never did understand exactly how or why. But suddenly I found myself turning down a side hall instead of going straight, walking twenty feet past the men's room, and opening the door to the Transmitter Lab.

It was deserted.

I crossed to the bench where my transmitter module, one-quarter of the complete unit, was set up. I set down my textbooks and turned on the instruments: pulsed power meter, digital scope, spectrum analyzer, signal generator, pulse modulator, oven, soldering stand. The ultra-miniature capacitors had come in the day before; I used a plastic tweezers to extract one from the package. With the soldering iron I tinned a grounded patch of circuit board at the base of Q7, laid the capacitor on it, used the iron to reflow the solder.

Next I took the wire loop inductor already on the transistor, nudged and flattened it so it literally hugged Q7's surface, then, my face about an inch away, tack-soldered it to the top of the capacitor.

I blinked and jerked back as the wispy curl of smoke from the iron got into my eyes and nose. I returned the iron to its stand, then peered down at my work. It was done. This was as close as any possible wire could ever get to the transistor. I turned on the power supply, watched the current reading on the face of the meter. Four percent below spec.

I looked over at the spectrum analyzer: a nice clean line at 1030 megahertz, no spurious over the seventy-decibel dynamic range, no sign of the half-frequency degenerate parametric. None. Power meter reading: fifty-one watts, peak. Excellent. I checked the pulse rise and fall times, the duration, the delays: all within spec.

I began to feel something not quite describable, a *lightness,* a chill, a certain *quietness.* I placed the module in the oven, tightened the cable connectors, then pressed the hot-cycle button that would increase the temperature to +85° centigrade. I sat on the stool and watched the LED readout gradually run up.

As expected, the power decreased a little at the hottest temperature and the pulse parameters changed, but still no spurious frequencies came up, the current draw remained low, and everything was still in spec.

Now the real test. I waited for the oven to return to room temperature, then pressed the cold-cycle button that would take it down to −40° centigrade. I watched the LED readout, then looked around. What the hell was I doing here? What was I doing? I was *laid off,* for chrissake, *canned, cut, let go,* no longer a part of the team. I was not being paid for this. No *kuh-chings,* nothing. It was irrelevant, supremely, totally, unconditionally irrelevant. The job staff had been terminated, and the very job itself! No one cared! Didn't I get it? *No one cared.* NO ONE CARED. NO ONE—

I watched everything at once as the temperature descended. Zero, where water freezes. Minus twenty, where a thin patina of ice would begin to coat the circuit board. Minus thirty, where the oven window whited over, where the plastic cases of the low-power transistors strained to let go of their metal leads. Minus thirty-three, where the most recent spurious frequency had popped out of the noise at the bottom of the spectrum analyzer.

Nothing. Current still good. Pulse still good.

Minus thirty-five, where the goddamned degenerate at 515 megahertz usually sprang up ten decibels like a rapist out of an alley, pulling away the power from the main frequency, sapping the efficiency, ruining the spectral purity . . .

Nothing.

Holy . . .

Nothing.

Minus thirty-seven. Minus thirty-nine. Minus . . . forty. Limit of the spec.

I quickly scanned the instruments: power, current, pulse rise-time, fall-time, width, delay. My breath seemed to match the train of pulses on the screen. I swallowed, looked around at the empty room, then back to the setup. The balloon. The balloon full of shit. I had pushed it in at ten different points.

I waited the fifteen minutes the oven lingered at maximum cold, then watched hypnotically as it came back up toward room temperature. Back through the minus thirties without a problem, up through zero where the ice would turn transparent before it liquified, back up finally to plus twenty-three, room temperature.

I opened the oven door and reached in. I ran my index finger along the edges of the board, along a path in the air a half inch above the components, stopping finally at Q7. The radio frequency transmitter module for the Advanced Interrogator/ Receiver. The Class-C power output transistor with the OMIT B–Zack Zaremba parametric suppressor. I checked the instruments a final time, then looked back at the module. Canceled or not, relevent or not, cared about or not . . .

It was working perfectly.

EPILOGUE

Careers in engineering, science, and technology
promise to be rewarding and plentiful up to the
year 2000.
— *CAREER INFORMATION CENTER* (GLENCOE
PUBLISHING CO., 1990) P. 14.

n 1991, the Soviet Union collapsed and disintegrated, a process soon mirrored by our own defense industry establishment, which—in its characteristic obscure and jargon-laden manner—referred to its particular crumbling and withering self-cannibalization as "downsizing" or "consolidation." It was a period where the weak ate the weaker in a Darwinian struggle to survive. Martin Marietta bought GE's Defense Division and General Dynamics' Space Division. Loral purchased LTV, Ford Aerospace, and Unisys. Lockheed merged with Martin to become Lockheed Martin, which promptly bought Loral. Northrup bought Grumman, Northrup-Grumman bought Westinghouse Electronic Systems, Hughes bought General Dynamics Missile Division, Raytheon purchased E-systems, and Boeing bought Rockwell.

During this time, hundreds of thousands of highly trained defense workers were laid off. There were newspaper stories of engineers who opened sandwich shops, engineers who drove taxis, engineers who became lawn service franchisees. While the rest of the country gradually climbed out of the economic abyss, while the Dow shot through eight thousand, while interest rates dropped and real estate recovered, the sky rained defense engineers who, mostly, splattered on hard concrete. And understood, in a way quite different from less technically adept friends, the meaning of the term "peace dividend."

Six years after the cancellation of AIR, I went to one of those "Computer Expo" shows at the Nassau Coliseum. I was on my way out of a men's room when I just about collided with someone in the corridor.

"Excuse m—" The jaw drops were simultaneous. "Lilah . . . ?"

"Zack. How are you?"

She smiled, the even rows of white teeth still the same, the (somewhat shorter) carbon-black hair framing the elongated oval face. She wore a tangerine dress and matching high heels and lipstick, and she was still so beautiful I could barely catch my breath.

"I'm good . . . just like you told me to be."

"You follow directions."

"When it suits me." People were streaming around us. "And you?"

"Same. When it suits me."

"I meant, how are you? How've you been? How's Kevin?"

"Oh, we're both fine. He's here, somewhere. He's become quite the computer nerd."

"Is that right? He's how old now? Let's see, he was . . ."

"He was thirteen last month."

"Jesus."

"Yes. A long time."

I became aware that we hadn't taken our eyes off each other. I glanced down quickly to see if she wore any rings, but one hand was behind her and the fingers on the other were folded. "So what's been happening with you? How, uh"—a bit awkward—"what went on with your lawsuit? Did you win?"

"You mean, are you talking to a millionairess?"

"Okay . . ."

She motioned to a spot alongside one of the concession stands. "Let's go over there. Less traffic." We walked a few steps, leaned against a wall. "This is better."

"Listen, I didn't mean to take up a lot of your time—"

"No, no, really, I'm . . . I'm just happy to see you." She reached out to touch my sleeve, then quickly withdrew.

I felt a familiar weakness shudder from my chest to my groin. The endocrine system, the limbic brain, the autonomic nervous system, apparently all were uneducable; all this time, after everything, they—and, I suppose, the part of me they constituted—had learned nothing.

"The answer is no," she continued. (For just an instant I thought she'd read my body's subconscious question.) "You're not talking to a rich person."

"You lost the suit."

"There never was one. Wonderboy beat me to the punch."

"Wonderboy?"

"Yup. Seems he got the idea the noose was closing, and just after you asked about his time card he hired his own lawyer and filed his own lawsuit under the False Claims Act."

"For what?"

"Fraudulent design. Fraudulent data reported to the Air Force. Fraudulent testing, falsification of STE calibration stickers, the whole nine yards."

"But he was the original liar about the system! He was part of it!"

"Yes. . . ." She grinned. "The process is not entirely fair."

"And what about your case?"

"Oh, they played around with it for a while—well, more than a while; three years, actually—but they finally decided not to go forward. My lawyer said the Justice Department was claiming that my case involved breach of contract rather than fraud, and that in any event they really don't like to rock the boat with private contractors because, whatever their behavior, it had been condoned by high-level government officials."

"So after all that, you got nothing."

"Right."

"And Wonderboy?"

"I heard from somewhere he ended up with about seventeen million."

I shut my eyes and rocked back and forth. "Makes you wanna simultaneously laugh and cry."

"Didn't do much laughing," she said, smiling now.

"What *did* you do? You're not still at II, I presume."

"Oh, no. No. I left about three months after the AIR layoff, worked for a while at Sperry, then finally, about a year ago, got a job at *Sky and Telescope* magazine as an editor. Matter of fact, that's why I'm down here from Cambridge. I'm supposed to interview this astrophysicist at Stonybrook."

"Is that right? But that's great. That's terrific. I remember you always liked astronomy."

"Yes. . . . So far, I'm really enjoying it." She strained to look down the wide corridor. "Oh, here comes Kevin." She waved, then returned her attention to me. "So how's things going for you? Do you keep up with any of the guys?"

"Some. Boulot writes me every once in a while from Paris."

"Really? That's nice. I remember you mentioned he wanted to open a bookstand."

"Maybe, but he certainly hasn't yet, can't afford to. He works for Thompson-CSF." I remembered his last E-mail.

"Hates it." A middle-aged woman dropped a hot dog wrapper on the floor; automatically, for some reason, I bent to pick it up and deposited it in a wastebasket. "Uh, Warren I see from time to time. He's a lawyer, works for New York State. Shopper Jim I lost touch with, although somebody told me he's a lawyer too. Patent attorney out in L.A."

A tall teenage boy bumped into her shoulder. I was about to give him a *Hey, watch where you're*—when Lilah said, "Zack, this is Kevin." And to the boy, "Kev, do you remember Zack?"

He looked at me, blinked, and then his face lit up as he extended a hand. "Yeah! Coach. How are you?"

"I'm good," I said, running my eyes over his nearly six-foot length. "You got . . . giant."

"He's bigger than nearly everyone in his grade. Idonno where he gets it."

I said, "It's good to see you, Kevin."

"Good to see you."

"You doin' okay?"

"Yeah, not bad."

"Still play soccer?"

"Mmm, not really. Now I stink at basketball. I like to stink at a different thing each year."

"You do not stink," said Lilah. Then, looking at me, "Maybe you just need a better coach."

A sudden surge of people headed for the exits. I glanced at the wall clock. "I gotta go," I said. "My wife's gonna worry."

"Oh," said Lilah, her voice a pitch higher, "you're married. . . ."

I nodded, "Three years in, uh, April."

"Well . . . that's terrific."

"And you?"

"Four months."

"Wow . . . congratulations. Wonderful."

She nodded. I imagined our facial expressions were the same: brittle masks of theatrically pleased surprise.

I found myself trying to fathom, as I had so many, many times over the years, the exact reason I'd caused her to leave me. Had it been simply a fit of stubborn pique? Or rather (as I kept telling myself) that she'd betrayed a trust, and so how could I ever trust her again? It was one of those closed-loop conundrums I'd never resolve. Better scar tissue on the brain than reexposing the wound.

"Well . . ." I began to move away. "I gotta run. It was really great to see you, great to see you both."

"Wait," said Lilah. "I forgot to ask. What about you? What're you doing now?"

"Oh. Well, I, uh, teach."

"Teach . . . That's very nice. A local college?"

"Actually, I teach third grade."

The lip-parting and raised eyebrows, as if I'd announced I'd just licked a turd, were not unfamiliar to me. When I'd made the decision to leave engineering, I was told by nearly everyone—other engineers; friends; my parents, of course—that it was a disastrous course of action. That I was giving up a job that paid wonderfully for a job that paid poorly. That I was cavalierly casting away all that academic achievement, that rigorous high-tech training for something that could be done by nearly anyone. That I was exchanging a transient disillusionment for a permanent one, since it was well known—just ask them—that all teachers burn out in five years anyway.

"Third grade . . ." echoed Lilah.

"I like the kids. They say funny things. And they're cute. And they have strange, interesting ideas. I didn't want to spend my whole life just listening for *kuh-chings*."

Her eyebrows furrowed in some complex blend of incomprehension and incredulity.

"Big shortage of teachers, you know." I grinned, then felt a pang I'd sounded too flippant. "I just, the kids . . . I try to fortify 'em a little before the world educates all the originality and sweetness out of them."

And the illusions.

I sidled away even farther, jostled now by the crowd. Lilah and Kevin waved. I remembered suddenly when she'd saved my coaching position, the moment afterward outside the school when we'd kissed so deliriously in the snow. And the overwhelming, drowning certainty that I'd love her forever.

For some of us, life is full of illusions, personal and professional. We never do get over them and are nearly always disappointed. And yet . . . and yet . . . I've come to the conclusion that maybe that's not so bad. That most of the things in life that've made a difference in the human condition were accomplished by Pollyannas and Quixotes, naïfs and malcontents and obsessives, people who didn't know any better, stubborn people who didn't listen, people swept up in a tornado of emotion, driven people who forced reality into the mold of their hallucinations. And that if *dis*illusionment is the ultimate fate of most of those people, to deny their nature would be worse, a loss of themselves, and a loss to everyone else.

My son Ethan is one year old now, and if (when) he someday asks my advice about becoming an engineer—despite my natural revulsion—that's what I'm going to tell him.

And of course, he won't understand.

APPENDIX 1
ACRONYM SOUP

RF   Radio Frequency

RFP   Request for Proposal

IFF   Identification, Friend or Foe

AIR   Advanced Interrogator/Receiver

WRL   Wire Run List

STE   Special Test Equipment

BM   Bill of Materials

PDR   Preliminary Design Review

CDR   Critical Design Review

SWR   Stock Withdrawal Request; also, Standing Wave Ratio

FTMP   Fast Track Management Program

PIDOOMA   Pulled It Directly Out Of My Ass

ECR   Engineering Change Request

ECN   Engineering Change Notice

REV   Revision (designator)

FUBAR   Fucked Up Beyond All Recognition

MHz   Megahertz, or million cycles per second

BIT   Built-In Test

TFR   Thin-Film Resistor

dB   decibel (ten times the logarithm of a power ratio)

LNA   Low Noise Amplifier

APPENDIX 2

THE ENGINEERING RULES, OBSERVATIONS, AND ADVISORIES OF SHOPPER JIM

RULE ONE: Don't take it too seriously.

RULE TWO: Your only security is your ability to get the next job.

RULE THREE: You can't make anything (at least not to spec).

RULE FOUR: You can't measure anything (at least not to required accuracies).

RULE FIVE: There's no such thing as a shortage, only a shortage at a price.

RULE SIX: To gain management's favor, tell them what they want to hear, which is invariably different from the truth.

RULE SEVEN: Always keep enough cardboard boxes under your desk to carry out all your stuff.

REGARDING ENGINEERS: The good ones get out. (Usually.)

MURPHY'S LAW: *Anything that can go wrong will.*

SHOPPER JIM'S COMMENTARY: *True but incomplete. For sufficiency we must add, Anything that* can't *go wrong also will.*

PARKINSON'S LAW: *Work expands to fill the time allotted for it.*

SHOPPER JIM'S COMMENTARY: *Incorrect. Work expands* beyond *the time allotted for it.*

PETER PRINCIPLE: *In a hierarchy, people are promoted until they reach their level of incompetence.*

SHOPPER JIM'S COMMENTARY: *This applies only to managerial personnel. A competent engineer is so valuable that he's kept at his position until he's laid off.*

Engineer Deficit Puts Military Readiness at Risk
—HEADLINE, *ELECTRONIC ENGINEERING TIMES*,
SEPTEMBER 25, 2000, P. 6

ACKNOWLEDGMENTS

For their contributions to this book, witting and unwitting, I'd like to acknowledge Joe Seinberg, whom I will always think of as a 10; Bob Schwartz, one of the nation's foremost toilet-burning lawyers; Harriet Bara, whose expert keyboarding proved that speed and accuracy are not mutually exclusive; my editor, Bryan Cholfin, who has my great gratitude for his many perceptive editorial suggestions (and whom I admire despite his lack of strength in differential equations); Hayes Jacobs, teacher and friend; the thousands of engineers, technicians, and engineering managers I've met, worked with, and worked against during four decades of employment in the defense/ aerospace industry; my mother, Mollie Simon, and father, Herman Grossbach, who lavished all their love, guidance, and wisdom on their sole mutual product; my wonderful children, Mitchell, Elliot, and Jennifer, who survived their childhoods despite my coaching in athletics, and who have taught and entertained me far more than I ever did them; and, finally, my wife, Sylvia, who unwaveringly supported me while career after career spiraled into the Event Horizon of Creative Writing, while my contemporaries became stars—Sylvia, who made it all possible, and without whom none of it would mean anything.